This book is dedicated to all the unbreakables out there. You are beautiful and strong and so very, very inspiring. Keep fighting.

what

unbreakable

looks like

kate mclaughlin

what unbreakable looks like

WEDNESDAY BOOKS
NEW YORK

First published in the United States by Wednesday Books, an imprint of St. Martin's Publishing Group

WHAT UNBREAKABLE LOOKS LIKE. Copyright © 2020 by Old Crow, LLC. All rights reserved. Printed in the United States of America. For information, address St. Martin's Publishing Group, 120 Broadway, New York, NY 10271.

www.wednesdaybooks.com

The Library of Congress Cataloging-in-Publication Data is available upon request.

ISBN 978-1-250-17380-5 (hardcover)
ISBN 978-1-250-17382-9 (ebook)

Our books may be purchased in bulk for promotional, educational, or business use. Please contact your local bookseller or the Macmillan Corporate and Premium Sales Department at 1-800-221-7945, extension 5442, or by email at MacmillanSpecialMarkets@macmillan.com.

First Edition: 2020

10 9 8 7 6 5 4 3 2 1

This book contains depictions of human trafficking, sexual assault, and violence. Please proceed with caution if you have been affected by any of these issues.

PART ONE

poppy

chapter one

Clean sheets. That's what I'm dreaming about when something wakes me up. I groan, swearing. Sleep is the only time I have to myself—the only time I'm free from the motel and the other girls in it. The sound grows louder, people coming up the stairs outside the room.

I force my eyes open. It's still dark, but there's always a sliver of light that comes through the window—neon blue from the vacancy sign, and yellow floodlights. Shadows pass, strobing the light. It's too late for business. If Mitch let us go to bed, it has to be not much before dawn. We're his nighttime girls.

I took some pills earlier, after the last john left, so maybe I'm imagining things. Mitch came by and gave us all a little "treat." I'd been greedy. I'm always greedy when it comes to my medicine, and Mitch spoils me. I'm his favorite—he told me.

There are six of us on the second floor of the motel. The manager gave Mitch a deal on the rooms for a cut of his take—and a piece of each of us. I wonder if that's what this is, the slimy piece of shit coming to get a little somethin' somethin' before work.

There's a crash, followed by a scream. I sit up, head swimming. Fear takes hold, sobering me. I crawl out of bed, stagger to the other one. Ivy is out cold. I shake her shoulder—it's bony. Too bony. "Wake up. Ivy, wake the fuck up." How can she sleep with all the screaming?

"Poppy?" She clutches at my hand. "What's going on?"

"I don't know, but you need to get up and put some clothes on." She's naked. I'm in a tank top and my underwear. I stumble to the dresser we share and pull out a pair of jeans that should have been washed days ago. I tug them on, fastening them low on my hips. I grab a sweater and shove my feet into a pair of sneakers. Behind me, I hear Ivy getting out of bed, the sheets rasping against each other.

More screams. I run—lurch—to the door and try to open it, but the manager locks us in after the johns leave. Most of us have nowhere to go even if we were straight enough to run, but every once in a while a girl tries to take off. They never get far before they turn around and come back on their own. Mitch has that effect on us.

"What is it?" Ivy asks as she stumbles into a pair of jeans. Her voice is slurred, her eyelids barely open.

"I think it's the cops," I say. Either that, or it's a rival of Mitch's. I don't want to think about what's going to happen to us if that's the case.

The door to our room flies open. I jump backward, putting myself between whoever it is and Ivy. The cops. We stand there watching them like cornered dogs, beaten and meek. We know the drill. Don't say nothin'.

"Are you girls okay?" a woman cop asks. She's tall with long, curly hair and dark skin. Beyoncé wishes she were this beautiful.

"We ain't done nothing wrong," I tell her. "You can't arrest us."

She gives me a funny look. "Honey, we're not here to arrest you. We're here to get you out of here."

"Yeah? Where you gonna take us?"

"The hospital, then home, if we can."

I snort. Home. Yeah right.

She holds out her hand. "Come on. You can't stay here."

Ivy clings to me as we inch toward the door. As soon as I cross the threshold, I start to run. Ivy's feet tangle with mine and we go down, hitting the cement walkway hard.

Ivy grunts. There's blood on her lips. A male cop hauls her up, carries her away.

"Hey!" I cry.

"Da fuck?" someone yells. I smile at the sound of Daisy's voice. She's gonna fuck somebody up. "Get off the floor, you stupid bitch."

I push up onto my hands. The female cop takes my arm and pulls me up.

"Ow!" My left ankle doesn't want me to stand on it.

"Lean on me," the cop says, putting her arm around me. Her hand is on my ribs. I wait for it to creep higher, but it doesn't.

My foot really hurts. I should have grabbed my pills. What am I going to do when these wear off?

"What's your name?" the woman asks as we begin walking. She's taking a lot of my weight, but she doesn't seem bothered by it.

"Poppy."

She smiles a little. "Your real name, sweetie. So we can let your parents know you're okay."

I'm not sure my mother would even care. "Alexa," I tell her. "Alexa Marie." It doesn't feel like mine anymore—it belongs to someone else.

"You're safe now, Alexa. You're going to be okay."

I laugh. Who does she think she's talking to? She don't know shit. "Bitch," I say. "We ain't *never* going to be okay. Never."

They say I'm safe. I don't feel safe. My skin itches and twitches like bugs are crawling underneath it. I've left fingernail scratches on my arms from trying to get to them— long, raw furrows in my skin that felt so good at the time, but burn like hell.

I'm in the hospital. Why doesn't Mitch rescue me? Why doesn't he come take me home? He's a bad guy, they tell me. I know, but he's *my* bad guy. He's all I got.

"How long have I been here?" I ask the nurse, but she doesn't seem to hear me, because she doesn't answer. It has to have been a while. I don't feel right. I need my medicine.

My clothes are gone. I'm wearing a thin cotton gown that smells weird. I've been photographed, poked, and prodded. They swabbed my mouth and got me into stirrups so they could swab down there too. They said they were going to check me for STIs, and would I consent to a pregnancy test? Sure. If I am pregnant, I want it out of me.

So many tests. So many questions.

"You okay, baby?" the nurse asks.

I want to ask her if I fucking look okay. "No," I say instead, scratching.

Her lips form a thin line and she nods, like she understands. "I'll see what we can do to take the edge off." She leaves the room, but she's back in a few minutes. She gives me a cup of water and a little paper cup with pills in it. I don't even ask what they are, I just flush them down my throat and start counting the seconds.

"Give me your arm, honey," she commands. She has a tube of lotion that she rubs into the scratches and dry patches. It feels good, takes away the sting and itch.

"You're pale as milk," she comments. "Skin that delicate needs to be protected."

I don't know what to say, so I stay quiet.

"I'll be back later to put some more on, okay?"

She smiles at me, and tears burn in my eyes. I blink—hard. No one is going to see me weak.

I'm watching cartoons on TV a little while later when another woman comes in. This one's wearing pants and a blouse and carrying a bag big enough to hold a small child. She has curly blond hair and blue eyes.

"Hello, Alexa," she says. "My name is Jill. I'm with DCF. Do you know what that is?"

"Yeah," I reply. They came by to talk to Mom once when I went to school wearing the same clothes three days in a row and didn't have lunch.

"Good. I work specifically with cases involving human trafficking. Are you aware of what that is?"

Does she think I'm a fucking idiot? Brain damaged, maybe? "It's when you're forced into being a ho."

She inclines her head. "That's part of it. I'm here

because you've been identified as a victim of human trafficking."

I stare at her. She doesn't seem bothered by my silence.

She walks over and sits in the chair by my bed. I push myself farther up on the pillows.

"Would you be okay if we talk about what happened to you?" she asks me.

"Ain't nothin' happened to me," I respond.

"Mitch Anderson didn't force you to have sex with strangers for money?"

"I didn't charge anyone money."

"No. Mitch did that, didn't he?"

"I don't know what you're talking about. Mitch is my boyfriend."

"That's what the other girls from the motel called him as well. You don't mind sharing your boyfriend with them?"

I'm silent. I want to tell her I'm his favorite, but I've already said too much. I forgot how much trouble Mitch could be in for having sex with young girls.

"Your mother's boyfriend, Frank, is a friend of Mitch's, isn't he?"

"I don't want to talk about him." What I want is my pills. I don't like the things I'm starting to feel. To think.

Jill gives me a sympathetic look. "Alexa—"

"Poppy," I correct her. "My name is Poppy."

"Do you really want to be called that?" she asks me.

Yes, but I give her the answer she wants to hear. "No." I'll tell her whatever she wants if it makes her go the fuck away.

I have to get out of here, but how far will I get in a hospital gown with my bare ass sticking out? I want to scream, but when I tried last night, nothing came out. Jill's still watching me. I want to punch her in the face.

"I want to see Ivy," I say.

Jill nods. "I'll see if we can make that happen."

"You don't have to see shit. She right down the damn hall." To prove it, I yell her name at the top of my lungs. "Ivy! Ivy!"

"Poppy!" comes the answering shout. "Pop-py!"

I grin, so fucking happy to hear her voice.

There's a knock on the open door. I turn my head and see the woman cop who found me at the motel.

"Detective Willis," Jill says, giving her a look I recognize from adults I've known my whole life. It brands me as "difficult," an asshole.

The cop smiles at me. A small real one that tells me she's known too many girls like me.

She ain't known *anyone* like me.

"Can I come in?" she asks.

Like I can stop her. I nod. I can't help but stare at her. She's probably one of the most beautiful women I've ever seen. And she's got this attitude—like she knows how to kill somebody with only two fingers, y'know? She's strong.

I hate her for it.

She stands beside my bed, watching me like she thinks I might bite—and she's prepared to take the risk. "How are you feeling?" she asks.

"Like a junkie," I rasp. I hold up my hand; it trembles.

Detective Willis looks sympathetic, but I wonder if she's ever felt like this before. "We're going to get you into a rehab program for girls who have been trafficked."

I startle. "I'm not going home?" I don't care if I see my mother, or Frank, but Mitch won't know where to find me if I don't go home.

She looks at Jill, who shakes her head.

"What the fuck are y'all not tellin' me?" I demand. "I'm right fucking here."

Jill sighs. "Alexa, your mother has given up her parental rights. You can't go home."

I look from her to Detective Willis. "She doesn't want me?"

The cop tries to take my hand. I pull it away. "She knows home is not a good environment for you."

"Bullshit," I say. "She just doesn't want her fucked-up kid back."

I am *not* going to cry.

"So, I'm going to be sent to prison, then, huh?" I ask. I won't be eighteen for almost a year. That makes me a ward of the state. "Where all unwanted kids go?"

"No," Jill says. "We found someone who very much wants to take you."

"Who?" I demand.

"Your aunt Krys," she replies.

I remember Krys—vaguely. We used to spend a lot of time with her when my grandmother was alive, back when I was little and Mom's drinking wasn't so bad. I liked her.

I frown.

"She'd like to visit with you, and if you want, you could maybe live with her and her husband in Middletown when you get out of the program."

"What does she want in return?" I ask. "She get paid to take me?"

Detective Willis doesn't look surprised at the question. "She doesn't want anything."

I snort.

"She told me your mother wouldn't let her see you when they broke ties. She says she's missed you."

My throat is tight. I swallow hard. I'm not the kid Krys

knew. I'm not a kid at all. "She's not going to want me when she sees what a mess I am."

"Maybe you should let me decide that," comes a voice from the door. My head whips around so fast, it hurts.

Standing just inside the room is a woman who looks like a younger, sober version of my mother. Softer. She's tall and slim with bright red hair and blue eyes. She's wearing a long sweater over leggings with tall boots. She looks like she stepped out of a catalog.

"Aunt Krys?" My voice sounds thin, stupid.

She's pale, her mouth tight and eyes watery as she nods. "Hi, Lexi-bug."

I burst into tears.

"Wake up."

Something pokes me in the face. I groan and push at it, grabbing a skinny finger. My eyes open, blinking against the corridor light shining into my otherwise darkened room.

A familiar face looms over mine.

"What time is it?" I ask.

"Time for you to get a Altoid or somethin'," Ivy replies. "Girl, whadafuck died in your mouth?"

I laugh. "You don't like my breath, get your face out of it," I tell her. "What are you doing up? It's late."

"Somethin's goin' on. The nurses ain't watching the station. Let's go."

Suddenly, I'm wide awake, throwing back the covers. They took my IV out earlier, so I'm not connected to anything anymore. I'm not 100 percent, but I'm better than I was, and I'm ready to get the fuck out of this place.

Yesterday, when one of the nurses opened the cabinet in my room, I spotted the clothes I was wearing when they brought me in. I go get them and pull them on. They smell like the motel and French fries. Ivy's dressed too.

"Where we goin'?" I whisper.

She shrugs. "Anywhere we want."

"What about your parents?"

She watches me pull on my sneakers. "I can't go back to them. They don't want my fuckin' broke ass. Like any of us can go back to how things were."

"Mitch will take us back," I tell her.

She gives me side-eye. "He's hiding from the po-po. He don't want us neither."

He will want us, eventually. She knows it as much as I do. Mitch will always want us.

We peek out the door of my room. The corridor is bright with a slightly greenish light, but Ivy is right—it's practically empty. Whatever's going on has the nurses busy.

All we need to do is make it to the elevator.

"C'mon," Ivy says, grabbing my hand. We run down the hall. Pain sparks when I put weight on my ankle. The elevator is right there—so close but so far. I run faster, ignoring the pain. Sweating.

Ivy hits the button when we get there. Nothing happens.

"Shit," I whisper. We have to wait for a car to reach our floor. Beside me, Ivy's twitchy.

"You okay?" I ask.

"I need to get the fuck out of here," she replies, scratching at her arm.

She needs a hit, but there's no point saying what we both know. I look down the hall as I chew on the side of my thumb. A woman walks out of the waiting room, rubbing her face.

She turns her head and our gazes meet.

"Aunt Krys?" My voice is a squeak. Has she been sleeping here?

Has she . . . been waiting here for me?

Her face is white. Her mouth opens, and there's a loud dinging noise. The elevator door opens.

Ivy tugs on my arm. "Come on."

I can run. I can leave this place and not look back. I can go back to Mitch and the life, to my pills. I won't have to worry about letting anyone down, and I'll be with people who love me.

"Poppy?"

I turn my head. Ivy's in the elevator, leaning against the door. She's impatient, wants to get out of there. I do too, but Krys is watching. She hasn't moved—like she's not sure what to do.

I know how she feels.

I also know there's only one reason she'd be sleeping in a hospital—me.

"Poppy, come on."

I glance at Ivy. She used to be someone else. She was the one who tried to hold on to that old self. I'd been the one to tell her to let it go, and now . . .

"That's not my name," I whisper. I take a step backward. If I don't move back, I'll move forward. As much as I want to, my body refuses to get on that elevator.

"Whatever," she replies. I can't tell if she's mad or sad. Maybe she doesn't feel anything—we're all pretty good at that. She waves at me as the elevator doors slide closed. I stand there like a stupid idiot, watching the numbers blink on the screen above.

"Lex?"

I turn. Krys is behind me. I didn't hear her approach. I'm taller than her, I realize. She used to seem so tall when I was a kid. Larger than life.

"Are you okay, sweetie?" she asks.

I nod, shuffling toward her. "I want to go back to bed," I tell her. What I really want is a hug. I want her to promise me everything is going to be okay, and I want to believe her. I want someone to tell me what to do. I want someone to fix me. Or maybe I want to go to sleep and not wake up. I don't know. I just know I can't stay like this.

We go back to my room, and I take off my sneakers before crawling back into bed.

"I'll have to bring you some pajamas," my aunt comments as she tucks the blankets around me.

"Why are you here?" I ask her.

She smiles—it's a pretty, gentle thing. I haven't seen anything like it in a long time. "For you, kiddo. For you." Her smile fades a little. "The girl who left. What's her name?"

She's going to rat her out. "Ivy," I say.

My aunt's head tilts to one side. "Her real name."

Maybe she understands more than I think. I close my eyes, because that makes it easier to betray my friend. Easier to remember things I am supposed to have forgotten.

"Jaime," I say.

"Go to sleep," she tells me. Warm fingers close over my cold ones. "I'll be here when you wake up."

I don't believe her. I keep my eyes closed and wait for her to let go.

When the nurse comes in to check on me in the morning, Krys is asleep in a chair by my bed. She kept her promise.

Part of me hates her for it, because that's going to make it worse when I disappoint her.

chapter two

I should have run when I had the chance.

I don't want to go to this "recovery house" that Krys and Detective Willis are so horny for. Who wants to hang around with a bunch of messed-up bitches? I just got done doing that—I don't want to do it again without my pills.

Krys comes to drive me there. She's been hanging around the hospital a lot. I don't know if she spent the night again, because I haven't left my room. Not since Ivy ran.

When Detective Willis comes by, I ask her about Ivy.

"I haven't seen or heard anything about her," she tells me. "If I find her, I'll let her know you're concerned."

I shrug. Like concern ever matters for much. As far as Ivy is concerned, I bailed on her. That's not easily forgiven. "You know this place they're sending me to?" I ask as I toss a T-shirt into my backpack. I'm wearing leggings and an oversize sweater that's soft and warm. Krys brought them for me.

She nods. "It's a good place. If you follow the program and stay out of trouble, you won't be there long."

"What kind of trouble you think I'm gonna get into?"

She gives me a look that says she knows me better than I do. I could get in a whole lot of trouble for punching a cop, so I don't.

"I brought you something." She hands me a gift bag.

The last time someone brought me a gift in a bag that pretty, I ended up giving a blowjob in return. I stare at it.

"No strings," Detective Willis assures me. "It's only a gift."

I take the bag. Inside, wrapped in tissue paper, is a plaque—the kind you hang on the wall. The background is light turquoise and written across in big black letters is: YOU SURVIVED THE ABUSE. YOU WILL SURVIVE THE RECOVERY.

My throat is tight when I look at her.

She smiles. "In case you need a reminder." She hands me a card. "This is my cell number. If you need anything—even if it's just to talk, you call me. Okay?"

I'm an ass for wanting to hit her. "Thanks, Detective."

"Marianne. Would it be okay if I gave you a hug?"

I nod. It's not a long hug, or even that tight of one, but . . . it's nice.

Krys arrives a few seconds later, right as Marianne is leaving. "All set?" she asks me.

"Almost." My aunt picks up the plastic bag of dirty clothes that sits outside my closet. "I'll wash this stuff for you at home. I hope it's okay, I picked up a few things for you. They're in the car. When you come home, we can go shopping and you can pick out your own clothes."

Home. Yeah, okay.

"Have you talked to Mom?" I ask.

"I left a message. A couple of them."

"Yeah, she hardly ever answers her phone. Does she know where I'm going?"

Krys shakes her head. "No, and you shouldn't tell her, okay? They don't want anyone to know where you are."

I nod. "In case she tells Mitch."

"I would hope that if he contacted her, she'd call the police, not tell him where to find you."

"He buys her booze," I say, and she nods. We both know what that means where my mother's loyalty is concerned.

"Let's go. The sooner we get you settled in, the sooner you can come home."

She keeps talking about "home." Like everything is going to be magically okay once I come live with her and her husband. But how long will it be before he starts telling me I'm pretty, expecting me to suck his dick? 'Cause I haven't met a man yet who doesn't go the same way once he finds out what I am.

Krys hands me a winter coat, one of those light puffy ones. "It should fit," she says. "It's one of mine. I hope that's okay."

The last winter coat I had came from Goodwill and smelled like an old woman. "It's cool. Thanks."

"Goodbye, sweetheart," the nurse at the desk says. The one who put cream on my arms. "You have a good life, y'hear?"

I smile at her and lift my hand in a wave. "Bye."

Krys thanks her and the other nurses for everything they've done, and then we're in the elevator, sinking.

It's cold out. The street, the sky, even the trees, are gray. The air is thick and heavy.

"We're supposed to get a storm tonight," Krys says as she puts my laundry in the trunk. "I got you some slippers and a fuzzy robe so you'll be warm."

"Thanks." I climb into the car. It's nice and clean. New, and it doesn't smell like cigarettes. I glance in the back seat. No beer cans or wine bottles either.

"How do you feel about this?" she asks. "Are you scared?"

I shrug.

"I would be," she goes on. "I don't know how you've been so strong through all of this. I'd be a wreck."

I look at her as she drives. "Once you lose control, it's easier to let other people take it."

Her knuckles turn white as she grips the steering wheel. "I don't want to control you, Lex."

"Not you," I say. "Other people. Like the doctors and the cops."

"And Mitch?"

"Don't talk about him." Mitch was there for me when no one else was. He took care of me. He sold me. Beat me. Told me I was beautiful and said I was an ugly bitch. He said he loved me.

Nobody else has ever said they love me.

"I'm sorry."

I shake my head. "I don't want to think about him, okay? Ain't your fault."

"Isn't," she corrects me.

I smile. "Yeah, okay." Is it weird that I like that she cares how I talk?

I haven't been outside in months, so I stare out the window as we drive. "Where are we?" I ask.

"West Hartford. The place we're going to is in Middle-

town, not far from where Jamal and I live. We got lucky—
they had a bed open up."

"How long before I can go out?"

"You can come home with me next weekend if you want.
We'll start with day visits and then overnights. It's whatever
you want."

Yeah, right. If it's what I want, she'd drop me off at a
bus stop.

"I'm new at this," Krys says. "I'm going to need you to
help me."

I look at her. "Help you what?"

"Be what you need."

"I don't know what that is."

She smiles, but somehow manages to still look sad. "I
guess we'll figure it out together, then."

I don't want to feel this hope in my chest. I want to shrug
and turn away from her, so she won't know she has power
over me. I don't want to trust her.

"Okay," I say. Fucking traitor.

Middletown isn't a city like Hartford. It's a town, and not
a really big one. It has Wesleyan University, though, which
is supposed to be, like, a top-shit school. The main street
is lined with shops and restaurants that look newer the farther south we drive.

"Is that a Thai place?" I ask, turning my head. "I like
Thai."

"There's just about whatever you might want," my aunt
replies. "Thai, Vietnamese, Japanese, Indian, Mexican,
Chinese, Italian. We can go to some of them if you want.
And I can always bring you takeout."

"You'd do that?"

She shoots me a glance, frowning. "Kid, I'd do that and so much more if I thought it would help you."

I swallow. Is she for real? "Thanks."

Sparrow Brook. That's the name of the place where I'm going. It doesn't have a sign out front or anything, but Krys has a pamphlet stuck in one of the cup holders and I recognize it from the photo.

It's an old hotel or something—red brick with white trim—not far from the river and down the street from a large mental hospital. That's where I would have gone if I hadn't had Krys. If she hadn't wanted me. If I'd been trouble. It's where I heard they were taking Daisy.

When we pull into the parking lot, there's a group of girls out by the stables, feeding horses. I can't see them that well, but they're different sizes and colors—the girls, not the horses.

Some of them are smiling, some of them aren't. It's easy to pick out which ones have been out of the life the least amount of time.

They're the ones I want to stand next to. The ones I know won't try to make conversation or be friends.

We're met by a woman named Song, who smiles at me and takes me up a wide staircase to my room. It's nicer than the room I had at the motel. There are windows on two of the walls that let early spring sunshine into the room. The curtains are light and airy, the walls painted cream. The bed I'm given is a twin, but it's a four-poster and the sheets and comforter are new.

Clean sheets.

I have a dresser and a small closet to myself. Krys begins

putting stuff away. My roommate comes in while she helps me unpack.

"Hey," she says. "I'm Sarah."

I nod. "P—Lex." Not Poppy. Not anymore. Not out loud. I size the other girl up and she does the same to me.

She gives me a binder that has my name on it. "It's got a schedule and calendar in it," she tells me. "Plus pages for you to journal or make notes, draw—whatever. It's part of therapy."

"Yay," I say, without any real enthusiasm.

She dares to smile at me. "Yeah, that's what I said when I got mine too."

I bristle at her tone. She doesn't know me. I don't want her talking to me like she understands or she knows what I've been through. She doesn't know shit. But I don't tell her that. Something keeps me quiet.

Sarah and Jill show me where the bathrooms are. There are three for the twelve girls that are living here at the moment. They also show me where the laundry is, the linen closet, kitchen, common area—the whole tour. After, we move outside. It's a damp, cold day. The sky is gray, and the air smells of snow and horse manure. I'm taken through the stables while the horses and other girls watch me. Song reappears in time to introduce me. I don't remember all their names. I don't want to.

I don't plan on being there long enough to get to know them.

I spend the rest of the day meeting the staff and being treated like an idiot. Everyone talking to me *sloooowly* and LOUDLY in case I don't understand. Like I'm a kid. That night, there's a group meeting that's like a twelve-step thing for those of us who are addicts.

It makes me wish I were stoned. Food's good, though. And they give us a lot of it, but this place isn't for me. I'm not into "higher powers," and I don't need to fix my problems by falling in love with a horse, which is kinda creepy if you ask me. Even if they are pretty.

There's a girl who stares at me all through the meeting. I've decided to punch her in the mouth if she keeps it up. I may be the new girl, but I'm not anyone's bitch.

She comes up to me afterward. I didn't speak throughout the entire thing. No one asked me to, which surprised me a bit, but maybe they like to listen to themselves talk.

"I know what you're thinking," she says.

I turn my shoulder to her. "You think?"

"You're thinking how stupid this is, and that you don't need it. You probably hate horses and have already made your escape plan."

I glare at her for being so spot-on. "You don't know anything about me."

She laughs. "Sure I do. You're here. That means someone took you from your home, put you on your back, and let people rape you for money while they kept you as numb as possible. Am I wrong?"

I clench my jaw, try to stare her down, but I'm the one who looks away first.

"Look, you don't have to play tough here. No one's looking to hurt you, so try to check the attitude and show the women who run this place some respect."

"Or what?" I challenge.

She shrugs. "Or you piss away the chance you've been given. You know how many of us never even make it this far?"

"No, and I don't care."

"Not yet," she says. "You will, and that's when it gets hard. Right now, it's easy."

I give a rough laugh. "Yeah, cause this is so fucking easy."

She tilts her head. "Would you rather be back with your pimp?"

"No." I say it before I can stop myself. I kick myself for giving anything away.

"Good. Maybe you'll be one of the ones who make it." She turns and walks away before I can reply. She walks with a limp—a heavy one.

Sarah comes up beside me. "That's Lonnie," she says. "She's been here longer than I have."

"What's up with her leg?" I ask.

Sarah glances at me. "Her pimp hit her with his car and left her for dead."

I look at her in surprise, then turn my gaze again to Lonnie, who's talking to one of the other girls. As if she feels the weight of it, she lifts her head and returns my stare. The scars on my back itch and pull.

Maybe she knows something about me after all.

I go to bed with every intention of sneaking out before dawn. No idea where I'm going to go, or what I'm going to do, but I can't stay here. This place freaks me out. Too many people getting in my head.

"Do you like to read?" Sarah asks. She's sitting on her bed in her pajamas and a pair of fuzzy socks. Her long, dark hair is back in a braid. She looks young until I look in her eyes.

"Yeah," I say. I used to read a lot.

She opens the door of her bedside table, revealing a

small stack of books. "Take one if you want. We're allowed to read before bed."

I hesitate. But the temptation is too strong. Not like a book is a magical thing that can make me stay if I don't want to.

Slowly, I ease off my bed and cross the distance to her side of the room. I crouch down and look inside the cabinet. There, second from the top of the pile, is the latest book in a series by one of my favorite authors. It came out while I was at the motel.

I hate the excitement that rises in my chest, but I take the book anyway. "Is it okay if I borrow this one?"

"Sure," Sarah says with a smile. "I've read that one already. It's awesome. Have you read the series?"

I nod. Clutching the book to my chest, I retreat to my bed.

I read for half an hour before we're told to turn out our lights. I haven't gone to bed this early in months, but I press the switch on my lamp and settle into the pillows.

There's a tiny night-light in the opposite corner of the room. It's not enough to keep me awake, but it's enough to break up the darkness. I like it. *It will make my escape easier,* I think as I close my eyes—just for a minute.

I don't escape that night.

The bed is too comfortable and warm. The sheets smell too clean. Outside, it's windy and cold. I fall into a deep sleep that turns into a nightmare. Mitch is there, and my mother. They're arguing over who gets to have me, but they don't want to love me. They want to chop me up and eat me.

"No!" I jackknife up into a sitting position on the bed. I'm panting and sweating. Sarah is there beside me.

"You're safe," she says, catching my hand in hers. "Lex, you're safe."

I gasp for breath, my gaze focusing in the gloom. I look up into her concerned face and relax.

"Sorry," I say, pulling my hand free.

"We all have them," she says, letting me go. "Eventually, they'll start to happen less and less."

"If you say so." And then, because I'm uncomfortable, "You can go back to bed."

"Here." She gets off my bed and goes back to her own, only to return a couple of seconds later. She presses something warm and fuzzy into my hands. It takes me a minute to realize it's a stuffed cat.

"It seems ridiculous, I know," she says, "but you'll sleep better with it. Trust me."

I'm doubtful, but I don't give it back. "Okay."

Sarah smiles. "Go back to sleep. I'll be here if you wake up again."

The idea of her hovering over me should be enough to keep me awake, but it isn't. Clutching the plush cat, I fall back to sleep almost instantly, and I don't wake up until Sarah's alarm goes off at seven.

"C'mon," she says, shaking me. "The others won't be up for half an hour. We can grab the showers."

"Fug off," I tell her, snuggling deeper into the cocoon I've made.

"Bro, you will be so pissed when there's no hot water left for you."

No hot water? Hell, one time at the hotel we didn't have water at all for a week. My ass was nasty.

"Lex," she tries again. "They've got body scrubs and lotions and professional shampoo. Face masks too."

What the hell is this place? "They got pumice stones?" I ask, peering up at her with one open eye.

She nods enthusiastically.

I throw back the covers. It's been too long since my ugly-ass feet got some attention. My toenails need clipping and my heels are cracking, they're so dry.

I grab towels and clothes from my closet and follow Sarah from the room. Someone else had the same idea and is using the bathroom at the far end of the hall. Sarah gestures for me to use the one closest to our room, and she hurries to the one in the middle.

She wasn't lying. Oh my God—the stuff in this bathroom! There's a basket of masks on the counter, the kind that have three or four applications in them. I pick a moisturizing and toning one. There's a note that says to check under the sink for shampoos and body lotions. I can't believe it when I open the cabinet.

"Jesus," I whisper. There are tons of small bottles of high-end stuff. I grab shampoo, conditioner, body wash, and a pumice sponge wrapped in plastic, and stand with my hands full. That's when I see the baskets on the stand above the toilet. They have names on them—mine is empty—but the others are full of different items.

I start the shower and clip my toenails with clippers I find in a small bottle of disinfectant. After getting clean, I wrap my hair in a towel, dry off, and dress, putting all the items I used, including a new razor, in my basket and setting it on the shelf. I put my towels in the laundry and return to our room. Sarah is already there, making her bed. She takes one look at me in my leggings and sweater and smiles. "You look like your aunt."

I glance down at my clothes. "Yeah, not really my style, but they're comfortable."

"Make your bed and you can come with me to help feed the horses."

Do I look like someone who wants to feed horses? I must, because I make my bed as fast and neat as I can and follow after her.

Downstairs, breakfast is cooking. My stomach growls at the smell of bacon and coffee as I pull on my coat and boots. I tug a cap over my damp hair and step out into the cold. There is a fine layer of snow on the ground, and our footsteps seem to echo in the quiet, the crunch of gravel sounding like a roar.

The stables aren't far from the house. A couple of women are working there, carrying bales of hay and shoveling manure. One of them looks up as we approach. Her eyes are bright and her cheeks pink. She looks older than my mother.

"Good morning, Sarah!" she says. "And you must be Alexa."

I hesitate. "How do you know my name?"

The woman smiles. "I'm Bev, dear. I help run this place. I'm supposed to know your name. You two are just in time to help feed the beasties, though I'm sure you know that."

The last time I met a person whose eyes twinkled so much, he was done up on cocaine. Bev doesn't seem high though. Just . . . happy.

She leads Sarah and me into the barn. It's darker in there, the air slightly damp with horse breath, and smelling of shit. Horse crap doesn't smell as bad as I thought it would. It's almost sweet.

Sarah names the horses off to me, but I'm not listening. My gaze is locked on a huge, black monster at the far end of the stalls.

"What is that?" I ask, pointing.

Bev laughs. "That's Joe, our Percheron."

"Percheron," I repeat. "Are they all that big?"

"That big and bigger," she replies. "Would you like to meet him?"

I shake my head.

"He's a big baby," Sarah tells me. "Come on, you can give him a carrot."

Hesitantly, I approach the giant horse. As we get closer, I notice the white blaze running down his nose and the shaggy fur—hair?—hanging over his forehead. His eyes are huge and dark when he looks at me.

"Here." Sarah puts a chunk of the biggest carrot I've ever seen in my gloved hand. "Open your hand and offer it to him on your palm. That's it. Open your fingers a little more. Now give it to him."

I hold my breath. Joe's giant head comes farther out of his stall. He snorts lightly, and the carrot is gone.

I stare at my empty palm. I didn't even feel him take it.

"See?" Sarah says, grinning. "A baby." She runs her bare hand along the horse's jaw. "You can pet him. He likes it."

I take off my glove and carefully set my hand on the side of Joe's face. He's soft, but not like a cat or dog. Solid muscle is right below the surface, and it moves and flexes as he chews the carrot. He turns toward me, sniffs my coat. Tastes it.

I laugh. The sound startles me.

Sarah offers Joe some oats and gives me a sympathetic look. "Pretty great, huh?"

I nod. I'm embarrassed, but that doesn't stop me from taking a handful of oats from the bucket and feeding them to Joe when she's done. This time, when he nuzzles me, I get closer. He rubs his muzzle against the side of my face. I smile.

Sarah shows me some of the other horses—all rescues or donations—but I go back to Joe before we have to return to the house for breakfast. Inside, we wash our hands in the small bathroom by the kitchen and join the others in the dining room. Breakfast is set up buffet style. We get to take what we want, and there's so much to choose from!

So far, I'm enjoying rehab.

I load my plate with scrambled eggs, bacon, and toast. I even take an orange. The only place at the long table left open is next to Lonnie and another girl whose name I don't remember. I sit down. Lonnie smiles at me.

"Been to the barn?" she asks.

I nod. "Sarah took me to meet the horses."

"Which is your favorite?"

"Joe."

She looks surprised. "Yeah? A lot of girls find him scary when they first come here."

"He didn't scare me." It's not really a lie. He didn't scare me for long.

"No. I'm not surprised." She smiles. "I don't think you're scared of much."

"What's there to be scared of now?" I ask her.

"A lot," she replies, her smile gone, and goes back to eating her eggs.

After breakfast, we're funneled into the living room to watch a documentary on human trafficking. The girls I saw with the horses when I first arrived are sitting together. They look bored and defiant. I take a step.

"Sit with me," Lonnie says.

I glance from her to the girls. I really want to be with them, the ones who look like they might explode at any second. But Lonnie just watches me with a faint smile, and the next thing I know, I'm sitting in the chair next to her.

The documentary is about girls who were trafficked, and the case their mothers are building against Stall 313—the website they were trafficked on. Stall 313 is where Mitch posted his girls. Us. Me.

I squirm in my seat. I can't get comfortable. This shit on the TV isn't helping. Mothers crying, dead-eyed girls talking about what happened to them, lawyers promising justice.

Ain't nobody promising justice for me, or for the girls sitting around me.

"Fry their asses," says a girl close to me. "Make them motherfuckers pay."

"Shut up," says another. "You know they ain't gonna pay shit. Bunch of old white guys are gonna buy their way out."

The people behind Stall 313 are three middle-aged white guys. You only have to take one look at them to see they're assholes. I want them to pay for what they've done, but I know they probably won't.

There's a woman on the screen, talking about her daughter, Shendea, who was sold on Stall 313, beaten, and left for dead in a motel room. She's crying. I can't imagine my mother getting sober long enough to cry over me. I don't want to listen to the list of things the johns did to her girl.

"They raped her, vaginally and anally. They beat her. They burned her. They whipped her with belts . . ."

If I could reach the TV, I'd put my foot through it to shut it the fuck up. Lonnie puts her hand on my left leg to stop it from twitching. She doesn't look at me.

The film cuts to a girl about my age. She's got scars on her face, on her arms and back and legs. Everyone in this room knows she's got scars in other places too, places the documentary can't show. She takes out her false teeth, showing how many the men who bought her knocked out. I run my tongue along my own teeth, thankful I still have them all.

On the other side of the room, the girls I belong with are agitated, saying shit. I could have been one of them, but instead, I'm watching them, and I see them. I see them like Lonnie sees them. They're scared little girls who don't want to deal. They don't want to see themselves in the girl on the screen.

I can't stop seeing myself.

"My pimp named us after flowers," says a new girl on screen. She's kind of hard looking, black eyeliner all the way around her eyes. Her hair is bleached blond. On the screen they call her "TS," but I know her as Iris.

"He was friends with a guy my stepfather knew. Started coming around the house, telling me how pretty I was. He bought me gifts—things my parents couldn't afford. Mom told him to step off, but it was too late. I loved him. He said he loved me too."

They ask her about the first time she was forced to have sex with a stranger. "He told me he owed this guy money, that he was going to get hurt—maybe killed—if he didn't pay the guy back somehow. He said he hated asking me to do it, but the guy thought I was pretty. Did I love him enough to save his life?" She smiles sadly. "I did."

I'm cold. Something prickly is crawling up the back of my neck, digging its claws into the base of my skull. My vision narrows so all I can see is Iris's face. Her words ring in my ears, bitterly familiar.

"Afterward," she says, "he put me to work with the other girls, but he always told me I was his favorite. I believed him. I still believed him when he tried to kill me, when he let two other girls be killed. Peony and Tulip."

I see their faces in my mind before their photos appear on the screen. They disappeared shortly after I arrived. This couldn't have been filmed too long ago. Mitch told us they'd left. That Iris had left.

I'm going to puke. I start to stand, but Lonnie grabs my hand.

"I can't," I whisper. Some of the other girls are watching me, but I don't care.

"You can," she says, squeezing my fingers.

I pull hard against her grip. "Let me go." I'm going to run. If I make it out that fucking door, I'm going to run as far as I can and I'm not coming back. Fuck this. Fuck her. Fuck it all.

"This is how you survive. You sit the fuck down and give them the respect they deserve, and you make a promise to yourself that they didn't die for nothing. You get mad, and you keep going. That's how girls like us get even, how we say fuck you to the people who did this to us. We live." She nudges me with her injured leg as she says this.

I sit. Every nerve in my body is on fire, twitching and thrashing. I swallow and taste vomit in the back of my throat. My stomach lurches. If I puke, I'm going to do it all over Lonnie, I swear.

Slowly, it begins to fade. On the screen, Iris is talking about how some organization that fights trafficking helped save her, took her in, and gave her purpose. I focus on her, on her face and her voice. I see her looking strong and healthy, going to school, and getting her diploma.

She looks so normal.

"I'm going to have that," Lonnie murmurs. She looks at me. "*You're* going to have that. Promise me."

I nod. Lonnie looks away, and so do I.

chapter three

I've never lived in a house, and I've never had what I would consider a home—not since I was a little kid and we lived with my grandparents. But I don't remember that part of my life very well. I remember some of the apartments that came later. Some of them my mom and I lived in alone, others we shared with her friends, or people she'd managed to con into letting us crash with them. When she had a boyfriend, we usually had a place to stay. Sometimes I even had my own room, but usually I slept on a couch.

I can't remember the last time I had any privacy.

"I hope you like your room," Krys says when she picks me up Saturday for my first visit to her house. After two weeks in the program, they decided I could have a day out. "It's pretty plain, but you can decorate it however you like."

"Does it have a door I can lock?" I ask, climbing into the car.

"Well, yeah," she replies. "Of course."

"Then I'll like it."

She winces. I don't mean to make things hard for her. I don't know how to say things so they won't affect her, and it's not like I can pretend nothing bad has ever happened to me. She already knows I had crabs and gonorrhea. The hospital told her before they told me. Luckily HPV and HIV were both negative.

Would she still have wanted me if I had AIDS?

She turns to me after pressing the button to start the car. "I can't imagine what you've been through, but I want to understand you, okay? I want to help you get through this. If you want to talk, I'm here. If you don't . . . well, I'm still here. Always."

My aunt hasn't asked me a lot of questions, but I know she met with Detective Willis and Jill. I assume they filled her in on my story. What they know of it, anyway.

"Okay," I agree. I'm not about to start telling her everything though. She might still change her mind. Who the hell wants to take in a seventeen-year-old who's been passed around and discarded like loose change? God, I could really use a little something right now.

Being clean is hard. I don't miss the drugs, really. I like being able to focus, but I miss being numb. Feeling shit is overrated. Feeling shit means it has to go somewhere— get out—and everyone at Sparrow Brook has sharp fucking eyes that'll notice new cuts, fresh marks, or missing hair. Even if you think you're being smart, Dr. Lisa always seems to notice. Yesterday, she noticed me rubbing a spot on my leg.

"Lex," she said. "Have you been self-harming?"

It's no good to lie. Bitch has some kind of superpowers when it comes to that shit. She doesn't like being called "bitch" or "bro" either. I have to remember that.

"It's just a scratch," I told her.

She looked at me a second, got up from her desk, went to a cupboard, and took out a small laptop. She handed it to me. "How about you try writing your feelings down on this rather than on your skin?" she suggested.

I grabbed the laptop like it was gold, or E. I could check my email, my Facebook accounts, my Twitter, my Instagram . . .

"It doesn't leave the house. Wi-Fi is available only at certain times, and social media sites are blocked."

I slumped. So much for having any kind of contact with the outside world.

"We can't take the risk of anyone finding you who might hurt you, Lex." Her expression said she was sorry. I got it, but I didn't like it.

So now, I'm writing stuff down when I feel like tearing into myself. I haven't made myself bleed once today. I don't share this with Aunt Krys, but Dr. Lisa will be happy when she sees me next week.

"Do you like shopping?" my aunt asks. "I thought maybe we'd get you some new clothes, stuff you can pick out for yourself. We don't have to worry about school for a few months yet."

School. Right. I agreed to summer school to catch me up to where I should be, and then I'll complete my senior year at Middletown High School. "A fresh start," Jill called it. A place where no one knows me or my story.

"Sure," I say. I do like to shop. I like clothes and nice things; that was how Mitch sucked me in. "Why are you doing all this? And don't say it's because you love me. You don't know me."

She looks surprised—and hurt. I refuse to feel bad. "You're right. I don't know you, but I don't have to know you to love you. We're family. I should have taken you when you asked me to. I've always regretted that."

I frown at her. "What do you mean?"

She glances at me. "You don't remember?"

I shake my head.

Her attention on the road, she says, "When you were seven, you asked if you could come live with me. I was barely twenty-one and enjoying life away from my parents. But I should have taken you."

I shrug. I still don't remember. "Mom wouldn't have let you."

She sends me a dubious glance. Yeah, okay, so maybe Mom would have helped me pack. "I'm sorry I didn't listen to you then."

I am too, but I don't say it. It's not her fault there's a part of me locked in a room that can't get out. I feel her in there, pounding on the door, but I can't be bothered to help her. It's like I'm sitting on a couch in my head, listening to that part of me screaming, but I'm too stoned to get up and open the damn door.

I stare out the window as we drive through Middletown. It's a nice town for the most part. Cute downtown. No mall, but lots of neat-looking restaurants and shops. Krys tells me the school where Jamal is a professor has all kinds of famous alumni. I try to look impressed, but it really doesn't have anything to do with me.

A few minutes later, we're in a fairly nice neighborhood— better than anything I've ever lived in before. I think maybe we're only driving through, but my aunt pulls into the driveway of a big gray and dark blue house with a veranda.

I stare at it. "This is your house?"

She looks almost embarrassed. "Jamal's parents gave us the down payment as a wedding present."

"Are they rich?"

"They do okay."

"Okay"? Obviously she and I have different ideas of what that word means.

Inside the house is even nicer. The kitchen is huge and the living room has a TV bigger than I've ever seen before. The sofas and chairs look comfortable and soft. We walk up a polished staircase, and she takes me down the hall to the last room.

"This is yours," she says, and opens the door.

There's a hard thump against the back of my ribs when I look inside. She's right. It's kind of bland. The walls are off-white, the floor polished wood, but there are large windows and a desk with a computer. The bed is a big four-poster that could probably fit three people, and there's a huge closet.

"Your bathroom is through the second door." My aunt points across the room.

My own bathroom? I don't have to share it with anyone? What's the cost of having all this luxury? What are they going to want from me? What happens if I don't give it? I can't . . . I just can't.

Krys frowns. "Lex?"

I try to breathe and I can't. It's like the air gets to the back of my throat and won't go any farther.

She grabs my shoulders and steers me to the bed. I'm plunked down onto the mattress, my head pushed between my knees. I suck in air as blackness crowds the edges of my brain. Who the hell panics over a fucking bedroom?

Me, apparently.

Once my breaths come steadily, I lift my head. Krys strokes my back with long, firm strokes. I don't pull away. "I'm sorry," I say.

"You've got nothing to be sorry for."

I've heard that a lot lately. Still not sure I believe it.

"It's bigger than the last apartment Mom and I had," I confess.

Krys nods. "It's a little overwhelming, I know. I thought maybe you were freaked out at the prospect of decorating." She smiles when she says it.

I look around at all the white. "It could use some color," I allow. But that's all I'm going to say. *Don't get attached,* inner me says. *This isn't going to last.*

"I want you to feel at home here," my aunt says, as if she can read my mind. She gives my shoulders a squeeze then releases them. "You're part of the family."

I want to believe that so much.

"I'm starving," she says. "I have Chinese leftovers in the fridge. You want?"

I follow her back downstairs to the kitchen and watch as she gets cartons out of the big, shiny fridge. I sit on one of the stools at the island.

"So, we'll need to get you a phone too. The computer upstairs should do—Jamal just bought it. We can get you a TV if you want."

"You don't have to spend all this money on me."

She straightens and looks me right in the eye. "You think we want something in return; is that it?" She smiles sadly and shakes her head. "Kid, I've had three miscarriages.

I don't know if I'll ever have a child of my own. Sometimes I think I don't deserve one. Then I find you again. I'm not a big believer in God, Lex, but I think you and I were brought back together because we need each other. I know it's not going to be easy, and we're probably going to have fights and we're not always going to agree, but anything I do for you is because I *want* to do it. Okay? I want to buy you clothes and give you a room. I want to give you the life you ought to have had. Will you let me try?"

I look at the door. If I'm going to bolt, this is the moment to do it. Get the fuck out of here and away from this crazy-ass bitch who doesn't even realize what she's asking of me. I've been beaten by men who didn't scare me half as much as my aunt does. What if she discovers I'm not worth it? What happens when she finds out I'm unlovable? Or that I can't love her the way she wants?

Yeah, I should bolt. My thighs twitch, my legs ready to jump up and starting running.

I stay where I am.

Krys and I go shopping in West Hartford. I get a few clothes and some things for my new room.

There's a comforter and sheet set on one of the display beds that's so pretty, I can't stop touching it. It looks antique in shades of ivory, rose, and tea—like something a Victorian lady might have had.

"Do you like that one?" my aunt asks.

I shake my head. It's so girlie I shouldn't like it, but I do. I really do. I open my mouth to tell her that, but what comes out is, "Yeah."

She smiles at me. "It's beautiful. Let's see if they have

it in a queen." We wander over to the bins on the wall that hold each style, and Krys quickly finds the one I like. "They have it! Want to get it?"

"No," I whisper hoarsely, even though every inch of me is screaming yes inside.

"What's wrong?" she asks with a frown. "Are you okay?"

"Please. Just . . . don't." Dread bubbles in my stomach, chilling my bones. If she buys that set for me, I know something terrible will happen. I'll die without ever sleeping on it. I don't deserve something that beautiful.

"Okay." She doesn't ask why, just links her arm through mine and starts walking. "Let's go get some dinner. Jamal's going to join us before I have to take you back."

It's easier to breathe when we leave the store.

"Maybe next weekend we can get pampered," Krys suggests. "Have you ever had a facial?"

I shake my head. "Not a real one. At the motel, sometimes we'd do masks and paint one another's toes."

She smiles, but it looks shaky. "Do you miss the other girls?"

I shrug. "Not really. I miss Ivy. Do you know where she is?" Has she forgiven me for wussing out on her?

"No, but we can ask Detective Willis if you want."

"Thanks."

We meet my uncle Jamal at P.F. Chang's. He's tall—over six feet—with a buzz cut and stubble on his face. He's good looking, and his face lights up when he sees Krys. I bet my mother had a shit hemorrhage when she found out her little sister married a Black guy. Mom has no problem dating a guy who'd fuck her own daughter, but she draws the line at anyone who's not white.

"It's good to finally meet you," he tells me after giving

Krys a kiss. He doesn't try to touch me, but he does pull out my chair before sitting down in his own.

"Did you ladies have a good day?" he asks, opening the menu.

"We did, I think," my aunt replies. "Why do you even bother to look? You always get the same thing."

Jamal laughs. Under the table his knee brushes mine. I tense, waiting for a hand to follow.

"Oh, I'm sorry," he says. "You don't have enough room." He moves his chair around the table, closer to Krys.

"He takes up a lot of space." Krys laughs. She trusts him—trusts that he won't screw around or betray her. Trusts that he won't touch the ho they're going to move into their house, because she's family.

Krys doesn't know men like I do. She doesn't know the nasty shit they're capable of. They think shoving their dick inside you means they own you. I wish I didn't know the things I do. I wish the thought of them didn't cause me to break out into a sweat and make me think about raking my fork down my forearm just to let out how fucking powerless I am.

I run the tines of my fork along the sensitive underside of my arm. The metal is cool and sharp against my skin. I shiver—only a little—but it's enough to catch Krys's attention. She smiles.

"Are you cold, Lex?"

I set down the fork and straighten up in my chair. "No. I'm good." I open the menu and start reading. Suddenly I'm starving.

A waiter comes to take our order. It's a stupid amount of food for three people, but neither Krys nor Jamal seems to notice.

"I'll be right back," my aunt says as she stands. My heart skips a beat as she walks away. *She's only going to the bathroom, psycho.*

I glance at Jamal, then at the bathroom door, then at Jamal.

"Is it because I'm Black, or because I'm a guy?" he asks casually.

I whip my head around to look at him. "What?"

"Do I make you nervous because I'm Black or because I'm a guy?"

"Bro, I don't care what color you are." We had the spectrum pretty much covered at the motel, and we were all the same there. Just goods and services.

He nods solemnly. "So, because I'm a guy. Okay. Listen, I don't know all the right things to do or say to make you feel comfortable, and you have no reason to believe anything I say, but let me give it a try. I love your aunt, and your aunt loves you. We both want you to come live with us, even though the idea of being a parental figure freaks me out. Sometimes I might say or do the wrong thing, and I'm going to need you to tell me when that happens. So, did I do something to make you uncomfortable other than the knee thing?"

He picked up on that? I shake my head. "I'm sorry I freak you out."

"It's not you," he says with a smile. "It's the responsibility of you. What if I do something or say something that scars you for life?"

I blink at him. "You really think you can compete with what's already happened?"

He starts to laugh but stops himself. I can't help but smile a little, and he smiles too. "Well put."

He seems like an okay guy, but I've been wrong before. Still, I'm willing to give him a chance because he and Krys are taking one on me. I'd have to be dense not to realize I'm not much of a catch in the daughter department. No one would pick someone like me unless they really meant it, or wanted to exploit me some more. I might not trust many people, but I'm pretty sure I can trust my aunt.

"Do you like horror movies?" Jamal asks.

I shrug. "I don't know."

He looks mortified. His dark eyes widen behind his glasses. "The first night you stay with us, we're watching something scary."

"Oh, God," Krys says as she rejoins us. "Maybe not the first night, Mal."

He looks disappointed. "Sounds fun," I hear myself say.

Jamal's face lights up. "I know just where to start—*Carrie*. Little scary, not much gore, and very satisfying. Lots of girl power."

I've heard of it, but I've never seen it.

Krys rolls her eyes at him and smiles at me. They're both so . . . normal. Sitting with them feels surreal. I don't know how to act or what to say. Luckily, neither of them have any trouble talking. They include me in as much of the conversation as they can. It's exhausting, all this talking. I'm glad when our food arrives so I can be quiet.

After we eat, someone calls Jamal's name as we're leaving the mall. We all turn. It's a woman with a cane walking beside a guy who's probably my age. He's really tall with dark hair and dark eyes. He's cute in a serious kind of way.

"Anna!" Jamal greets her with a kiss on the cheek. I look at the hand holding her cane—her knuckles are huge, the fingers twisted. I've never seen anything so deformed that wasn't broken. Do they hurt? Does she have painkillers in her purse, and is there a way for me to get to them if she does?

"Zack." Jamal shakes the guy's hand. I look up, right into his dark gaze. He's caught me staring at the woman. I should probably be embarrassed, but I'm not. I stare at him instead. He doesn't look away. He's not threatening, but . . . he's not going to back down.

"This our niece, Alexa," Jamal says to the woman. I have to look away now, or be rude. I can't afford to be rude. I turn to the woman, who smiles at me.

"Nice to meet you, Alexa," she says. "I'm Anna Bradley and this is my son, Zack."

We look at each other.

"Hey," he says.

"Hey," I repeat. This time he's the one who breaks the stare. He looks bored, like he'd rather be anywhere but here. Get in fucking line, buddy.

The adults talk for a minute before saying goodbye. I cast another glance at Zack, but he's not paying any attention to me; he's focused on his mother.

"Anna looks good," Krys says as we cross the parking lot. "I think Zack's even taller than the last time we saw him. You'll probably be in some classes with him, Lex."

I shrug. "Okay." I hope she doesn't hold her breath waiting for us to become friends.

We leave Jamal at his car—a silver SUV—and Krys and I return to hers.

"So," Krys begins after we've been driving for a bit. "What do you think? You want to take a chance on us?"

Is she trippin'? "You sure you wanna take a chance on *me*?"

She doesn't hesitate. "Yes."

"Okay, then." I glance out the window and back at her. "What if I said no? Would you let me go?"

Her hands tighten on the steering wheel, knuckles turning white. "I would have asked for another chance, gone home and cried a bit, and tried again, because no—I'm not giving up on you."

"You might not be able to fix me," I warn her.

"I don't want to fix you, sweetie. I want to give you the opportunity to have the life you deserve. You can fix yourself, if you think you need fixing."

My throat is tight. I swallow, but the lump won't go away. "Thank you." I say it because it's the right thing to say. Part of me even means it. But another part of me? That part wants to unbuckle my seat belt, open the door, and roll out into traffic. That part of me would prefer pain and death over this small shred of hope I'm hanging on to. Pain and death rarely let you down, but hope? Hope's a heartless bitch.

That night, I lie in bed and think about Mitch. I miss him, and I hate him. I'm scared that I don't know what I'll do if he shows up. What if he tries to take me back?

The police haven't caught him. They're looking for him, but Mitch is a snake—he knows how to hide. He's got a lot of places where he can lie low. I've been to a few.

The first time I met him was at a party. Mom's boyfriend, Frank, had people over. There was a lot of booze and pot and other stuff. I was in my room with my headphones on when he opened the door and walked in.

I took off my headphones and looked at him. He was tall and lean with longish dark hair and dark eyes. He was almost pretty, like Ashton Kutcher on *That '70s Show*, but older.

"Sorry," he said. "I thought this was the bathroom."

"It's not," I said.

He grinned and walked in anyway. "I'm Mitch."

"Lex."

"What's a pretty girl like you doing home on a Saturday night, Alexa?"

I frowned. I didn't like being called by my full name. A name he apparently already knew. Still, he thought I was pretty. "There's nothing going on."

He leaned against my dresser. "When I was your age, there was always something going on." He inclined his head toward the door. "Want to come out and join us?"

Party with a bunch of old people? I'd rather chew off my own toe. The guys always got grabby. "No, thanks."

He nodded. "Okay. Maybe next time. Nice talking to you, Alexa."

I wrinkled my nose as he left the room. He was hot, but that was it.

The next time he came over, he brought me new headphones—good ones. They were expensive. He grinned at me and said, "They're noise-cancelling."

I wasn't sure what to say. "Thanks."

My mother beamed. "That's a real nice gift, Mitch. Give him a hug, Lex."

I froze. Hug a guy I didn't know? She didn't think that was creepy?

"She doesn't have to do that," he said, and I smiled at

him. It wouldn't be the last smile he manipulated out of me, but it was the first, and the one I regretted the most.

I bolt upright in bed, a silent scream tearing from my throat. Gasping for air, I clutch at my neck but there aren't any hands there but mine. No one's trying to strangle me.

I'm in my bed at Sparrow Brook. Sarah is asleep a few feet away. Moonlight shines through the window, illuminating everything. My gaze darts around the room, searching . . .

Mitch isn't there.

My heart slams hard in my chest as I squeeze my eyes shut. I suck in air. In . . . out . . . in . . . out. The pounding slows.

When I open my eyes, Sarah is sitting in bed, hair standing up. She's in pajamas, like me. "You okay?" she asks.

I nod, wishing she'd at least pretended to still be asleep.

"Want to talk about it?"

I shake my head.

"I have nightmares too," she confides. "I was forced into the life by my stepbrother and some of his friends."

Is it wrong that all I can think is how glad I am that Krys and Jamal don't have a son my age?

"They got me all done up at a party—cocaine, E in my drink. Passed me around and took photos, then threatened to show my parents if I didn't do what they wanted. When that didn't work, they threatened to show my grandparents. That worked."

"Assholes," I say.

She smiles slightly. "Anyway, I keep having this one nightmare that I'm back in college and I have to write an exam, but when I get to the exam room, there's a bed in the middle of the room and a line of guys around it—professors, students, strangers . . . The exam is that I have to be fucked by all of them, and if I don't do it, they'll fail me, and my grandparents will not only find out I'm a ho, but all the money they gave me for school will be wasted."

"What do you do?"

She tilts her head. "You know what I do."

Once you've been hurt and survived, you'll almost always do it again to protect people you love. To protect them from you.

"I dreamed I was being strangled," I confess.

"By your pimp?"

"No. He made one of the other girls do it." Ivy. Mitch had told Ivy to kill me. And she did.

"That's harsh." She throws back the covers. Her stuffed cat, Mr. Whiskers, is tangled in the blankets. "Hey, come on."

"Where?" We're not running away, because she's not getting dressed.

She grins. "I know where they keep the hot chocolate."

Seriously? Hot chocolate? Are we in a sitcom or something? Hot chocolate's not going to fix either of us.

But it sounds good.

I slide out of bed. Together, we tiptoe downstairs with nothing but moonlight and streetlights to guide us. It's not until we're in the kitchen that she finally turns on the dim light over the sink.

"Can I help?" I ask.

"Yeah, get the almond milk out of the fridge," she instructs. I watch as she gets out a grater and two large blocks of chocolate from the cupboard.

"Old school," I say.

Sarah smiles. "There's never been a mix that's as good as the real thing. That's what my gran says. She taught me how to make it. You mix milk and dark chocolate together, add a tiny bit of sugar and some vanilla. You'll see. Girl, you'll be spoiled rotten after this."

I don't think I've ever been spoiled before, so I'm kind of looking forward to it.

"Where are you going when you get out?" I ask. Obviously, she can't go back to where the stepbrother lives.

"Gran's. She lives in Hartford. You'll meet her if you're here Tuesday night. She always brings me dinner and we eat together."

"What about your grandfather?"

She grates chocolate into a pan. "Dead, I guess. She doesn't really talk about him. I don't think he was a good man."

"Are there any?" I ask with a snort, but the minute I say it, I think of Jamal.

"I think so," Sarah replies, reaching for the other block. "There has to be, right? They can't all be fuckwads."

I guess not. I watch her work. "Why are you being so nice to me?"

She shoots me a crooked smile. "Don't trust niceness, do you? None of us do. So how else are we going to trust it if we don't show it to each other? Doesn't cost me nothin' to be nice to you. I'm going to be real nice to you and tell you to stay away from those messed-up girls."

I know who she means. "What's wrong with them?"

Measuring vanilla, she gives me a pointed look. "They're messed up. Not like you and me messed up, but serious. One of them was top girl for her pimp and shopped for other girls for him. Dude, she was bringing in twelve-year-olds."

"That's not right."

"You know it. I ain't trusting no pimp-ass bitch. Bad enough men pimp us, we can't be pimping each other too."

"Does it get easier?" I ask. "Right now, I don't know if I should stay or run, be straight or high."

Sarah puts water in another pan and sets the one with the chocolate in it on top of the stove. "It does, but you have to do the work, y'know? There's no getting high and then trying to live straight." She turns on the burner. "It's a lot easier to believe you don't deserve better and run back to what you know."

Her words are like a magical truth to me. All I can think is that if Krys, who hasn't seen me in years, and Jamal, who doesn't know me at all, both think I'm worth taking a chance on, why can't I take that chance too? Two years ago, I had plans for my life that involved more than getting pills and not getting killed.

"I want better," I say.

"I know, I can see it. That's why I'm making you hot chocolate instead of pretending to be asleep." She smiles. "I'm glad they put you in with me. You remind me why I need to keep workin' too."

"You might change your mind after a few more night-mares," I joke, but I'm not really joking.

"No," she says, adding the milk to the pot with the melt-ing chocolate. "I don't think I will. You might ask for a transfer when I have one of mine though."

I nod toward the stove. "I guess you'd better give me the recipe."

She grins at me as she begins to stir. I grin back.

chapter four

Narcotics Anonymous. Is it really anonymous when you all live together? I mean, we all know each other's stories, for the most part. Some of us are more open than others. I'm not one of the open ones, but I like to listen. Makes me feel good about myself to hear about the shit lives of other girls.

At least Mitch wasn't into the hardcore stuff. He liked to give us stuff that made us feel good or want to party. Then pills to bring us down easy. No heroin or crack. Though, I guess drugs is drugs, right?

I've been at Sparrow Brook for almost three weeks, which means I've been clean a little longer. Sarah says she found it easy to be straight in here, but for me, not so much. The first two weeks were hard. Being around all these hot messes made me want something to take the edge off, bad. But the difference is I wanted pills—I didn't *need* pills.

"I miss pot," says Treena, one of those girls I wanted to

join up with when I first came here. We're not supposed to mention drug names, especially not in a way that makes them sound yummy. Feeding the addiction is not a good thing.

A couple of other girls make noises of agreement. I roll my eyes. She did this last week too, got everyone riled up.

"Oh, I'm sorry. Did I offend your delicate white feelings?"

Fuck. Here we go. Treena's been sniffing around a fight with me for the last few days. I'm not sure why. I don't think she needs a reason other than she seems to think that white girls and brown girls aren't supposed to like each other. I guess no one ever taught her that we're all the same with our faces pressed into a pillow and our asses in the air.

Lucky bitch.

"No," I reply. "But maybe let Sarah finish talking before you start shootin' off that fool mouth of yours."

"You think 'cause you talk like us that you one of us? You ain't, little snowflake."

A few of the girls laugh, but the rest are silent and tense. The woman leading the meeting, Vesta, sits up a little straighter. "Girls, this doesn't need to escalate," she cautions.

Yes, it does. I don't need a frigging degree to see how angry and hurt Treena is. She kind of reminds me of Daisy that way. Violence is Treena's answer to cutting or pulling out hair.

My scars itch.

I don't stand up because I'm a good person, offering myself to her as some kind of douched-up sacrifice. I stand because I've been wanting to punch someone—anyone—in the face for a long fucking time. I curl my hands into fists.

Treena comes at me. Girls start yelling and cheering. Sarah shouts at me to stop.

I let Treena take the first swing. She hits me in the side of the head. Stupid cow. It doesn't really hurt, not nearly as much as when I slam my knuckles into her nose. Oh, that satisfying crunch. *Mm-hmm.* Warm blood on the back of my fingers.

Someone gasps. Someone else hollers gleefully. Vesta shoves tissues into Treena's hands and takes her away to get medical attention. Bitch is probably going to get taken to the doctor. Everyone wants a trip outside.

I wipe my hand on my jeans.

"That was stupid," Sarah tells me.

"Felt good though." I'm smiling and I can't stop. Eventually, she smiles a little too.

Treena's girls don't bother me. They don't know what to do with their top girl gone. A couple of other girls congratulate or thank me, even. Others stay quiet as they leave the room. I guess the meeting's over.

"You're going to lose privileges," my roommate tells me as we head back to our room. I'll face consequences in the morning.

"It was worth it." Seriously, I can handle no TV or even no group activities. I probably will lose access to the horses too, but that's okay. I feel lighter than I have in . . . I don't know how long. That punch—that one fucking punch— opened a window inside me and let the sun in. It's almost poetic.

"What if it messes up you going home?" Sarah asks once we're in our room.

I glance over my shoulder at her. "What?"

"Will that punch be worth it if it fucks up your chances of being able to live with your aunt?"

I don't have to think about it. "No."

The other girl shakes her head. "You gotta be more careful, Lex. You act out like that again, and they're liable to send you to a facility—a real one. Not a nice one like this."

From the tone of her voice, I know that she's been in one of those "facilities" before. I don't know what to say.

"Yeah, thought that might shut you up," she remarks, but there isn't any meanness in her voice. "Next time you want to hit something, there's a punching bag in the basement."

"There is?"

Sarah's expression is pure exasperation. "Yeah, where all the gym equipment is?"

Heat fills my cheeks. "I haven't been down there since orientation."

"Pfft. Bitch."

She means because I haven't put on weight. Well, I have, but I'm still skinnier than I probably should be. My hip bones stick out, and I can feel my ribs just under my skin. Mitch liked us thin. Said we photographed better, so we looked sexier when he put our pictures up online.

I think he liked us frail and weak. Unable to run. How can I know how awful he is and still miss him sometimes? To me, that's real weakness.

If there is a God, I hope he makes me not feel that way someday. As for the rest of it . . .

I turn to Sarah. "Show me that punching bag."

After several brief visits, I go to Krys and Jamal's for an actual weekend. In another couple of weeks—if Sparrow Brook thinks I'm ready to leave—I'll be living with them. After punching Treena, I've been on good behavior. Turns out breaking her nose really wasn't worth the punishment. I was bored stupid, and after a while, looking at her swollen, bruised face wasn't even satisfying.

Jamal takes my bag into my room. I follow him but only so far. He sets the bag near the closet. "I'll let you get settled," he says, and leaves me there alone.

The room is the same as it was when I first saw it, except the bed set I liked and wanted that day at the mall is on the bed. Krys went back and got it.

My hand trembles a little when I touch the quilt. It's so pretty. I blink as the pattern blurs before my stinging eyes. None of that shit. It's just a bed.

"Do you like it?" My aunt's voice comes from the doorway. "I think it really makes the room."

I nod. "Thank you."

"Here. This is for you." She comes into the room and hands me a small box.

I frown. "Aunt Krys, you really don't—"

"I wanted to. I don't want to make you uncomfortable, Lex. I just . . . I just want to give you everything you deserve."

I swallow, try to think of the right words. "He bought me a lot of gifts." I can't say his name in front of her. Not yet.

Her face blanches, leaving nothing but freckles and horrified eyes. "Oh, sweetie."

"I know it's not the same, but . . . it's overwhelming."

For a second, I think she might cry. She shakes her head slightly. "I hadn't thought of that. I'm sorry. Do you want me to save it for another time?"

I glance down at the box in my hand. It would be a rejection if I said yes, and she looked so excited when she gave it to me. "No. I want it."

She watches me as I open the lid. Inside, on the fluff, is a gold wire bracelet with a couple of flat disk charms hanging from it. One says, YOU DESERVE TO BE LOVED, and the other reads, YOU ARE BRAVER THAN YOU BELIEVE, STRONGER THAN YOU SEEM, AND SMARTER THAN YOU THINK.

I run my finger over that charm. "Why does this sound familiar?"

"Winnie the Pooh," my aunt replies. "I used to tell you that when you were little. You used to get me to read the books to you, remember?"

I don't, but there's hope in her voice I can't bring myself to squash. "Thank you," I whisper, and I slip my hand through the bracelet. Mitch bought me a lot of things, but never something as thoughtful as this. Mom never bought me anything so nice.

I turn to my aunt. I feel awkward and disjointed. A light touch on her shoulders, a brief nearing of my body to hers. Her hand gently touches my back, and I know she understands. How can she understand?

"Jill tells me you've discovered a love of kickboxing," Krys says, lightening the mood.

"Yeah?" God, she knows about Treena, doesn't she? She must, but she hasn't mentioned it. I lost privileges for it, had it written up. They had to have told her.

"I like it too. I have a Wavemaster in the basement if you want to use it, but I thought maybe we'd take some classes together—if you want."

Another nod. I can't handle all of this, I don't think.

"Hey."

I look up, meet her gaze.

"You're going to be okay." She says it with a confident smile.

"How do you know?" I challenge. A pulse behind my right eye is making my lid twitch.

"There's an old saying: That which doesn't kill us makes us stronger. Have you heard that before?"

I nod. "I don't feel very strong."

"Honey, you're here. Sometimes that's all the strength you need." She smiles again. "Why don't you unpack? I was thinking tacos for dinner. You like those?"

"Yeah. I can help."

"Unpack first. Take a few minutes to yourself."

And then I'm alone. I glance around the room. How is this real? At our old apartment, my room was half this size. My bed was a twin that sagged in the middle and had a spring that poked me in the side if I didn't position myself just right. The walls had been stained by cigarette smoke and age, and forget having a desk. I'd been lucky to have a dresser with drawers that stuck.

Was it any wonder Mitch had been able to seduce me away? That's what my therapist, Dr. Lisa, said he'd done. He'd seduced me. It's a nice way of saying I let him buy me. How else was he going to justify selling me?

Krys and Jamal aren't trying to buy me, I remind myself. There are good people in the world. I have to believe that, otherwise I'm as bad as the rest of them.

There are velvet hangers in the closet—so my shirts don't slide off—and special hangers for pants and skirts. The drawers on the dresser move smoothly and are lined with cream-colored paper. In the bathroom, I set my small makeup bag on the counter along with my skin care products. My own freaking bathroom.

I laugh. Just a little. Is it happiness, or am I about to lose my shit? I can't tell. Instead of waiting to find out, I go downstairs to the kitchen, where Krys and Jamal are making dinner. I watch them for a second. Jamal sings along with a song on the radio that I don't know as Krys laughs and dances.

Is this normal? And what the fuck is it going to do to me?

"Can I help?" I ask.

"Yep!" Jamal says. "Come mash these avocados."

And just like that, I'm helping. I've never made guacamole in my life. I would have, if I'd known how simple it was.

"Seriously," I say a few minutes later. "This is all there is to it?"

My uncle tosses some cilantro into the bowl to go with the onion and garlic he added before. Then, he squeezes lime juice over it. "Pretty much." Then, he throws some tomato and diced-up peppers in as well. "Stir that all up, please."

By the time we have everything ready, my stomach is growling, which is good, because we've got enough food to feed everyone at Sparrow Brook, I think.

We eat at the kitchen table. It's all so good that I eat until I feel like I'm going to puke. I have no regrets.

We go to the living room afterward. Jamal turns on the TV and calls up a screen with movie posters on it. "Pick which one you want to watch," he says.

"*The Autopsy of Jane Doe, Get Out,* or *Happy Death Day*?" They all sound crazy.

He nods excitedly. "Since you're new to the genre, I'm thinking either of the last two. They're all fairly current. The last few years, anyway."

I pick *Get Out* and hand it back to him. He arches a brow. "You didn't even read the descriptions. Did you just pick this one because it's got a Black guy in it?"

Heat fills my face, and he starts laughing.

Krys whips a dishtowel at his leg. "Don't tease her, Mal."

My uncle stops laughing, but he's still smiling. I guess I didn't offend him. "Okay, we'll start with this one, but I'm going to make you watch the others too."

"I've been made to do worse," I retort with a hint of a smile. His face falls, and I realize what I've said. "That was supposed to be a joke."

Jamal smiles again, but it doesn't look quite right. "Ten bucks says you'll be a fan before the end of the night." He turns to get a drink from the kitchen. Krys touches his shoulder and gives him a loving look. I've watched people have sex, but this exchange between the two of them seems more intimate than any other I've seen. I can't look away.

"I didn't mean to upset him," I say, when it's only my aunt and me. I scratch my thumbnail along the skin of my wrist.

She catches my hand, stopping me from drawing blood. "*You* didn't. The situation you were in upsets him." She turns my other hand over in hers. We both look at the red marks I've made. "I used to pull my hair out. It didn't leave the scars that cutting does, but I had a bald patch I had to cover up."

"You did?" She nods. "Why?"

She strokes her thumb over the welts. "A long time ago, I was at a party and some boys decided to have some fun with me. I didn't think it was fun. Let's get you some cream for that."

My chest feels like my heart is trying to squeeze out between my ribs. I leave the room with her, stupid and silent. I don't know what to do or what to say. I stand by the bathroom sink and let her rub the antibiotic ointment on my wrist like I'm a little kid who can't do it myself. It feels nice.

"Let's go watch that movie," she says when she's done. "Jamal's already watched them all."

"Why would he watch them again?"

She looks at me like I'm an idiot, but not in a mean way. "Because he wants you to like them. And him. He wants to have something in common with you."

Well, I don't want to like *him*. I don't want to trust him and be disappointed when he comes into my room at night.

But what if he doesn't? What if he really is as nice and decent as he seems? What if he protects me rather than hurts me?

I glance toward the living room. "Okay." My aunt takes my hand and leads me into the room.

The sofas have built-in recliners so I get way too relaxed. It's hard to relax when you're watching a freaky movie though. It's so good, but *so* messed up. A couple of times I'm on the edge of my seat, yelling at the TV. Krys and Jamal laugh at me.

Afterward, I look at the two of them. "What is *wrong* with you guys?"

"Admit it," Jamal urges. "You liked it."

"It was awesome," I admit.

"Ready for the next one, or are you done?"

It's only nine o'clock. "Do it up."

He puts on *Happy Death Day*. It doesn't mess with my head like *Get Out,* but there are a few good scares. It's a fun movie, more about how the character needs to change than horror.

"Okay," Krys says after that one. "It's been a long day. Time for bed."

I'm not really tired, but I've got a few books I want to read in my room. Before I go, I turn to Jamal. "Can we do this again next weekend?"

His grin is huge, like the biggest, whitest smile I've ever

seen. "*The Autopsy of Jane Doe,* next Saturday. Maybe even *Carrie.*"

I smile and say good night. In my room I put on my pajamas, use the bathroom, brush my teeth, and wash my face. Before climbing into bed, I check my door. There's a lock on the knob. I turn it to be safe.

I crawl into bed. Oh, God—the sheets are so soft and clean, and the bed is so big and comfortable. I close my eyes. It can't be real. This is all too good to be true. Something terrible is going to happen.

But nothing happens while I read my book. I turn pages until my eyes are heavy and my head starts to swim, then I turn off the light.

There's a soft glow coming from the far corner of the room. It gives off enough brightness that I can just barely make out my surroundings. A night-light. How did Krys know I don't like the dark?

I roll onto my side, facing the door, and tuck up into a ball on these impossibly awesome sheets that smell like summer and feel like a dream. I stare at the doorknob for as long as I can, but my eyes keep drifting closed.

Finally, I fall asleep. No one tries to get in. There aren't any screams in the night. I don't even dream. Nothing bad happens.

But I know it's coming.

"What are you writing?" I ask my uncle the next morning. We're at the table having breakfast like a family on TV or something.

Jamal smiles. His teeth are perfect, I realize. Mine are okay, but a little crooked. He obviously grew up in a family with more money than ours. What would it be like to grow up that way? A john once knocked out one of Jasmine's teeth. Mitch bitched and moaned about having to take her to get it fixed. Good thing he knew a dentist that would take payment in trade.

"I'm making a list of movies for us to watch," he replies. "You want some more bacon?"

He plops a couple of pieces onto my plate, and I dip them in the yolk of my egg before eating them. As I chew, I think about the motel and how long ago it feels.

Where's Mitch? He's out there, somewhere. The cops haven't arrested him, and I haven't seen him—yet. What happens if he comes for me? What if he doesn't?

I don't know how I'd react if I saw him. Part of me misses him, as fucked up as that sounds. Another part of me wants to kill him. Slowly, so he suffers.

My mother's boyfriend, Frank, told me it was my fault I ended up at the motel. If I hadn't been such a horny slut, it never would have happened. I made all the decisions that put me there, he said. I believed him, but now . . . I don't remember ever saying yes. Not once. I don't remember being asked what I wanted at all.

"I've been thinking," Krys says as she refills our coffee cups. "You might need a tutor to help get you caught up on school."

Yeah, right. School. Is it too late to bail on that shit? "Okay."

"You know, I'm beginning to realize you say 'okay' whenever I bring up something you're not really keen on." She gives me a smile. "So, yeah, I'm thinking maybe Zack could tutor you. He's a ridiculously smart kid."

"Great idea," Jamal says, looking up from his list. "You want me to ask him?"

"To tutor me?" I ask.

"Who else?"

I glance at my aunt. They're both watching me, waiting. Neither one of them is going to make the decision for me. I can't explain it, but I kind of wish one of them would.

"Maybe see if I need help first?" Mostly because I'm pretty sure Zack thinks I'm a douche. And I'm not convinced he isn't one either.

"Sure thing," Krys replies and takes the coffeepot back to the counter. As soon as she sets it down, the phone rings. I go back to eating as she talks. She sounds excited about something.

"I'll be over later, Maria. Thanks!" She hangs up. "The Diazes' puppies are ready!"

"Save me, Lord," Jamal mutters.

Krys grabs my hand, almost pulls me out of my chair. "Let's go get one!"

"What?" I stumble to my feet.

She looks stupidly happy. "They're giving us first dibs. Let's go!" A puppy? We're getting a puppy? How did I end up here of all places?

I put on my sneakers and follow her out of the house. It's a warm morning for March, so I'm fine in my hoodie. We walk down the paved driveway and take a right when we reach the sidewalk. The Diazes live two houses down in a big white house with a huge veranda.

Krys rings the bell. The door is opened by a very short girl with long, brown hair, huge hazel eyes, and a tiny bow-like mouth. She looks like an anime drawing come to life.

"Hey, Krys," she says. "We're loaded with puppies."

"Hi, Elsa," my aunt replies. "This is my niece, Alexa."

"Lex," I say.

The girl looks up at me and smiles. "El. I'll take you to the pups."

The house is gorgeous—even more than Krys and Jamal's. It's like walking through a magazine that someone actually lives in. It's clean but doesn't look like anal people live there. It actually feels welcoming. There's even a pool out back.

We follow Elsa to a door with a baby gate across it. She lifts the gate and lets us into a room that I guess is a sunporch. A noise makes me look up. I make eye contact with the biggest pit bull I've ever seen.

There's two of them.

My heart jumps into my throat, but the dogs don't lunge. They don't do much of anything. They're both lying on the floor, looking exhausted, while what has to be at least ten puppies run around them, tripping over their own feet.

"They're big babies," Elsa tells me. "Really. The only time you'd ever have to be afraid of them is if you were like, breaking in or something."

"I'll remember never to do that," I reply.

This makes her laugh. "Sit on the floor. They'll come to you."

I glance at Krys, but she's already plunking herself down in the middle of the floor, not far from the dog parents. The larger of the two comes over and sits beside her, leaning into her shoulder.

"He's such a flirt," Elsa says. "Especially with Krys. Aren't you going to sit?"

Okay, if it's such a big deal, I'll frigging sit. The puppies have already started coming over to check out Krys, their tails wagging so hard, their little butts sway back and forth. They are the cutest things I've ever seen.

I sit, feeling the clear blue gaze of the mama dog on me. It's like she can see right through me, and I'm not sure I like it. What if she doesn't like what she sees?

She gets up and pads over to me. Sitting right in front of me, she puts her paw on my knee.

"She wants you to scratch her ears," Elsa says. She's on the floor now too, cuddling a little brown puppy that licks her face like she's covered in ice cream.

I scratch the pit bull's ears. She closes her eyes and makes a noise that sounds like a groan. After a few minutes of this, she decides she's had enough and goes back to her previous spot. I guess I passed her test because a few seconds later, four puppies decide they want a piece of my action.

"They're adorable," I say, because numb as I am, I'm not so far gone that I can resist furry cuteness. "How are you going to pick one?"

"I'm not," Krys says, grinning at me. "You are."

My jaw drops. "I can't!"

Elsa laughs, but it's not a malicious sound. "You don't have to. One of them will choose you."

I'm not sure I believe her, but as the puppies get bored or tired and wander off, I see what she means.

Only one of them stays with me—a gorgeous little girl with fur so sooty it's almost black and blue eyes like her mama. She's sturdy and strong and a little bit sassy. I rub her velvety ears, and she looks at me like I'm the most incredible thing she's ever seen. It hurts, her looking at me like that, but I can't look away.

"I think we found our winner," Krys says with a smile. "We'll pick up what we need for her and take her home later today or tomorrow, if that's okay?"

Elsa shrugs. "I don't see why not, but I'll go get Mom to make sure."

When she leaves the room, I look at my aunt. "We're seriously taking her?"

Krys nods. She scoots closer across the polished boards. "She's your dog, Lex. I want you to have someone you can trust and love without anything getting in the way, someone who will love and trust you unconditionally. Plus, no one's going to mess with you when you're walking a pit bull."

I can't imagine the little ball of warmth against my leg would ever inspire fear in anyone, but I glance at her mother again. Okay, maybe. I rub my chest to ease that strange pinch. Happiness isn't supposed to hurt, is it?

My eyes burn. The puppy chooses that moment to climb into my lap. It takes her two tries. "You're so good to me," I say to Krys. "I don't know how to deserve it."

I notice her eyes are a little bright too. "You don't have to know how, just know that you do."

I'm not sure I believe it, but I believe that she does, and that's good enough. I lean into her. She hesitates before leaning into me. It's not quite a hug, but it's the second time I've initiated contact with her. And that means something.

chapter five

Krys keeps her word. All day, I keep thinking she's going to change her mind about the dog—the dog I've already named in my head. The dog I'm already half in love with. I feel more for that puppy than I do for Jamal, or even Krys, for that matter.

But Krys hasn't changed her mind. After we do some clothes shopping at the mall, she looks at me and says, "Ready to go puppy shopping?" We make a run to the pet store for everything she'll need: food, a bed, training pads, a leash, bowls, toys. We sign up for behavior classes too.

"Have you decided on a name yet?" Krys asks as we drive home.

"Isis," I reply.

"Like the Egyptian goddess?"

I glance over at her. "She watches over slaves and the downtrodden, and she's a friend to children."

Krys doesn't ask me how I know this, so I don't have to

tell her Ivy told me. I think about Ivy a lot—what happened to her when she escaped from the hospital, if she's okay. Is she home with her parents? Or is she back with Mitch? I was dumb enough to trust Mitch, but I'm smart enough to know that without Krys, I'd probably be on my back again somewhere. I'd be stoned and used, and I probably wouldn't live to see eighteen.

I still might not.

"Isis is a perfect name," my aunt enthuses. "You're going to have to walk her a few times a day and train her to go outside. It's a lot of responsibility."

"I don't mind," I say quickly. Krys flashes me a smile.

Elsa is there when we arrive. I'm five-foot-seven and the top of her head is below my chin. She's gotten her nose pierced since yesterday, and she's wearing a Hanson T-shirt and shorts, so I can see she's got several tattoos, two of which are quotes on the inside of her forearms. I can't read what they say. I've always wanted a tattoo.

She catches me staring and holds up her arms. "Perfect way to hide the scars of my tragic youth," she quips.

Her left arm says: RAZORS PAIN YOU and the right says: YOU MIGHT AS WELL LIVE. I don't recognize the quotes.

"Dorothy Parker," she supplies at my blank stare. "It's a poem about suicide."

"Did you try to kill yourself?" I ask.

"Haven't you? All the kids are doing it these days." She laughs. "Sorry. That was stupid."

I shrug. "I say stupid stuff all the time."

She looks at me from underneath impossibly long eyelashes. "Yeah? Because you don't really seem to say much at all."

"I don't always do it out loud."

She laughs again, her eyes crinkling at the corners. "You can bring her over any time to play with her sibs," she tells me. "I'm only working part-time this summer, so I'll be around."

I nod. "Thanks."

Her laughter fades to a smile. "So, are you like, super awkward, or is it me?"

I blink. "It's not you."

"Good to know," she replies, bobbing her head. "So, you want to hang out sometime?"

"Seriously?"

"Yeah, why not? I kinda dig super awkward, y'know? You'll make me look way cooler than I am." She smiles when she says it, so I know she's joking. I think.

"I don't know . . ." I glance at Krys, but she's talking to Elsa's mother about Isis's papers and habits. Stuff I should probably be listening to.

Elsa shrugs. "No pressure. It's just that Cleo doesn't immediately take to a lot of people, so I figured maybe you'd want to be friends."

I stare at her like she's speaking a foreign language. "Cleo?"

She points down, and I follow her finger with my gaze. There, sitting next to me is Mama Pit Bull. Just sitting there, looking at me. I pat her on the head and her tail thumps.

"I named my puppy Isis."

"I know. It's like kismet or something."

I swallow. "So, they're called American Pit Bull Terriers, right?"

"Yup. A lot of breeders get all freaky about it, but I don't care. I call 'em pitties because it's fun to say."

She's the oddest girl I've ever met. I kind of like her. "I might be able to hang out sometime."

She looks at me. I don't know what she sees, but she gives me a quick nod. "Cool. I'm babysitting the puppies next Saturday. Probably get pizza around seven and watch a movie. If you like pepperoni, come on over."

"Okay. I'll see if I can make it."

A little smile curves her tiny lips, like she knows I'm BSing and is okay with it. "Awesome."

Krys plunks Isis into my arms and says, "Okay, let's get this little girl home."

The puppy licks my chin, and I can't help but smile.

"Bring her with you if you come over next weekend," Elsa suggests. "She might be lonely without her sibs."

Krys looks surprised when she turns to me. "The two of you are hanging out?"

"Maybe," I say, hoping she sees the warning in my eyes. "If I can."

"Right." My aunt doesn't miss a beat. "We'll have to check and make sure there's nothing already planned." I blush slightly—nothing like making it obvious.

"Sure," Elsa says. "No worries."

I snuggle my dog and meet the other girl's gaze. "Thanks," I say.

She smiles. "You won't want to thank me the first time you have to pick up warm dog shit with a plastic bag around your hand."

I shrug. "Aren't all the kids doing it these days?"

She laughs a little, still holding my gaze. "Right. Hey, I hope you're free next weekend."

Isis licks my face, and I feel a smile stretch my face. "Yeah," I say, and at the moment, I mean it. "Me too."

Sarah's leaving.

After a few months at Sparrow Brook, she says she's ready to go home. It amazes me that even though all of us have been through a lot of the same stuff, we all handle it differently. I really don't understand the ones that are crying all the time, or always looking for a fight, like Treena. Dr. Lisa says I "dissociate" so that makes the emotional stuff easier for me because I refuse to feel it.

She says it like it's a bad thing. I'm pretty sure it's what keeps me alive, what keeps me doing the things they say I'm supposed to do. I must be doing something right because I'll be leaving Sparrow Brook a couple of weeks earlier than they first thought. Some of that has to do with the fact that they don't think I'm a high risk for readdiction.

I miss my pills sometimes, but there's not one part of me that *needs* them. Not anymore. Maybe if I felt more, I would.

We have a little party for Sarah. Apparently they do this every time a girl leaves. They get a cake and give her a present that's supposed to be from everyone, but is really picked out by the staff.

"Ten bucks says it's a journal," Lonnie whispers near my ear as we watch Sarah open her gift. "With something inspirational on it."

"A journal," Sarah says, holding up the book. I see the quote on the front says BE THE YOU THAT YOU WANT TO BE in swirling script.

"Puke," I whisper.

Lonnie laughs. "It's meant well."

I turn to her. "Why are you still here?"

Her smile fades. "My sister smuggled in some Percs for me a month ago. Put me on a spiral again. She thought she was helping. My leg hurts a lot."

"I thought you couldn't abuse painkillers if you're actually in pain," I say.

She gives me a look that makes me think I don't know shit.

The cake is good, and we rip into it like a pack of starving wolves. Sometimes I think sugar is the best drug of all.

When it's time for her to go, we all line up to say goodbye. Well, some of us. Treena and a couple of others leave the room. I hope they know Sarah's not going to miss them either.

When it's my turn, I hug her. It's a one-armed hug and a little stiff, but I'm getting better at it. Touching people is . . . weird.

"You're going to be fine," Sarah tells me. "I left you everything you need." She hugs me and turns to leave. Her mother smiles at me, at all of us. We all stand there, a sad little group watching out the window as Sarah, now outside, gets into the car, takes one last look at us, and drives away. She's gone.

Just like Ivy. You'd think I'd be used to people leaving me, given how many girls came and went at the motel, but I'm not. See, Dr. Lisa? I'm not entirely without feeling. She's going to tell me it's because I have abandonment issues. No shit.

I go up to our room—my room, now. There, on my bed, is Mr. Whiskers, and underneath him is a recipe for hot chocolate. I don't know whether to smile or cry, so I do a little of both. Just for a second. After I go to see if there's any cake left. People come and go, there's no point crying over it.

Not like it's going to bring any of them back.

"Your mom called last night."

Krys tells me this when she brings me lunch the next day. We're sitting at a small table in a room separate from the normal dining room. I don't feel the least bit bad having Indian food while everyone else has to have soup and sandwiches.

"What did she want?" I ask, dipping naan into the sauce on my plate.

My aunt watches me closely. "To ask if they could visit you."

"*They?*" I repeat. I shake my head. "No."

"Okay." She doesn't ask why. I know she wants to, but I'm glad she doesn't. I don't want to talk about it. "Have any new girls come in?"

I shake my head. "Not yet. Another few days, I guess." It's strange having the room to myself. It will be even stranger when someone else moves into Sarah's bed.

"Have you heard from Sarah?"

"When I checked my email this morning, there was one from her." It wasn't really "my" email. It was an email sent to the patient inbox with my name in the subject line. I'm pretty sure the staff read it before I was allowed to see it and respond. That's the extent of what we're allowed to do when it comes to the outside world, other than phone calls. They don't want pimps or johns or whatever finding us.

"How's she doing?"

I shrug. "Good, I guess. She didn't say much, just asked about the horses and if I was looking forward to going home with you."

"Are you?"

I look at her. "Is that a trick question?"

Laughing, my aunt shakes her head. "Just want to make sure you're happy."

"I'm . . . happier," I reply. It's the best I can do.

Her smile fades. "What can I do to help you?"

"You're already helping me."

"It doesn't feel like enough."

I hate the frustration in her gaze. "Krys, a few months ago, I was in a motel, high and dirty and getting raped by strangers. You don't think you're an improvement over that?"

I can't tell if it's laughter or a sob, the sound that comes out of her. She knows what happened to me. She has to. "Jesus," she whispers. "I am so sorry. Lex, you know none of that was your fault, right?"

"Yeah." And the funny thing is, I mean it. The only thing I'd done wrong was to trust Mitch, and I'm not the first girl to have made that mistake. What he did to me wasn't my fault, but there are times, even now, when I still miss it. *God, I'm so fucked up.*

"What's in the bag?" I ask her, wanting to change the subject.

"They're some books Zack gave me to pass on to you. He says they're the ones you'll need for your classes this summer."

"Oh. Great." Yeah, not really.

"Look, I know summer school sucks, but soon, you'll be in your senior year and after that you can do whatever you want."

It's hard to imagine myself in college. It's hard to imagine myself doing anything but being a ho. What the hell am I going to do with my life? Who would hire a broken-ass piece of shit like me? Some guy who likes to screw his secretary? I could be a sugar baby, I suppose. This time, I'll decide who I do and do not have sex with, and I'll keep all the money.

"Okay," I say.

"Do you mean that, or are you trying to shut me up?" she asks.

"Is that possible?" I ask with a little smile.

She throws a chunk of naan at me. I pick it up and eat it, and that's the end of talking about school.

After Krys leaves, I take the books from Zack up to my room and start looking at them. *To Kill a Mockingbird*, *The Crucible*, *The Scarlet Letter*, and *A Raisin in the Sun*.

I have an hour to kill before group, so I lie on my bed and start reading *To Kill a Mockingbird*. It's pretty good for a school book. Zack made notes in the page margins. I saw his name written in the front of the books and the penmanship matches. His thoughts are like a one-sided conversation, like he's the teacher.

"You never really understand a person until you consider things from his point of view . . . until you climb into his skin and walk around in it," I read out loud. It's something Atticus, Scout's father, says to her in the book. In the margin of the book is scrawled: *As if anyone in this godforsaken place would even try.*

What does he know about it? I wonder. His mother's a professor. He's obviously smart, and I saw for myself that he's not ugly. Fuck, I don't want anyone to try walking around in *my* skin. I can barely handle it myself. And who says things like "godforsaken" anymore? I have to admit, though, I'm intrigued by his thoughts. Some of them mimic my own.

When I read, I like to watch the story unfold in my head, like a movie, and I'm the director, star, and whatever else I want to be. Or, I just watch as it all unfolds, sucked into a world that hopefully turns out better than this one.

Before I know it, we're being called to dinner. I'm still pretty full from lunch, so I don't eat much. I'm at the table with the others when I hear a car with no muffler rumble by.

"That's the third time that car's slowed down as it's driven by here," Lonnie comments, looking out the window. Her knuckles are white as she grips her fork.

"What color is it?" I ask. My voice is little more than a rough whisper. I know that car.

"Brown," she says. "An old boat."

"Rust spot over the passenger front wheel?"

They're all looking at me. "Alexa?" Song asks, her voice tight with concern. "Who is it?"

I can imagine Mitch in the passenger seat, looking for me in the windows as they drive by. I could push back my chair, walk out the door, and be gone in a matter of minutes. He'd take me back. I'd see Ivy. I'd be his girl. With Daisy gone, maybe I'd be top girl.

But I don't push back my chair, and I don't go outside, because the car doesn't belong to Mitch. It belongs to Frank. It's not a coincidence that he's driving by the day after my mother calls to see if they can visit me. I don't think Krys told them where I am, but they managed to figure it out.

That it's Frank's car is what keeps me in my chair. It's

what makes me stay where I am while the bit of food I've eaten churns in my stomach and threatens to come back up. I look up at Song.

"Call the police."

Krys is furious. Jamal is furious. Detective Willis is furious. Even gentle Song is furious. The only person not furious is me.

I'm afraid. Afraid Mitch will come for me, because I've realized I don't want him to. I've thought about going back. I wouldn't have to go to summer school. I wouldn't have to worry about disappointing Krys, or fucking up, or Jamal not being the nice guy I want him to be.

I'd rather worry. I'd rather take my chances at a new life than ever go back to that one. I can always run later if I want to. At least now I have some say in what happens.

We're all in the living room. The other girls have been sent to their rooms, but I know they're listening, or trying to. There are a couple of uniformed officers there as well, and cop cars driving up and down the street. They're looking for Frank. Why don't they just go to my mother's apartment and wait?

Aunt Krys leaves the small group of people she's talking to—Song, Jamal, and some woman I don't recognize—and sits beside me on the sofa. "You okay?" she asks.

"I'm a little freaked out," I reply honestly. I think it surprises her.

"There is some concern about the safety of the other girls here," she begins.

I nod. "They're sending me somewhere else."

"If you want, you can come home with us."

My shoulders straighten. "But that's not supposed to happen for another couple of weeks."

"Given the circumstances and your progress, they're willing to give you an early release."

It's not because I'm awesome, I remind myself, *but because my being here could be dangerous for the other girls. Upsetting.* Not to mention Mitch might grab up one of them. Treena would probably go off with him in a heartbeat.

"What if he comes to your house?" I ask.

"Detective Willis is going to have someone watching our place. And I'm not going to make the mistake of telling your mother where you are. The next time she calls I'm *not* answering."

"You're pissed," I say. There are red splotches on her cheeks.

She nods. "And I'm disappointed. She's your god-damned mother, for fuck's sake. She should be better than this shit."

My eyes widen.

Her jaw is tight when she looks at me. "I'm not going to apologize for swearing. I meant every fucking word."

I smile. I can't help it. "O-fucking-kay."

We laugh a little. She takes my hand and squeezes it. I squeeze back. Whatever happens next, Aunt Krys has my back. I know my judgment is shit, but I really want to trust her, so I'm going to. Because taking me on doesn't benefit her in any way. In fact, I'm probably more of a pain in the ass than she ever wanted.

I go upstairs to my room. Lonnie is waiting on my bed. "What's going on?" she asks in a whisper.

"I'm leaving," I tell her. "I guess it's not safe for me—or you guys—if I stay."

She nods. "Keep going to meetings, okay?"

"I will." I mean it.

She stands and limps toward me. Stiff arms jut around me and she pats me on the back with one hand and then keeps walking.

"Take care of yourself, Lex."

"You too." She doesn't ask me where I'm going. Lonnie knows better. She's been in the game a lot longer than I have.

I pack up my things. It only takes a few minutes. I come downstairs with my small suitcase, Mr. Whiskers, and the bag of books.

I don't get a cake or a party. The other girls are still in their rooms and won't know I'm gone until long after I've left. It's better this way, because none of them will know what's going on or where I'm going. They can't tell what they don't know. I should have told Lonnie I'm going to another facility. But I'm not important enough to Mitch that he'd sneak onto the property and ask one of the girls about me.

At least, I don't think he would.

My chest buzzes, like a whole beehive is in there. Am I ready for this? Do I want this? What's going to happen? Am I ever going to feel like a whole person again? What if I fuck up?

Krys gives me an encouraging smile. "Ready?"

No. "Sure."

Detective Willis puts her hand on my shoulder. "I'll check in with you in a day or so. It's going to be okay."

I nod. "Okay."

Jill is there too—everyone had to meet to decide what to do with me, I guess. She tells me she'll come by the house in a few days to check on me.

"Okay," I say again. The buzzing subsides, giving way to . . . nothing.

I say goodbye to Song, and we leave the building. I glance toward the stables. I probably won't ever see Joe again. My throat tightens. I'm going to miss that horse more than any person here.

As Jamal puts my stuff in the back of the vehicle, a city bus lumbers along the dark street. I could run out in front of it and end all of this shit right here and now. I could just die and be done.

It's a weird thing, contemplating suicide but not caring enough to actually do it. I watch the bus go by. A kid about my age in the back seat gives me the finger. Loser.

When we get to the house, the first thing I hear is Isis yipping from her crate. As soon as Krys lets her out, she runs across the kitchen floor toward me and pees. I'm so happy to see her, I don't care I have to clean up her mess. She squirms in my arms and howls at me as she tries to eat my face.

Krys and Jamal laugh at the two of us. "I'm glad you'll be the one picking up her poop now," Jamal tells me.

"I don't even care," I tell him. "Her poop is precious."

He shakes his head. "She's definitely your niece," he says to Krys. "Y'all are too weird."

I smile. I love this dog so much. What I can't seem to feel for the rest of the world is all balled up and directed solely at her. Did Krys know that would happen when she decided to get us a puppy?

"So," my aunt begins, leaning against the kitchen counter, "you'll still have therapy with Dr. Lisa once a week, and at least one NA meeting a week as well. During the day, we'll work on getting you caught up and ready for summer school. Zack will come here to tutor you, like you decided. You can help me out around the house and in my studio. Sound good?"

Isis licks my neck. "I'm sorry things got messed up," I tell her.

Krys frowns. "Sweetie, this isn't your fault. It's mine. I'm the idiot who let your mother know you were in Middletown. They figured it out from there."

"What if he comes here?" I can't help but ask.

Jamal's face hardens. "He'll be sorry for it if he does."

My uncle's a big man—bigger than Mitch—with broad shoulders and muscular arms. He could seriously hurt someone if he wanted to. It makes me feel safe, even though it scares me a little.

After a while, they go to bed. It's after ten, and I'm starting to get tired too. I take Isis into my room and put pee pads on the bathroom floor for her, along with food and water.

I read for a little while before turning out my light. My dog snuggles into the space between my neck and jaw and starts to snore. I stroke her soft, warm body and lie there, staring up at the ceiling, listening.

I fall asleep waiting for the rumble of Frank's car. I know I'll hear it sometime soon. It doesn't matter if Mitch is with him or not. He found me once; he'll come again.

chapter six

"I thought maybe I scared you off," Elsa says to me when I walk into her house on Saturday night. Even though she lives down the street, Krys walked me to her door—just in case. It took longer than it should have because Isis had to stop and smell something every five steps. Or pee.

"Nah," I say. "You didn't scare me."

"You like pizza?" she asks, shutting and locking the door.

"Doesn't everybody?"

"You'd think, right?" She bends down to pick up Isis. "But there are actually people out there who don't like the most perfect food on the planet." She lets my dog lick her cheek.

"Aliens," I say, because it's the first thing that comes to mind. I don't think Elsa thinks much about what comes out of her mouth either.

She grins at me. "Yeah, that's it. Now, tell me you like Hawaiian and we're set."

"Actually, I do, yeah." She mentioned pepperoni before, but I guess she changed her mind. I don't care—pizza is pizza.

"Awesome. I'll order it. Let's take this little one to her fam."

When we get to the living room, there are fewer puppies than last week. Isis yips excitedly as she rejoins her family. Cleo comes over and nudges my hand with her head, wanting attention.

"You wanna watch a movie?" Elsa asks as I rub Cleo's ear.

"Sure." If we watch something, then there's not as much pressure to talk, right?

"What do you feel like?"

I shrug.

Elsa gives me a wry grin. "Help me out, girlfriend."

"I don't know. Something fun?"

"Oh! I know just the thing."

"The thing" turns out to be an action movie with a female lead who kicks some serious ass. I love it. We sit on the couch, surrounded by dogs as we eat pizza and guzzle cola. After begging for and failing to get pizza, Isis falls asleep on the floor in front of me, Cleo beside her.

"That was so fucking good," I say when the movie's done.

Elsa slumps. "Oh, I'm so glad you swore," she says. "I've been watching everything I say!"

"Girl, you don't have to watch nothin'," I reply with a little smile.

She leans back. "So, I'm guessing you've had some crazy shit happen to you or something?"

That's unexpected. "What have you heard?" Did Krys tell her mother?

A shrug. "Nothing, but people don't move in with their aunts unless something's fucked up at home, right? Plus, those marks on your arm don't look accidental."

I frown. I don't want to talk about it, but I don't want to lie. She seems really nice, and she was open about trying to kill herself with me. "You know that trafficking ring they busted up near Bridgeport?"

Some of the color leaves her face. "Yeah."

"Yeah."

"Oh. Oh, shit." She looks like I punched her in the head. I want to apologize, but I'm feeling a little light-headed. I can't believe I told someone my secret. What if she tells other people?

"No one around here knows," I tell her. "At least, I don't think they do."

She jerks her chin. "Right. You don't have to worry about me telling anyone. Wow. I don't know what to say."

"You don't have to say anything. I just want you to know why I'm weird."

"I said awkward, not weird."

"Same thing."

"Not really."

I stare at her. "I just told you I was whored out, and you want to argue semantics?"

"I'm arguing word choice, not meaning."

Maybe I shouldn't have used the word "whored" either. "I freaked you out, didn't I?"

"Yep," she replies honestly. I'm disappointed. I thought maybe she could be a friend.

"There's only one thing to do," she says, slapping her hands on her thighs. "Come with me."

Hesitantly, I stand and follow after her as she hops to her feet and leaves the room. She takes me to a doorway, snaps on a light, and begins descending the stairs to the basement. I balk at following her into the unknown.

I need to decide whether I'm going to run or take a chance on trusting someone other than myself.

I draw a deep breath.

"Coming?" Elsa calls up the stairs.

I grab the railing tight, forcing one foot in front of the other, slowly following her down.

The basement is fully furnished with couches and a TV with a game console. There's a drum kit in the corner.

"Your brother's?" I ask.

She grins as she turns on the TV. "Mine."

I'm impressed. She shoves a microphone into my hand. "What's this for?"

"Karaoke, baby," she replies, a mic in her own hand. "We're singing the weird away."

"I can't sing," I tell her, horrified.

"Neither can I," she says with a laugh. The music for an ABBA song starts, and I begin laughing.

"Come on, Dancing Queen!" Elsa urges, bumping her hip against my thigh. "Work with me."

The words come up on the screen and she begins to sing. She's not bad. I join in—I'm not bad either. We smile at each other.

When Krys comes to pick me up, my throat is sore from singing, but I feel strangely light and free. Isis is still asleep, so I pick her up and carry her out to the car, singing under my breath. The puppy doesn't seem to mind.

"Are you singing ABBA?" my aunt asks when we pull into the drive, and I laugh.

I think maybe Elsa is magic. Or maybe this is what having a friend feels like.

Since I'm out of Sparrow Brook early, Krys signed me up for online classes to help me catch up on school. Mom never really cared if I went to school or not, so at the end of grade ten—when Mitch first started sniffing around—I started fucking off on classes. I never finished the year, but I did some testing, and it was decided I basically had the sophomore stuff down, so I just have to catch up on grade eleven and I can start this coming school year as a senior.

I've always kind of hated school. I don't expect that to change, but Krys is determined to make me some kind of brainiac.

"You're going to college," she says. "You're having every opportunity you can get to have your best life."

"Okay," I say. Whatever. I don't really care either way. The idea of "best life" isn't something I can wrap my head around.

"What do you want to be?" she asks me.

I blink. "I don't know. A stripper?"

The horrified look on her face makes me laugh. "I don't know," I say truthfully. "When I was little, I wanted to be a singer."

She smiles. "So did I. What do you enjoy doing?"

I shrug. "I like taking care of Isis. I like writing about stuff. I like makeup."

"Well, there are three options right there. You could become a vet, or a writer, or a makeup artist."

"Okay."

Her face tightens. I frustrate her sometimes.

I try again, thinking about it. "I couldn't deal with dying animals, so maybe a writer or makeup person."

A tiny smile curves her lips and eases the tension in my chest. "There. Something to think about, anyway."

She's right. Now that those ideas are in my head, I do think about them. I kind of like the idea of being a writer. I always feel better after I journal and write down how I'm feeling or what I'm thinking.

Not that I feel a whole lot still. Every once in a while, I still get overwhelmed. I've been with Krys and Jamal a couple of weeks—no sign of Mitch or Frank, and nothing horrible has happened—but I woke up sobbing last night. I cried for, like, ever, it seemed. Cried myself back to sleep. I woke up feeling like ass, but also strangely better, like I'd been carrying around all those tears and just needed to dump them.

A few days before that, I lost my temper over something and had to go a few rounds with the Wavemaster. My arms and shoulders are still sore. Again, though, I felt better. Dr. Lisa thinks it's good I'm finally letting my emotions out. I only wish when they happened, they weren't so . . . *much*. It makes me feel crazy.

It would be easier if I had my pills. Easier to go back to Mitch and not try to be anything other than what he made me. I can't do that, and I know it. I hate him for the fact that I even think it.

It's after dinner and I'm reading a book I got the other day at the bookstore. Krys lets me get as many books as I want, but I try to keep it in check. This weekend, we're getting me a library card. It's the most exciting thing in my life right now. I'm such a nerd.

The doorbell rings. A few seconds later I hear Krys talking to someone. A guy. My heart seizes up.

"Hey, Lex?" she calls upstairs. "Zack is here."

Riiiight. My tutor. Like I need one. I'm not stupid. But, hell, if he makes getting through these online classes and summer school easier, I guess I can eat it.

"Be right down," I call back. I get off my bed and look at myself in the mirror. My hair's piled up in a messy bun. I'm wearing sweatpants and a long-sleeve shirt. It's April, but it snowed yesterday. I hate the cold.

Should I change? Maybe put on some lip gloss? He is a guy, after all. It's amazing what shiny lips can do. Maybe put on something that shows more cleavage? Or take my bra off altogether? That might be fun.

I can't be bothered to do any of it. Besides, Krys will notice.

I grab my notebook and head downstairs. Zack is in the kitchen, drinking a glass of soda. He's taller than I remember, and his shoulders wider. His hair's a little longer, his eyes a little darker. Intimidating—that's what he is. I don't like it.

"Hey," he says.

"How frigging tall are you?" I ask, frowning.

"Six-three," he replies. "Four, actually. Is that a problem?"

"Why would it be a problem?"

He arches a dark brow. "'Cause you're looking at me like it's a problem."

I force my forehead to relax. "Sorry."

"We don't have to do this if you don't want to."

"Yeah, we do. My aunt set this up. I assume she's paying you for your time." Imagine that, and no pimp to hand it over to.

He lifts his chin, like he needs to make his head any higher than mine. "I'm not going to work with someone who has a problem with me."

"I don't have a problem. *You* have a problem with me. I saw how you looked at me at the mall."

Now he's frowning. "Because you were staring at my mother's hands. Looking at her like she's a freak and less than you."

Less than me? Asshole, *no one* is less than me. "I don't give a fuck about her hands. I was wondering if she had any pills I could steal."

"Oh."

"Yeah. Oh." Shit, I'm angry. Not needing-to-hit-something angry, but pissed.

"You an addict?" He sits down at the table, like he's planning to stay awhile.

"I'm going to NA meetings, so yeah, I guess so."

He looks at me with those dark eyes. It's like he can see inside me. "My dad's a drunk."

"Yay, him."

Instead of getting mad, Zack smiles a little. "Exactly. I don't have a lot of sympathy."

"Not asking for it."

"Fair enough." He glances at the books he's set on the table. "You want help with school shit though?"

I'm tempted to say no, but that would be giving in. "Yeah. I do. You want to give it?"

A single nod. "I do."

I pull out a chair and sit, slapping my notebook onto the polished wood. "Bring it."

"Where do you want to start?"

"I dunno. You tell me."

"English is always a good start," he says. "Did you read any of the books I gave Krys?"

I nod. "I read *To Kill a Mockingbird* and *The Crucible*."

His eyes light up a little. "What did you think of the Miller?"

"Bitches be crazy. Accusing people of witchcraft and shit."

Zack stares at me for a minute. "Seriously?"

I want to slap him with my notebook. I want to slap myself. That was something Poppy would say. "I liked it—kind of. Part of me admired Abigail for how she manipulated all those people, but I don't like that she did it just because of a guy."

"Most people don't sympathize with Abigail. Proctor is considered the hero of the story."

"John Proctor fucked someone he shouldn't have and got all bent out of shape when there were consequences. He knew what he was doing."

He's silent for a second and leans back in his chair. "Yeah. He did. What about all those people Abigail accused of being witches, though? Did they deserve what they got?"

I shrug. "That's not really how life works, is it? People don't really get what they deserve. If they did, only bad people would ever be hurt."

"You're right. Abigail doesn't have to face the consequences of her actions, does she? She runs away."

"And becomes a whore. I think she probably paid for her choices."

A frown brings his dark brows together. "That's not in the play."

"It's what happened to the real Abigail. I looked her up."

Zack grins, and it startles me. His smile is so . . . big. His teeth are almost perfectly straight and so freaking white. I have a dentist appointment next week. I want to take a picture of Zack's mouth and take it with me. *Give me teeth like that.*

"I knew English was the right place to start," he says. "Mr. Bent is going to love you. He's our English teacher."

I just smile. Of course Mr. Bent will love me. Every man I've met has said he loved me—at least until he came.

"How was the tutoring session with Zack?" Jamal asks me that night at dinner.

"All right," I tell him. "I didn't catch him looking at my boobs once."

Jamal blinks. "Well, that's good, I guess. Not what I meant, but good."

"He's smart." I reach for the mashed potatoes. "Really smart. I didn't understand some of the things he talked about."

"His mother's a professor," Krys reminds me. "But you're smart too. You remember that. You just haven't had the same advantages."

"But you will," Jamal adds. "You have your own in-home professor now too."

"What do you teach?" I ask. I'm embarrassed I never asked before.

"African American Studies. You can sit in on a class sometime if you want."

I glance at Krys. She's smiling. "Sure," I say.

"So, do you like Zack?" my aunt asks.

I start to shrug, but stop myself. "I guess he's okay. He's really defensive about his mom, though. He thought I gave her stank eye in the mall."

Jamal nods. "He's very protective of Anna. I get that."

"Anyway, I wasn't looking at her like that at all, so I guess we're good." By the time he left, I felt more comfortable with him, especially after we started talking about *To Kill a Mockingbird.* He seemed to like that I appreciated his notes.

"He's top of his class, so I'm glad you're working with him," Jamal remarks.

"I'm not dumb, you know."

He looks surprised. Hell, I'm surprised. "I know you're not. You just have some catching up to do."

"Have we made you feel dumb?" Krys asks, a worried frown on her face.

"No." I shake my head. "I . . . I guess I assume people think I'm stupid, because of what I let happen to me."

Krys reaches over and grabs my hand. She doesn't seem to care there's a knife in it. "You did nothing wrong. I'm going to keep telling you that until you believe it."

Good luck.

The phone rings. Krys gets up to answer it, even though she hasn't eaten half of what's on her plate. Mom always used to swear when the phone rang during meals. Once, Frank ripped it right off the wall.

I keep eating. Jamal flashes me a small smile. I try to smile back.

A few minutes later, Krys returns to the table. She's paler than normal.

"What's wrong?" Jamal asks.

My aunt sits down. She takes my hand again—this time my fingers are empty. Hers are cold.

"What?" I whisper.

"Sweetie, that was Song from Sparrow Brook. She thought you'd want to know. Sarah Winters died."

Who the fuck is Sarah Winters? "Wait . . . Sarah? My Sarah?"

She nods. For a second I think she might cry, which is stupid because she never knew Sarah.

"How?"

Krys glances at Jamal. "Suicide."

The word slams into my soul like a brick. "No."

My aunt nods, pressing her lips together. "I'm afraid so."

I shove my chair back from the table so hard it scrapes the floor, and I bolt from the room. I run up the stairs to my room, closing the door behind me. I lean against it, breathing hard. I know it's true. I know she's gone, but I don't want her to be. I'm so . . .

Angry. Sad. Hurt. I want to put my fist through the wall. I want to cut myself to let this feeling out. I want to hurt someone. I want to hurt me.

I grab Mr. Whiskers off the bed and throw him across the room. I want to rip his legs off. Rip him to shreds. I stomp over and pick him up again. I look into his plastic eyes.

A tear slides down my cheek, followed by another. They're fat and hot, scalding my skin. It's like someone turned on a tap—I can't make them stop. I fall against the wall and slide down to the floor, clutching the stuffed cat in my arms. I'm so sorry for hurting him.

Isis wiggles out from under my bed and waddles over to

me, her head down. She climbs up onto my lap, front paws on Mr. Whiskers. She stands up, licking at my wet face. I hold her in one arm, the stuffed cat in the other, and cry until I think my head's going to explode.

Why couldn't I have stayed numb?

chapter seven

Days go by and turn into weeks and before I know it, it's the first of June. Thoughts of Sarah drift to the back of my mind. It's not like I really knew her. Not like I could have helped her. I can barely help myself. Thinking about her doesn't do me any good, so I stop thinking about her. Dr. Lisa keeps wanting me to talk about it, but I'm done.

I would have been done with everybody if they'd only let me. Krys and Jamal won't let me stay in my room. Elsa won't let me mope and sulk. Even Zack, who isn't really a friend, keeps showing up. Sometimes I think that's all life is—just showing up. I've known too many people who have decided to fuck off instead.

But it's Elsa who has been the most relentless. She calls me almost every night and tells me about her day. Sometimes, she just shows up. Once, she joined in on the tutoring session with Zack. On weekends, she comes over or invites me over there. She has become my friend whether I want her or not, and I don't want her. That's not true. I do want her, even though I figure someday she'll be gone like everyone else.

"I can't believe you have to go to summer school," she says, not for the first time, as we're walking Caesar and Cleo one evening after dinner.

"I'm kind of looking forward to it." I'm surprised to hear the words come out of my mouth. "At least it will get me out of the house."

She shoots me a narrow glance. "Freak."

I laugh as I pick up Cleo's lead. All the puppies have found new homes except for the ones Elsa and her brother got to keep. The two of them are curled up with Isis asleep, which is good because they'll howl like crazy if they discover their parents are going for a walk without them.

I haven't explored the neighborhood much—not alone. Krys and I have gone for walks, but I get nervous if we're too far from the house. I keep looking for Frank or Mitch, even though there's been no sign. I feel personally safe with Elsa, but not so much physically. I mean, she's like a pixie. Still, having the adult dogs with us helps. Caesar and Cleo are totally sweet with us, but they're fiercely protective of their humans, and I am now included in that group.

It's just beginning to get dark as we leave the house. I'm a little nervous as we start walking, despite Cleo's reassuring presence. I suppose I'll always be this way—more leery of potential dangers than other people. I'm not worried about someone trying to grab us; that kind of stuff doesn't happen as much as people think. The real danger is from people who have gotten to know you, earned your trust.

I'm afraid Mitch will find me, or that I'll run into someone from the motel.

"Are we still on for Saturday?" Elsa asks as we walk. She knows that talking helps ease my anxiety, and she is really, really good at talking.

"Yep! Krys said she'd drive us if we want."

"Okay. I don't think I'll be able to get the car, so sure." She glances over. "You going to get your learner's permit soon?"

"I have an appointment next week." Something else to be nervous about. What if I smash up the car and Krys decides to get rid of me? I know it's irrational, but I can't help but think it. I keep waiting for her and Jamal to decide they made a mistake. Every time DCF checks in, I think they're going to tell the case worker to take me with her when she goes, but they haven't yet. I'm starting to believe they're not going to ask. That's even scarier than expecting them to bail.

Why is it so much easier for me to believe the worst about people, but not the good? I've known good people. Haven't I?

We're only a few blocks away from the house when a car pulls up beside us. I hear it before I see it—loud bassline thumping. They're listening to rap, what Daisy used to call "angry white boy music." It makes me smile a little to think of her. Is she okay? Is Ivy? What about Jasmine or Rose? Are they safe?

"Hey, Elsa," a boy yells from the passenger window of an old Volvo.

Caesar growls. Elsa frowns at them. "Turn down the music, moron."

To my surprise, the music is lowered to an almost-quiet level. The car has three guys in it. The one leaning out the window is cute, and I'm pretty sure he knows it. Nothing really threatening about any of them, but I take a step back regardless. Cleo doesn't make a sound, but she puts herself between me and the car.

"Who's your friend?" the boy in the window asks. He has blondish hair and bright blue eyes.

Elsa turns to me. It's up to me to decide if I want to know him. "Lex," I say.

He grins. "Hi, Lex. I'm Mike."

I smile slightly.

He turns back to Elsa. "I'm having a party Saturday night. You guys should come."

I haven't been to a party in forever, at least not a normal party. The kind of "party" I've become used to is something these guys have probably only seen on TV.

Elsa shrugs. "Maybe."

Mike is still smiling at her. "You're not going to get a better offer." He looks at me. "You'll come, won't you, Lex?"

I shrug too. "If I don't have anything better to do." The way it comes out of my mouth surprises me. Elsa too. I sound flirty.

Mike doesn't seem to notice. He really is cute. "I'll cross my fingers nothing else comes up. See ya."

They roar off. Caesar growls again.

"Do you want to go?" Elsa asks me.

"I don't know. I'm not sure it's a good idea." The way Mike looked at me . . .

"He was definitely flirting with you, but hey, you're hot."

"Ha. Thanks. I don't know if Krys will go for it."

She shrugs. "I'd go with you. It might be a good way to meet some people before school. Make some friends."

I give her a pointed look. "I have a friend."

She smiles. "You can have more than one."

"One's all I need," I say as we start walking. "But I'll think about it."

Actually, I'm thinking about Mike and how nice it was to have a cute boy smile at me. Mitch didn't completely destroy that part of me. Besides, boys are safe. After all I'd been through, I can handle boys. Right?

When is the last time I thought a guy was cute? Or wanted a guy's attention? I can't remember. One party wouldn't hurt, especially if Elsa is with me.

And Mike is very, *very* cute.

"You're not going to run away, are you?"

I'm putting on makeup when Krys appears in my bathroom doorway. I look at her in the mirror. "What?"

"This party, you're really going to it, right? You're not running away to meet up with him, are you?"

Him. She means Mitch. I stare at her, mouth slightly agape. "No."

She nods, and I can tell how worried—how scared—she is. "It's just . . . I know sometimes girls who have been through what you have, they run away—like your friend at the hospital."

Ivy. We've never talked about that night she saw me at the elevator, ready to bolt.

"I almost ran away at the hospital. I thought about running away at Sparrow Brook, but I haven't thought about it since coming here."

Are those tears in her eyes? "Good. It would break my heart, you know. If you ran."

I nod. My throat's too tight to form words.

She smiles a little. "You look pretty."

"Thanks." It's a rough whisper.

"I remember watching your mother get ready to go out when I was younger. You look a lot like her."

I'm not sure if that's a good thing or bad, but I have to assume she wouldn't have said it unless it was a compliment.

"I thought she was so beautiful, like a movie star. Do you ever miss her?"

I shake my head. "No." It's horrible, probably, but it's true. "Should I?"

"I don't know."

"Has she called again?"

"No."

"Then she doesn't miss me either." I pull a tube of mascara out of the organizer. If I could wear only one kind of makeup, it would be mascara. My eyelashes are next to invisible without it. I coat the top and bottom, swirling the wand as I go. It's relaxing. Centering. The kind of thing Dr. Lisa says is good for easing anxiety.

Talking about my mother makes me anxious, because I can't think of her without thinking about Frank.

Still no sign of him, but he's out there. So is Mitch. They probably took off to Mitch's brother's in upstate New York to avoid the police. Mitch likes to recruit girls from up there. He likes to recruit girls everywhere, but New York is where he found Daisy and Jasmine. I think Holly came from there too, but she left shortly after I was brought in. I don't know where she went.

Where is Ivy? Is she okay? It's not like she'd know where to find me even if she wanted to. Not like I can reach out to her. She'd tell Mitch. He'd take it as a sign that I want to go back. I don't. Even if I think about it sometimes, I don't want to go back there.

"I think your mother misses you as much as she's able," Krys says, bringing me back to now.

"Maybe." I put the mascara away and get my lip gloss. "It's nice of you to think it."

"So, Elsa is picking you up and bringing you home?"

I nod. "I told her I need to be back by midnight."

"And you'll call me if you need anything, or something happens?"

I turn to face her with a slight smile. "Nothing's going to happen."

She doesn't look like she believes me. "Promise you'll call."

"Aunt Krys, I promise." I walk over and give her a hug. I'm slowly getting better at it, but I still suck. "Please don't worry."

She bobs her head, but doesn't say anything. God, she's really a mess.

"Do you want me to stay home?" I ask.

"Yes," she replies with a shaky laugh. "But no. I want you to go and have fun. I'm just . . . scared." She clears her throat. "Is your phone charged?"

I hold it up. It's still plugged in. "One hundred percent."

The doorbell rings. She jumps at the sudden sound. "That's probably Elsa. Do you want me to send her up?"

"No. I'm ready." I shove the lip gloss into the small cross-body bag Krys bought me a few days earlier, along with my phone. There's twenty dollars in there for emergencies. I wouldn't be surprised to find a tracking device sewn into the lining.

It's not me she doesn't trust, not really. She's worried I'll make a shitty decision, and I can't blame her. I'm great at shitty decisions.

We go downstairs together. Jamal has answered the door, and Elsa is in the kitchen with him when we appear. She's wearing torn black jeans and a dark red top with black wedges. There's a fresh streak of dark purple in her hair and she's got her nose piercing in.

I wonder if Krys would mind if I got my nose pierced.

We say goodbye and Elsa promises my aunt and uncle we'll be home by midnight. She even makes sure they have her cell number. I'm starting to wonder if I should be insulted by all this. I mean, I've been in more dangerous situations than the three of them combined, and I'm not nearly as worried about my safety as they seem to be.

"You look awesome," Elsa tells me as we get into her car.

I'm wearing a new outfit I got at the mall a few days earlier—jeans, a teal top, and flats. Nothing too flashy. I don't know how people around here dress, and while I'm not interested in being a fashion clone, I don't want to stand out either. I'm going to stand out enough as the new girl.

"Thanks. So do you."

She starts the engine. "So, I should probably warn you there's a good chance my ex is going to be there."

"Is he an asshole?"

"She, and she can be."

My eyebrows jump halfway up my head. "Dude, I told you about being fucking trafficked, and you're just coming out to me now?"

She lifts one shoulder. "I thought you figured it out."

"How? It's not like you have a pride flag in your bedroom. You don't even have posters of girls." She doesn't really have posters at all—just a few band shots and some weird-ass art.

"I told you I thought Chloë Grace Moretz was hot."

"I agreed with you," I remind her. "That doesn't mean I want to go down on her."

"Well, I would!" she shoots back. She starts laughing, and so do I. "I'm sorry," she says after a few seconds.

I wave it off. "It's no big deal. Not like I felt the need to tell you I'm straight." Well, mostly. I wouldn't choose to be with a woman, but I have had sex with them. Not many, but a few, and it wasn't that bad—as far as forced sex with strangers went.

"I kind of figured that out after watching you drool over Mike," she teases as we pull out onto the street.

"I didn't drool. I flirted a little."

"You still like guys after all you've been through?"

It's an honest question, and not a surprising one, really. "Yeah. I do. I really want to believe they're not all bad, you know?"

"Yeah. I guess I'm lucky. Women are safer."

I cast a sideways glance at her. "Girl, don't fool yourself. I've known some fucked-up chicks."

She holds up her hand. "I don't want to know. I mean, you can talk to me about it whenever you want, but I don't get off on other people's pain."

"I know. That's why I trust you. You'd never hurt anybody." Except herself, but I don't say that out loud. She would think I was being cruel, and that's not how I'd mean it.

She flashes me a toothy grin.

Mike only lives a few streets away. His giant house is red brick with white trim. Very bougie, Daisy would say.

There are three cars in the paved drive and probably a dozen more on the street. We can hear the music from outside and see people laughing and dancing through the large front windows.

Suddenly, I'm frozen on the sidewalk. My feet refuse to move.

"You okay?" Elsa asks.

"I'm not sure I'm ready for this," I admit. My heart is pounding like crazy. My scalp is sweating. What was I thinking, coming here? Willingly walking into a house full of strangers is fucking nuts.

"We'll stand out here until you're ready," she says. "And if that doesn't happen, we'll go back to my place and watch a movie." She doesn't sound like she'd mind either outcome.

"Thanks," I whisper.

"Hey," comes a familiar voice. I turn my head to see Zack walking toward us. In distressed jeans and a dark button-down, he looks more like a man than a high school kid. "You just get here?"

I nod.

"Lex is a little nervous," Elsa tells him. I shoot her a dirty look.

Zack shoves his hands into his pockets. "I don't blame you. I know everyone in there, and I'm nervous. It's like walking into a piranha tank. You never know which one's going to try to eat you alive."

"Aw, poor Zack doesn't like the girls falling all over him," Elsa teases.

I glance at him. Yeah, I can see why girls would hit on him. He's not as pretty as Mike, but he's got that dark and brooding thing going for him. He looks down at his feet. "It's embarrassing," he says.

"Is this the point where you come out to me too?" I ask dryly.

He looks at Elsa. "She didn't know you're gay?"

"Nope. She's not terribly bright." She winks at me to let me know she's joking.

Zack turns to me. "You think *I'm* gay?" He looks down. "I know it's not because of my fashion sense."

I sigh. "Apparently my gaydar is off. I can't tell who's straight and who isn't."

Elsa slaps him on the arm. God, even in heels, she barely reaches his armpit. "Oh, Zack is one hundred percent straight, much to the disappointment of half the guys in the gay-straight student alliance."

He rolls his eyes as he looks at me. "She's exaggerating. And I'm only popular because I'm on the basketball team. If it weren't for that, everyone would think I was a nerd."

"You are a nerd," Elsa informs him. She looks to the noisy house and sighs. "What do you guys think?"

"Let's go in," I say, surprising even myself. I'm more comfortable with the idea now that Zack is with us. Even if he abandons us when we get inside, at least there will be two people I know there.

"All right," Zack says. "Let's do it."

We walk up the steps and ring the bell. No one answers, so Elsa turns the doorknob—the door swings open.

"Come on in, guys!" someone inside the house yells.

Zack gestures for me and Elsa to go first. It's my last chance to change my mind. Go home and be safe, or step inside and take my chances. Mike turns his head and looks right at me. He smiles. He is so incredibly hot.

I smile back and step inside.

There's booze and pot. I stay away from both. It's really not that hard to do when I see other people staggering around and acting like idiots. Not the potheads—they're slumped on the sofa, laughing and covered in chip crumbs. I wish I were joking. None of them make getting wasted look appealing. They're not doing it to escape or be numb, they're doing it to be more than what they think they are. No one's taught them that it's supposed to make you feel less.

The red plastic cup in my hand has nothing but cola in it. I know better than to set it down anywhere. It's in my hand the entire time there's anything in it. The first time Mitch drugged me, it was in a glass of root beer.

It's hot and loud. I've met a lot of people, but it's almost impossible to talk to anyone without yelling.

Elsa's talking to a pretty little punk girl a few feet away, just far enough that I can't hear anything they're saying, which is probably for the best. Zack is surrounded by some of his basketball buddies, and yeah, several girls who seem eager for his attention. I'm tempted to tell one of them to talk to him about books if they really want his attention, but I don't. I kind of like knowing what they don't know.

I'm bored. I'm pretty sure I don't have anything in common with most of these people. What am I going to say if someone asks where I went to school before this? They start talking about the trip their family took last Christmas and I tell them what? That I spent Christmas Eve getting fucked by not one, but two guys dressed like Santa? And that both of them told me what a naughty girl I was? They'd probably think I was joking. Or maybe they wouldn't. Regardless, they'd probably laugh. What else are you going to do when someone tells you a story like that?

Finishing my drink, I set the cup down and go upstairs looking for a bathroom. The first door I open reveals a couple making out. I close the door. The next one is the bathroom. There's not even a line, which makes me think there must be another one downstairs. I lock the door and use the toilet. After, I wash my hands and check my makeup. It's a little melted, but not bad. I touch up my lip gloss and stand there for a second, staring at my face in the mirror. Sometimes I look at my features and don't recognize them, or wonder if they've changed.

I sigh. I can't hide in the bathroom for the rest of the night. Maybe I'll go tell Elsa I'm ready to go. I can always get an Uber or call Krys if she doesn't want to leave. I just don't belong here.

When I open the door, Mike is standing there, smiling.

"Hi," I say.

"Hi. I've been looking for you."

"Why?"

He kisses me. "Because I haven't stopped thinking about you since we met." He kisses me again. My heart jumps when his tongue touches my lips. When he takes my hand, I don't pull away, not even when I see Zack walking toward us. Mike pulls me down the hall to a room. It's his room, I guess. It looks like a boy's bedroom.

He locks the door.

"You're beautiful," he tells me, kissing me once more. "Is this okay? I wanna spend time with you."

I nod. I want to spend time with him too, so when he leads me to his bed, I go. I lie down with him and let him kiss me some more.

"You're not like other girls, are you?" he asks as he slides his hand under my shirt.

"No," I say. Then I kiss him so he'll stop talking.

I know what he wants. When his fingers unbutton my jeans, I don't try to stop him. And when those fingers slip inside my underwear, I show them where to touch me so there's a chance I'll enjoy what comes next. He pushes my pants down. I kick them off one foot.

I don't have to do this. I know I don't, but . . . I don't know what else to do. It's not like he's trying to hurt me. Not like he isn't cute. Not like I don't want him to want me. I do want him to want me. To like me. To think I'm special.

"You're so fucking hot," he tells me, unzipping his fly. On my back, I let Mike shove himself inside me. A little sigh escapes me as a door in my mind opens, and I walk through into someplace else. I stare up at the ceiling. I barely feel it. I'm not there anymore. There's no party, no hot breath in my ear.

For the first time since walking in his front door, I finally feel comfortable. I feel like I'm where I'm supposed to be.

I'm Poppy.

chapter eight

"You had sex with Mike?" Elsa wrinkles her nose. "Why?"

Is she judging me? "Because I wanted to." I lean back against the bench. We're at a neighborhood park with the dogs, who are lying in the sun after exhausting themselves. A slight breeze drifts through my hair and cools the back of my neck.

"Was it any good?"

I laugh. "It was okay."

She turns her head toward me. "He didn't force you, did he?"

"No." I shrug. "I wanted to. It felt right." Now I wonder if it was wrong.

"Okay."

"What's the problem?" I demand.

"Nothing." She shakes her head. "I'm surprised, that's all. I assumed you didn't like sex after what happened to you."

"It's just sex," I say. "Sometimes it's nice."

She looks at me, but I can't read her expression. "Yeah, well, what do I know? I don't do penises."

I laugh. "He wants to hang out Friday night."

"You're on the pill, right?"

She sounds concerned. "Yeah. Don't worry, Mom. He used a rubber."

"I don't want you to be taken advantage of."

"I can take care of myself." I sigh. "That was bitchy. Sorry."

"I know you can take care of yourself, but you're my friend, and I'm allowed to worry about you, so fuck off." She smiles.

I smile back, but I seem to have developed a habit of losing friends. First Ivy and then Sarah . . .

"You okay?" Elsa asks.

"Yeah. But we should probably get home. Krys will have dinner ready soon." As we stand, so do the dogs. The adults get up quicker than the puppies, who look at us with sleepy eyes.

Elsa gives me a hug when we reach my house. My house. That seems so weird. I hug her back. I'm getting better at it.

"I'll see you tomorrow," she says. I watch her and the dogs as they walk back down the drive. She is my friend. My only friend. Mike is just a boy. There will always be boys and men. I need to remember that.

After dinner, the phone rings. I hear Krys say, "She's not here. Can I take a message?" Jamal and I exchange glances.

"Who was that?" he asks when she returns to the table.

A small frown puckers the skin between her eyebrows. "Do you know someone named Ivy?" she asks me.

"Yeah," I say. "I used to. Why?"

"That was her. She said she got the phone number from your mom and the two of you are friends?"

"That was her at the hospital," I explain, heart pounding. "The one who left."

Krys nods. She's still frowning. "She left her number."

"Can I call her?" Why is she still using the name Ivy? Why not her real name? Unless she's back in the life?

Her gaze locks with mine. "Is it safe for you to be in contact with her?"

"Yeah. Ivy wouldn't do anything to hurt me." She doesn't look convinced. "I won't tell her where I am." We both know how easy it would be for her to find the address anyway.

"Okay." Krys slides a small piece of paper across the table to me. "I trust you, but I don't trust her, so be careful, all right? And call her from the house phone. I don't want her to have your cell."

I nod, snatching up the paper like it's gold, or pills.

After dinner, I grab the cordless and take it up to my room. I punch in the number on the paper and wait, like, forever as it rings.

"Yeah?"

"Ivy?"

"Poppy! My favorite bitch. How the fuck you doin'?"

"Who you callin' bitch?" I grin. "I'm good. You?"

"Hangin' in. Look, we need to get together."

We do? Doesn't she want to know what I've been doing? I want to know what she's been doing, how she is. *Where* she is.

"Can you meet me tomorrow?" she asks. "There's a park by the high school. You know it?"

"Yeah." How does she?

"Meet me there at three."

"Iv—" But she's already hung up.

I sit there, on my bed, staring at the phone. A worm of uncertainty—dread—coils in my stomach. I dial another number. The worm squirms.

"Detective Willis."

"It's Lex," I say.

"Honey, is everything okay?"

"Ivy called me. I'm not sure how she got the number, but she wants to meet tomorrow." Actually, I'm pretty sure she got the number from Mitch, who I'm sure got it from my mother. "I think she might be setting me up."

"Tell me when and where." After I do, she says, "I'll be close by, okay? I'll be there with you."

"Okay."

Krys knocks on my door. I tell Detective Willis I need to go and hang up.

"Everything all right?" my aunt asks.

I tell her what Ivy wanted, and that Detective Willis is going to be there.

She shakes her head. "No. I don't want you to do this. It could be dangerous. What if he's there?"

She means Mitch. "Then they can arrest him."

"You're not going. Give me the phone. I'm going to call Marianne and tell her you're not doing it."

I hold the phone tight in my hand. "No. I'm going to do it."

Her eyes are damp and wide. "If he hurts you . . ."

"He won't." I can't promise that, obviously, but what's another lie on top of all the others I've told? "I want to do this. I want to stop him from doing what he did to me to someone else." And if I talk about it or think about it too much I'll change my mind. I'll chicken out, I know I will. Because as much as I want revenge, I don't want to hurt him.

That's how I win her over—I can see it in her eyes and how her shoulders sag. "Fine. But I'm going to be there too."

I don't want her anywhere near Mitch, but I can't tell her no, not after convincing her to let me go. "Please stay out of sight."

She nods, and I give her the phone.

"It's just me meeting a friend in the park," I tell her. "Not a firing squad. It'll be okay."

She smiles and touches my hair. "Brave girl."

Stupid girl, more like it. It doesn't matter how many times or how many people tell me it's not my fault, I'm the one who made the decisions that got me here. Ivy and I both got ourselves into the life. But maybe—just maybe—I can get Ivy out.

He came at me slowly, gently. It wasn't like I met him one day and was working for him the next. No, Mitch slithered into my life like a snake with an apple, offering me the most delicious bite.

And I was dumb enough to take it.

"I got you something," he said to me one night, and handed me a small box. Inside were the prettiest earrings I'd ever seen. They sparkled under the light.

"Diamond," he said. "You deserve to shine."

"Mitch," my mother said. "You're too generous."

He smiled at her and handed her a bottle of Southern Comfort.

His gifts weren't always this expensive—sometimes he showed up with iTunes gift cards. Once he came by with a pair of sneakers I'd been drooling over. Said a friend of his had a connection. They were expensive, but I didn't care because I'd wanted them.

It never occurred to me he was setting me up. Never occurred to me he had any reason to be nice to me other than being nice.

It didn't take long for me to start crushing.

One night, he showed up at the apartment while Mom was passed out and Frank was gone. "Have you eaten?" he asked.

I shook my head. I didn't tell him we didn't have any food. Mom and Frank drank their calories when they were on a binge.

"Come on. I'm taking you out."

I expected McDonald's, not a nice place like the one he took me to.

"Get whatever you want," he said. "Price doesn't matter."

I got steak, and dessert after. We walked around town. He held my hand.

It was after ten when he dropped me off at the apartment. "I had a really nice time," he said.

"Me too."

He leaned over and kissed me. My heart jumped into my throat. I'd never been kissed like that before.

I didn't see him for a few days after that, then he stopped by and told me he'd gotten tickets for a concert that coming weekend.

"Want to go?" he asked.

I looked at Mom. She sat slouched in a chair, a glass cradled in her lap. "I don't fucking care," she slurred.

The concert was in New York. Madison Square Garden. Mitch got us hotel rooms for the night. It was amazing.

I was in my room getting ready for bed when he knocked on the connecting door. He came in with a bottle of wine and two glasses. I got tipsy. Hell, I was pretty drunk. When he kissed me, I didn't stop him. When he touched me, I didn't stop him. I didn't want him to stop. He made me feel things I'd never felt before.

It was him who taught me how to give blowjobs. He taught me that night. Only he didn't pull my hair or push on the back of my head. Not that time, anyway.

"You're so good at that, sweetheart," he said. "You make me feel so good."

His mouth was all over me. His hands too. By the time he slipped between my legs, I was practically begging him for it. It hurt, but just for a bit. He kept doing things to make it better, kept whispering in my ear. Things like, "Sweet baby girl. You're so beautiful. So perfect."

We showered together afterward. He went down on me to make up for the fact that I hadn't come during sex. We spent the night in my hotel room bed, and the next morning we had sex again before going to breakfast and driving home.

By then, I was in love with him.

I'm not sure my mother even noticed when I started spending more time at Mitch's house than I did at home. She certainly didn't care I was missing school. Meanwhile, he kept buying me gifts and treating me like his queen.

A month or two into our "relationship" he turned to me. "Baby girl, you'd do anything for me, wouldn't you?"

"You know I would," I told him. "I love you."

He looked away. "No. I can't do it."

My heart skipped a terrified beat. "Do what?" Was he going to leave me?

There was pain in his gaze. "I can't ask you to help me."

"Mitch, I'll do anything." The words he'd been waiting to hear.

"I owe money, baby girl. To a guy who isn't very nice. He's threatening to hurt me."

I was so scared, I started shaking. "What can I do?"

"He says he'll forget the debt if you . . ." He turned his head. "If you have sex with him."

Oh my God. "What?"

"He's seen how sexy and beautiful you are and he wants you. Just once." He took my hands in his. "I hate asking you. I don't want to share you, but you'd be saving my life, sweetheart."

That's all it took—at least that's how I remember it. Mitch gave me some pills to make it easier, before he presented me to the man. He was a big guy with a gut and a unibrow. His breath smelled like garlic as he panted on top of me, drops of sweat dripping onto my chest and stomach. It was horrible, but it was over fast, and Mitch was so thankful that it was worth it.

A week later it happened again with another guy, another life-threatening reason. More pills. It wasn't long after that he took me to the motel and told me I needed to repay him for all he'd done for me.

"No," I said. "I'm not doing it anymore."

That was the first time he hit me. "You're breaking my

heart," he said. "Why are you doing this to me?" It was all my fault. So, I did it. He took photos and put them on Stall313.com. He changed my name. After that it was a fairly steady stream of men in and out of my bed. A steady stream of pills and E and whatever else he made us take. A steady stream of humiliation and violence and being treated like I wasn't a person.

There was one guy who was amazed that I could speak because I asked him to get off me.

I guess by then Frank had told my mother I was living with Mitch. I don't know if she even cared. It didn't really matter. I had already discovered the escape hatch in my mind. Still, I was proud when Mitch complimented me, when he told me I was a good girl—that I was his favorite. I believed the lies, until one day I didn't believe them anymore. I knew what they were.

I do have to thank Mitch for one thing, though. He taught me a valuable lesson: What people say doesn't mean shit. It's what they do that counts.

I leave the house first just in case anyone's watching. I leave Isis at home. It feels weird to walk and not have her leash, or Cleo's, in my hand. Vulnerable. But I don't want my sweet dog anywhere near the life I used to have. She's better than that.

It's an overcast day, humid and sticky. My T-shirt clings to my back and my scalp is damp. Gross, but fairly typical for Connecticut.

School's let out for the day, and small groups of kids around my age walk together, backpacks jostling. They talk and laugh as though they don't have any problems, except for the one guy who shuffles along a few feet behind one of the groups. He looks like he has a lot of problems. Is that going to be me come September? The sad loser walking by herself?

"Hey."

I turn my head just in time to avoid walking right into Zack. Fuck me. What if he'd been Mitch? My heart starts to panic just thinking about it.

"Hey."

"You okay?" he asks with a frown.

I focus on his chest and how his T-shirt pulls across it. He's big for a seventeen-year-old, isn't he? He seems big to me. Was his father a giant? "Yep. You?"

"Sure." He drawls it out way longer than it needs to be. "Where you off to?"

I gesture up the street. "The park."

"Want company?"

"No." He looks hurt. "I'm meeting someone."

"Right." His lips twist a little—it's not quite a smile, but not really a smirk. "Mike?"

"Uh, no. Look, I gotta go." I start to walk by him.

"Your dealer?"

I turn. "What?"

His hands are in his shorts pockets as he shrugs. "Are you buying drugs?"

"What the fuck business is it of yours if I am?" I demand, stepping closer—right in his face. "Do I look like a fucking junkie to you?"

"No, you look scared."

I am scared. "I'm fine. Don't worry about it." I brush past him and keep walking, and I don't look back even though I want to. He doesn't say anything else, and he doesn't try to stop me. I'm a little disappointed even as I'm relieved.

The park isn't much. It's the same one Elsa and I bring the dogs to sometimes. It's small with a couple of walking paths through it, a few benches, picnic tables, and a small playground. A woman and a toddler are at the swings as I walk toward the girl sitting on top of one of the tables. Her hair is stringy, her roots dark. She's thinner than the last time I saw her, and puffing on a vape pod. She's got fresh scars on her right arm, I notice as I get closer.

"Bitch, that's my table," I say in a gruff voice.

Ivy's head whips around. She's wearing huge sunglasses that almost cover her black eye, but there's no concealing her grin. "Poppy!"

It feels like a code name now—not real. Like I'm a spy or something. A secret me. She jumps off the table and throws herself on me in a fierce, tight hug. Funny, I don't hesitate to hug her back, even though she smells like dirty laundry and BO.

"Bitch, I missed you!" she cries when she pulls back. She puts the pod in her pocket.

"I missed you too. Nice kicks." The Nikes had to have cost a few hundred. She can't afford shampoo, but she can afford those?

"Thanks. They were a present." She lifts her eyebrows, and I know exactly what kind of present they were. Probably stolen, as if that matters. Ivy doesn't care.

"Someone needs to gift you with some deodorant," I tell her before I can stop myself. We were always brutally honest with each other at the motel.

She lifts her arm and sniffs. "Fuck me," she gasps, making a face. "I smell like ass!" She laughs. I don't.

I used to be this. Strung out, dirty, thinking I'm all bougie and shit, despite stinking and looking like hell.

"Who hit you?" I ask.

Ivy takes off her sunglasses so I get a good look at the purple puffiness that is her eye. "Who do you think?" she asks.

"The same guy who bought you those sneakers." Mitch always likes to make grand apologies.

She grins. "You look good, Pop. I wouldn't have known you at first."

"Thanks. What's going on, Ivy? Where've you been?"

"With friends. You know. Rosie says hi."

Bitterness spreads across my tongue, even though I expected it. There's only one way she could be hanging out with Rose, his most obedient of girls. "Where is he?"

"He who?" comes a new voice. I stiffen, but I can't just stand there with my back to him. I turn slowly.

"What the fuck are you doing here?" I demand. I would have preferred Mitch, I really would.

Frank smiles. He's got a gold tooth in front that he loves showing off. "Why, I brought Ivy here to see you, doll."

He might have been good looking once, but he's heroin-ripped and tanned like leather. His brown hair is slicked back, or maybe just greasy. He's so skinny, I can see the muscles under his cheek move when he talks.

"Come with us," Ivy pleads. "Mitch wants to see you. He wants you back."

I knew it was a setup, but the fact that she's trying to play me still hurts. She let him use her against me. "No."

Frank's smile fades. He really is a mean son of a bitch. I wish I had Cleo with me—I'd let her use him as a chew toy. "It wasn't a request, girl. Mitch's got a lot of money invested in you, and you ain't earned out yet." That's a lie and we both know it. I never owed Mitch anything. You don't pay back "gifts."

"Fuck you." My voice is strong despite how I'm trembling. I shake my head. "I'm out of here."

Bony fingers, strong as steel and stained with nicotine, clamp around my wrist. Frank yanks me backward. He's skinny, but strong. His tobacco breath is hot and sour against my ear. "You ain't goin' nowhere."

"Let her go."

Out of the corner of my eye, I see a tall figure approach. Zack? He followed me. Asshole. I'm so happy to see him.

Frank releases me. I rub my arm as I back up toward Zack, putting as much distance between me and Frank as I can. Over Ivy's shoulder, I see Detective Willis walk toward us. Krys isn't far behind.

Look at all the people coming to rescue me. If only they'd all been around when Mitch first started grooming me. My life might have turned out completely different.

Frank notices as well. "Time to go," he says to Ivy.

"Don't," I tell her. "Come home with me."

She looks disappointed—that's the only way I can describe it. "See ya, Pop."

"My name is Lex," I tell her.

She shrugs and moves closer to Frank.

"Mr. Granger," Detective Willis says when she reaches us. "What a coincidence. Ivy."

Ivy looks away. Frank stares at Detective Willis like she's a bug he wants to squash. "Look at that, Ivy, they're lettin' darkies be police now."

Detective Willis makes a face. "This isn't Mississippi in the sixties, Mr. Granger. What are you doing here?"

He hitches his jeans. "I brought Ivy to see my stepdaughter. No law against that, is there?"

My teeth grind together. "I am *not* your fucking stepdaughter."

Frank grins, flashing that stupid tooth. Zack takes a step forward. His hands are clenched into fists.

"What are you all about, boy?" Frank demands. "You think you're her boyfriend? Shit, anyone can have her for the right price. I—" He stops. I guess he remembers I'm underage and there's a cop beside him.

Zack doesn't look at me. He stares at Frank, silent. Frank twitches. Zack might be twenty years younger than him, but he's several inches taller and at least thirty pounds heavier.

"Let's go, Frank," Ivy says. "I'm bored." Yeah, right. She's jonesing for a hit is what she is.

"Whatever you say, doll." He grins again. "You all have a lovely day."

I don't try to stop Ivy. There's no stopping her. I knew in the hospital and I know it now. If I brought her home, she'd steal whatever she could carry from Krys and Jamal, and take it all back to Mitch.

"Why are you letting him go?" Krys demands. Red splotches stain her cheeks as she faces Detective Willis. "Goddamn it, Marianne, he's a friend of that pimp."

I cringe at the word. Zack doesn't seem to notice. He's watching Frank.

"I can't arrest him for being in a park," the detective argues.

"She's a minor—and stoned," I say.

Detective Willis glances at me, a sad expression on her face. "Jaime's eighteen now."

"Well, fuck."

"My guys will follow them," she tells us. "Hopefully they'll lead us back to Mitch."

Right, Mitch—the big fucking prize.

I sigh. "Can I go home?" I'm so tired.

"Sure, sweetie," Krys says, putting her arm around my back. "Come on."

Detective Willis smiles at me, and I smile back. I get that she couldn't arrest Frank, that's not what matters. What matters is that she came when she said she would. I glance back at Zack. He turns his head and meets my gaze. I don't know what he sees when he looks at me now that he knows my secret. But when I look at him, I think I see a friend.

That makes two. Yay, me.

My gaze jumps down the street to Ivy as she gets into a car I don't recognize. Frank's driving. She doesn't look at me. Doesn't look back at all.

I don't think I'll ever see her again.

PART TWO

Lex

chapter nine

"C'mere," Mike whispers. His breath is warm and damp against my ear. I shiver. He smiles because he thinks I like it. He's wrong. We've been together—sort of—since his party back in June. We get together when we want, hang out, have sex, and don't talk for a couple of days. It works. To be honest, I'm surprised it's lasted this long. I figured he'd broom me as soon as school started.

The bell has rung for fourth period, and we're all shuffling through the hall like zombies. I'm one week into my senior year, and yeah, it's weird being back in school. My sort-of boyfriend pinches the sleeve of my shirt in his fingers and pulls me toward the boys' bathroom.

"What are you doing?" I ask. My heart speeds up a bit. I've been in enough bathrooms with guys to know what he has in mind. Mike likes making out and having sex in dangerous places. I don't know if it's the thrill we could get caught, or if he wants to see if there's anything I *won't* do.

He doesn't understand sex is meaningless to me. It's like flossing my teeth, but slightly more intrusive. He thinks I'm into it.

Or maybe he doesn't care if I am or not.

He pulls me into the bathroom. The lights are bright and harsh, giving the white walls a slight yellowish cast. There are a couple of stalls opposite the wall of sinks, and against the back wall, a row of urinals is lined up like we used to be every night at the motel, waiting to be chosen. Taken.

There's a guy at the sink. I recognize him as Trent, one of Mike's friends. He looks surprised to see us. "Oh," he says, backing up against the porcelain.

Mike grins at him, and the bottom falls out of my stomach. Elsa warned me that Mike's using me for sex. I know he is, but at least I've had a say in whether or not he gets it.

I begin to think that's changed when Kyle, another friend of Mike's, walks in. He's followed by Ethan and Tyler. They line up across the room, blocking the exit. A couple of them look nervous, but the others . . . the others look at me like I'm a rabbit and they're starving dogs. I turn to Mike. He's still smiling, like we're about to go on a roller coaster or zip-lining.

I haven't gone to a theme park with Mike. He hasn't taken me zip-lining either, though I know he's done both with his friends. I've never really hung out with any of his friends.

Until now.

"You don't mind, do you, Lex?" he asks, touching my hair. "I've been telling the guys how hot you are, and they're jealous. They want to find out for themselves. I told them you'd be cool."

There's a switch inside me that falls down, hard. Suddenly, I'm as numb and unfeeling as a stick of wood. I'm stronger than wood, though. Wood can splinter and break. I'm steel. Screw breaking, I won't even bend. I'm not afraid—these boys are nothing to be scared of. I'm disappointed.

But not surprised. I knew confiding in him was a mistake, but I did it anyway. He asked about my scars and I told him. *Stupid.*

"Yeah," says Ethan. "We want to find out for ourselves how hot you are, Lex."

They move closer, crowding into the bathroom. I smell bleach, urinal cakes, and their cologne. They're all wearing too much of it, and they mix together into something skunkish. There's no escape—I know it. The path of least resistance is always the one that keeps you safe—keeps you from getting beaten. Keeps them from using you so hard you bleed.

Mike stands in front of the urinals, but he faces away from them instead of toward. *How many teenage boys piss on this floor every day?* I wonder absently. *How many do it because they can?* Most men, I've discovered, have little to no regard for the mess they make for someone else to clean up, or the damage they do that someone else has to repair.

If it can be repaired.

I stand there, silent and waiting. It's better if I don't speak. Mike puts his hand on my shoulder and pushes. I don't need to be told what to do; I sink down. I'm on my knees on the hard tile floor as he unzips his jeans. Oral, then. That's better. I've been out of the life long enough to know how surreal and sad it is that I think letting them use my mouth is somehow okay. Behind me, I hear one of his friends says, "Oh, shit" like he can't believe this is actually happening. I was like that once—a long time ago. It's better to accept it and let it go. It's happening but it doesn't matter.

That which doesn't kill us makes us stronger, my grandmother used to say.

Mike's hand wraps around the back of my neck. He pulls me closer. I don't feel like this is going to make me stronger.

"She's gonna do it," another voice whispers.

"She's going to do us all."

I smell sweat and skin and all that awful cologne. My jaw opens. I almost gag, but I catch myself in time. I force myself to take a deep, acrid breath. I close my eyes and go somewhere else.

Anywhere but here.

The boys leave when they're done. Not like there's any reason to stick around. They don't want to be that late to class, I guess. Good thing they're boys—the whole thing hadn't taken longer than four or five minutes. Some old guys take forever.

I stand at the sink, brushing my teeth. The harsh light shows me too clearly in the mirror—my lips red and chafed, eyes watery. The back of my throat burns, and I scrub the inside of my mouth with the disposable toothbrushes my aunt likes to buy. It's not enough, but it will have to do.

Mike leans against the sink beside mine. He's smiling at me like I'm a puppy that just crapped outside. If he touches me, I'm going to shove this toothbrush through his eye.

I'm angry. It's like a slap to my forehead. *I'm so fucking angry.* Not annoyed or even mad. This is rage, and it's ugly. What am I supposed to do with it? I can't let it out. Someone will get hurt if I let it out, and historically that's always been me.

"That's a hundred," I tell him, spitting.

He blinks, smile fading. "What?"

"Five blowjobs. That's a hundred bucks."

Color drains from his cheeks. Because of the money, or because what he did is finally sinking in? "I thought it was a favor."

I almost gag on the toothbrush as I scrub the back of my tongue again. More spit. "That's what every pimp says at first. You planning to rent a stall?" I gesture at the row of partitioned toilets behind us. "It's cheap and dirty—like me, right?"

"Lex . . ."

"Don't." I toss the toothbrush in the trash. I can still taste them—but now it's cinnamon mixed with shame. "Do me a favor, Mike. Lose my number." I walk toward the bathroom exit. I'm going to skip class. I'll get Krys to call in for me, and go home. She can tell them I have cramps or something. I don't fucking care.

"*You're* breaking up with *me*?" His tone is incredulous, like it's the first time it's ever happened. Maybe it is.

Breaking up? Were we dating in his mind? How fucked up is that? I turn and look over my shoulder. "Yeah, I am. We're done."

He takes a step toward me, face red. A little boy on the verge of a tantrum. "You bitch."

I stand there, holding his gaze. "What are you going to do?" I ask softly. "Hit me? You think I haven't been hit before? I have, and by bigger guys than you. I've had lots of guys *bigger* than you, Mike."

His mouth falls open, but no words come out. I turn and leave the bathroom on trembling legs. The corridor is practically empty, so I go to my locker, get my things, and leave the school as quickly as I can. It's sheer luck that I don't get caught.

I walk home. I'm not scared that Mitch is going to show up. I don't care if he does. It would be the perfect time. I'd probably let him take me.

Or try to kill him. Maybe both.

Krys is at the counter when I walk in. She's prepping a roast or something for dinner. Her red hair is pulled up in a messy bun that matches her boho personality. She's wearing a long, knit dress and no makeup.

She looks up, takes one look at me, and turns even paler than normal. "What's wrong? Why aren't you in school?"

I think about the bathroom, about the smell of the urinal cakes, and the boys. The heat of their skin, the hair-pulling, the moist clutch of their fingers. My stomach suddenly rolls, acid flooding the back of my throat. I drop my books and purse to the floor and run. I race to the downstairs bathroom. My sore knees hit the tiled floor in front of the toilet hard. I yank the lid up and retch so hard, my diaphragm cramps. I'm sitting on the floor when Krys comes in.

"What do you need?" she asks me.

I pat the floor beside me. She doesn't hesitate, just sits down and opens her arms. I lean my head on her shoulder as her arms close around me. The rage is gone. All that's left is shame.

It's all I'm good for.

chapter ten

Krys cries when I tell her what happened. After we get off the floor, she calls my shrink and leaves a message. Dr. Lisa calls me back ten minutes later. She has to be on her lunch break, or between patients, to call back so quickly.

"Are you all right?" is the first thing she asks. "Do you want to talk about it?" The sound of her voice is enough to make me feel a little better.

"Some boys cornered me at school."

There's a pause. I know she's thinking of all the things I'm not saying. "Do you need to see a doctor?"

I'm on my bed, music playing low. Krys is downstairs. I can smell the roast starting to cook and it smells good. My mother thought cooking was microwaving a can of something, but my aunt can actually put a meal together. I've gained at least ten pounds since moving in. "No. I'm good. It was only oral." The back of my throat feels raw and bruised, but nothing serious.

"That's still assault, Alexa."

I sigh. "Yeah." But after all those months in the hotel, the days when sometimes it hurt to pee or worse, it seems insignificant. So why am I so fucked up over it? "I didn't say no."

"If you'd said no, do you think it would have made a difference?"

The side of my thumb is in my mouth. I'm chewing on it. "I don't know." I'd like to think it would have, but . . . "I think Mike would have kept on me until I broke."

"Mike?" The concern in her voice is sharp in my ear. "The boy you've been dating?"

"Yeah."

Silence. An exhale. "Oh, Alexa. I'm very sorry to hear that."

I blink back tears. Since becoming my therapist, Dr. Lisa has also become something of a friend. A confidante. She has experience in sexual exploitation, meaning she's been in the life. I can't hide shit from her. She understands all of it too well. Sometimes, the line between therapist and patient and friends gets blurred, and we both let it.

"I was surprised." That means I was stupid. I should have known better. I should have been smarter. I am so naive. I thought Mitch cured me of that. I don't want to be stupid and gullible anymore. "I'm pissed."

"I know you are," she replies. "And I want you to direct that anger away from yourself. There's nothing wrong with wanting to trust people. It's good that you are able to."

"I wanted to hurt him after, make him bleed."

"So, you are mad at him."

"I was starting to forget what it was like to be a whore, and he reminded me of what I am."

"You were never a whore."

"If you say I was a victim, I'm hanging up."

"I won't say it," she promises softly. "But it wasn't your choice. I want you to remember that."

"I had a choice today."

"Did you?"

I hate when she asks me questions instead of giving me statements. If I had the fucking answers, I wouldn't need her. "Yes."

"You said you thought Mike would break you down until you gave in. That doesn't sound like a choice." No, it sounds like the definition of trafficking they gave in that documentary we watched at Sparrow Brook.

I stare at the smooth white ceiling. The ceiling in the motel had been a weird yellowish color, with dark rusty splotches where rain leaked through. I used to make pictures out of them sometimes. "I could have fought." A little voice in my head laughs maniacally at that.

"How many boys were in the restroom, Alexa?"

"Five, including Mike."

"Did they seem like they would let you leave?"

I think of the other boys. They looked nervous, but they'd lined up across the bathroom, blocking the door. Had they done it on purpose?

God, I'm so tired.

"No," I reply honestly. "I don't think leaving was an option." Maybe it had been, but it doesn't matter. In that moment, I'd been taken back to a time when I hadn't had a choice. Five teenagers turned me into that mess, and I hate them for it. I hate myself more.

I'm tired of hating myself. Lately, I've started liking certain things about myself, and to be reminded of all that bad . . . "What should I do?"

If she turns the question back on me, I'm going to scream. "Are you asking my honest opinion?"

"I am."

"To begin with, I think you should report them to your principal."

I laugh—harsh and raw. Like there is anything remotely funny about this. "Like anyone will believe me."

"Why wouldn't they believe you?"

"You know why."

"Because you're such a terrible, awful person?"

A tear leaks from my eye. I wipe it away so hard, my skin stings. "Yes."

"*Alexa.*"

I sniff, wipe away another tear. They're becoming harder to hold back. "Will I ever stop feeling this way?"

"I think so."

She doesn't make promises, which is one of the things I like most about her. "I'll think about it." But we both know I won't report it.

"Did you break up with Mike?"

"Yes."

"And if he asks, you won't go back with him?"

I'm not insulted; she knows how these things go. She's known more girls in the life than I have, and she knows how many of them go back to it because it's what they know. I think of Ivy with Frank. What he might have done to her. Disgust slithers over my skin.

"No. Me and him, we're over." There has to be someone out there who thinks I'm special. Who won't use my past against me. There has to be. Otherwise, what is the point? "Thanks, Dr. Lisa."

"Are we done?" She sounds genuinely surprised.

"I need a shower," I confide. "And a nap." And Krys, but I don't say that. I don't want to admit to needing anyone.

"Okay. We can talk more when I see you." My regular weekly appointment, right.

"Sure. Thanks again."

"You're welcome. Goodbye, Alexa."

She makes a point of calling me by my name when we speak. I think it's to remind me I'm not Poppy anymore. I need the reminder. "Goodbye," I say, and hang up. I lie there for a minute, trying to get the energy to go to the shower. Finally, I get up and grab my pajamas.

In the bathroom, I take off my clothes and look at myself in the mirror. I try to look at myself like I'm not me. How would I react if I saw a naked girl with scars on her pale back from being beaten with a belt? I'd feel bad for her. And if I saw a brand burned into her hip—a simple letter *M*—I'd wonder who had been cruel enough to treat her like an animal. I trace the satiny flesh with my finger. Mike had said the *M* stood for his name. That I was his. I'd thought he'd meant it as something sweet, now I know better.

I know inside me that it was a good thing I believed him because it means I'm not completely broken, but God . . . I feel so stupid.

I look at myself some more. My hair is like rust against my shoulders. There's a scar from a bite on my left boob. I don't remember the guy who did it. I remember the antibiotics gave me the shits. The scars on my side and ass are from cigarettes. I don't remember who made them either, but I know they thought they had the right to burn me. I touch my throat, remember the guy who used to like to strangle me. Mitch banned him after he almost went too far one night.

If only he'd finished the job.

I look at my face. Can you tell by looking at me that I've been used up? Do people see me and know what I am? I've been told I'm lucky I got out, lucky I've stayed out. Lucky I didn't get killed.

Lucky. Lucky I wasn't pregnant. Lucky they used a condom. Lucky to be alive. Lucky we had Mitch. Lucky to have a place to live. Lucky to have a motel manager who'd hide our stuff if the cops came. Yeah. We were real lucky to have *him.* He held our things ransom until we fucked him.

I turn on the shower and step inside. Fuck lucky. I wasn't lucky then and I'm not lucky now. I'm tired, used, and dirty, and there is no way I'm ever going to get clean again. I've tried and tried, but I can't get the stink to wash off. I scrub and I scrub and all I get is raw.

When I first got out, I was numb and that was good. I thought I was doing okay, but now that I'm not so numb, I feel worse. Like I'm sliding back rather than going forward. So what if I don't talk street so much? I might sound different, look different, but I'm not different. I'm the same sad mess I've always been. Lucky, yeah, right.

If I were lucky, I'd be dead.

Zack doesn't tutor me anymore, but sometimes we do homework together. I've gotten used to seeing him a couple of nights a week. I'm on my bed snuggling with Isis when he knocks on the frame of my door.

"Krys said you left school because you weren't feeling well."

I nod.

He comes in and sets some papers on my desk. "I got your English and history homework. You missed a good discussion in Bent's class."

"Yeah?" I rub my face against my dog's ear.

He shoves his hands in his pockets.

"Are you okay?" he asks. He seems to ask me that a lot.

I sit up. Isis yawns and stretches. I look at him—as a guy, not as a friend. "If I shut the door and get naked, will you have sex with me?"

His mouth drops open. "Are you high? Why would you ask me that?"

I stand. Poppy's creepin' around the edges of my mind, and she wants to play. I guess what happened in the guys' bathroom wasn't enough for her. "Because you're a guy."

He looks confused. "I'm not *that* kind of guy. You're my friend."

"What if no one ever had to know?" I stand right in front of him and stare up into the darkness of his eyes. "What if I went down on you first?"

He swallows. I want to lick his Adam's apple. *Oh, Poppy.* "Lex . . ."

This acting all nice is pissing me off. I walk over to the bedroom door and shut it. I lock it too. Zack looks at me like I'm a tiger and he's a gazelle. I like it. I pull my T-shirt over my head and stand before him in my bra and sweats. "Come on," I say. "I won't tell."

Zack stares at me. For a second, his gaze flickers to my chest, but it locks with mine again. "Oh, Lex," he says, his voice a pained whisper.

I glance down. The bite on my breast is almost completely visible outside the edge of my bra. He's already seen the marks on my forearms, but now, he can also see some of those burns.

He sees *me*. Isn't this what I wanted? No, I realize. No, it's not.

I pull my shirt back on. "Look, you wanna fuck or not?"

He doesn't hesitate. "Not."

My lips twist into a sneer. Am I more surprised that he rejected me, or that it kinda hurts? "Why? I'm not perfect enough for you? Too slutty?"

Too damaged?

His hands cup my shoulders. God, his fingers are so warm. "Because you deserve better than a hookup."

I look up at him. "How do you know what I deserve?"

He looks so sad. I could hit him. Or kiss him. Both. "Because I know." And then, "I'm going to hug you, if that's okay."

I nod. He comes closer, wrapping his arms around my shoulders. I put mine around his ribs. My head is at his shoulder—perfect to lean into. I melt. Our bodies fit together like puzzle pieces. I hold him as tight as I can. He squeezes back. His chin rests on my head.

"You're a good person," he tells me. "I wish you could see that."

"You don't know anything about me."

"I know you better than you think."

I don't have it in me to argue. Besides, he's been nothing but nice to me, even when I've been a dick to him. Even when he found out the truth that day in the park. He's never made me feel like less of a person. "Okay."

Zack's arms tighten around my shoulders. "Someday you'll believe it too. You wanna go over the English assignment? It'll be easy for you."

I sigh and pull back. I'm cold where his body touched mine. And I can't quite look him in the eye. It's not because he's seen me, but because I'm starting to see him.

And I like it.

When I arrive at school the next day, Elsa's waiting for me at my locker.

The edge of a tattoo peeks out of the neckline of her shirt—it's the crow she has on her upper right shoulder. Sometimes, I see people—teachers too—looking at her like they're trying to figure out what other secrets she has on her body, and it makes me feel sick.

"What happened with Mike yesterday?" she asks.

Stupid me. I thought Mike wouldn't say anything because I wasn't going to. Should have known he'd blab. "He and his friends cornered me in the boys' bathroom." I manage to look her in the eye as I confide the truth. "They wanted blowjobs."

Her cheeks turn red. "Assholes."

I shrug, opening the locker door. "Dr. Lisa wants me to tell Mr. Case about it."

She nods—a sharp dip of her head. She looks so angry that I want to hug her. "You should. What they're saying . . ."

"Is probably true." I'm not trying to defend them, but I want to prepare her. "I did it, El."

She glances at me, scowling. "Do you think you blowing some guy—guys—would matter to me if I thought you *wanted* to do it?"

I smirk. "I think you'd want details." Seriously. I can't remember the last time I *wanted* to have sex.

Zack in my bedroom doesn't count. I wanted the power, not the act. I wanted to feel valued, but I didn't offer myself to him because I wanted him.

"Well, yeah." She's still frowning. "I almost kicked Mike in the balls when I saw him."

"He might like it."

Elsa shakes her head. "How come you aren't mad?"

"I was, but this doesn't change anything. People will think whatever they want of me. I have no control over it." And really? Part of me doesn't care.

She doesn't like this answer, and I don't know what else I can say to make her understand. "You shouldn't be punished for some guys being assholes. I'm coming to the office with you." She closes my locker.

I look at her. "I'm not going to the office."

"I thought you were going to talk to Mr. Case?"

"I said Dr. Lisa thinks I should report it." I make a face. "Not that I'm going to. It's not like he'll do anything about it. What if he kicks me out?" I might not like all the people at my school, but I like school itself. I like a lot of my teachers. I don't want to disappoint Krys and Jamal.

Fists on her hips, my friend glares up at me. "Oh, you're going to report it."

"No. I'm not."

She closes my locker door, putting herself between me and it. "Yeah, you are. If you don't, I will."

I shrug. "Go for it."

Frustration rolls off her like a perfume. "He's going to hear their lies. He needs to hear your truth."

I'm pretty sure she's going to be a lawyer someday. "I'm not doing it, and you're going to drop it."

Her nostrils flare when she looks at me. I try to smile. "Please," I say.

Elsa nods, but she doesn't speak. She's too pissed—at the boys, maybe at me, I don't know. What I do know is she won't betray me and run to Mr. Case. Ivy and Sarah might have been my friends, but Elsa reminds me what it's like to have a *best* friend. I haven't had one of those in a long time.

We walk together toward homeroom. We have to walk past the boys' bathroom, and I try not to look at the group of people standing around in front of the door. They're looking at something on their phones and making those noises guys make when they see tits. It's a sound that makes my stomach roll.

"Hey, Lex!" Mike calls out. "I got a stall with your name on it."

So he wants to be my pimp after all, huh? I don't look at him.

"I have mouthwash," he adds. His friends laugh.

This, I realize as I keep walking, is what happens when you break up with a guy. He gets mean. Or maybe I have a habit of picking rotten guys.

Elsa glares at him. "Fuck off, asshole."

Mike smirks at her. "There's room for you, Shopkin. Come on, Poppy. It's not a motel, but it's better than noth-ing. I'll give you half the profit. All we have to do is tweak your ad." He shakes his phone at me.

I should never have confided in him about the name Mitch gave me, or the ad he placed on Stall313.com. Some-how, Mike's found it—maybe it was never taken down—and he's shown it to all his friends. They look at me like

I'm something for them to jerk off to—or on. How many of them have copies of the photos from the ad on their phones now? Those pics don't exactly leave much to the imagination.

I have no control over anything. Nothing except how I let them see me react. And I've gotten really good at being completely blank.

Elsa marches up to him as though she is six-foot-four and not four-foot-eleven. "You're a real douche, you know that?"

Suddenly, I'm afraid for her. I know it's irrational—Elsa is one of the bravest people I've ever met—but I'm afraid of what he'll do to her. It's stronger than my desire to stay out of his way. I walk up to her and lightly grab her arm. "He's not worth it."

"You liked it," he says with a sneer.

Liked what? Him? The blowjobs? Being Poppy? How stupid is he?

I tug on Elsa. "Let's go."

Mike bends down. "You should try her out. You know she's done girls too, right?"

She spits on him. I can't believe it, just hocks up a huge loogie and lobs it right into his face. His hand comes up to block it and pushes her out of the way. He strikes me in the shoulder, shoving me back against the wall. If he'd hit her, it would have gotten her in the face.

"Hey!"

Oh, shit. It's Zack. His eyes look almost black as he approaches Mike. He looks tough and mad, nothing at all like the guy who hugged me yesterday.

Mike takes a step back, despite the cocky look on his face. "This isn't your business, man."

"I'm making it my business," Zack says. He glances at me. "You okay?"

"Yeah," I say, looking away. Physically I'm fine, but inside . . . I'm going to have to change schools. I can't stay there. I need to run.

But . . . I like my school. I like my classes. I like seeing Elsa every day. Fuck that noise; I'm not going anywhere unless I have to. I don't want to run and hide.

I've done nothing wrong.

"She's fine," Mike tells him. "She's had worse. Haven't you, Poppy?"

His friends aren't laughing, though. They look uncomfortable. I guess they're fine with looking at pictures of me, fine with knowing what Mike made me do, but they draw the line at him hitting me. Whatever.

I look Mike right in the eye. "Sure, I've had worse—I've had you." That gets a few laughs.

"You slut," Mike sneers, taking a step toward me. He's so full of hate, and only yesterday I thought he liked me.

Zack stops him with a hand on his shoulder. "You touch her, talk about her, fuck, man, if you even *look* at her, you and I are going to have a problem you don't want. Understand?"

Mike shrugs him off. "You think I'm afraid of you, *jefe*?"

Zack's scowl deepens. "I'm half Hawaiian, not Spanish, asshole. And I don't care if you're afraid of me or not; I will fuck you up."

The bell rings for class, but that's not why Mike backs off, and we all know it. I watch him slink away.

"Come on," Zack says. He puts me between him and Elsa as we walk down the hall. My bodyguards.

My friends.

chapter eleven

I'm in my second to last class of the day when Ms. Schnei-der, my teacher, tells me Principal Case wants to see me. It's almost a relief after being stared at and talked about all day. Maybe he'll expel me and save me from the stares and smirks and not-so-subtle remarks. The ad has been shared all over the school by now—at least I think it has. They all know what I am.

What I was. I'm not Poppy anymore, even though some-times she shows up.

Tyler texted me at lunch. It was an umbrella emoji fol-lowed by a question mark. On Stall 313 ads, that emoji is used as a synonym for condom. I didn't respond, though I was tempted to write back, "Only if you're still fucking your mom" because attitude is armor. All the girls knew that.

Mr. Case's office is on the first floor. When I check in at the desk, the secretary tells me to sit in the waiting area.

I'm only there for a few minutes before she calls me to go in.

"Are you comfortable being alone with me in the office?" Mr. Case asks after he says hello. He's probably in his fifties. Not bad looking. He reminds me of a cross between Will Smith and Denzel Washington, but his voice sounds like it comes from his toes, it's so deep.

I sit in a chair in front of his desk and look up. "Are you asking me that because I'm a girl, or because I'm me?"

His eyebrows raise—impressive because they are already fairly arched. "I promised your aunt and uncle I would do everything I could to make you comfortable for the duration of your time at our school. If you're not comfortable, I can have Mrs. Johnson join us."

Mrs. Johnson is a guidance counselor. She might be *the* guidance counselor—I don't know since I haven't spoken to her. I haven't given much thought to my future. There wasn't a point when I was with Mitch, and now, I'm just trying to deal with the present. I'm too exhausted from trying to figure out who I am to even think about what, or who, I want to be.

"No," I say. "I trust you."

He looks so surprised and honored that I don't clarify how I trust him as far as I'd trust any man in a room with people on the other side of the wall and furniture between us.

Mr. Case folds his hands on top of his desk and clears his throat. "I received a visit this morning from Detective Willis of the state police. She told me you were assaulted on school property yesterday. Is that true?"

I stare at him. He found out from Detective Willis? Not

gossip? "How did she know?" That's as good as admitting it, isn't it?

His frown deepens. "I assumed you told her."

I shake my head. "I haven't seen her." *Dr. Lisa. Shit.* In Connecticut, it's law that if a minor tells a teacher or therapist—someone in a professional position of authority—they've been assaulted, that person is obligated to report it to the authorities as well as DCF. DCF has to alert the school board.

Well, fuck.

"Alexa, we take this sort of allegation very seriously here. I understand you may not want to discuss it with me, but I do need to know if you were assaulted."

My first instinct is silence. Defiance. Put on that tough-girl face and tell him to fuck off. That's what Poppy would do. But I'm done defending guys who want to use me.

"On Tuesday, Mike Fischer and four of his friends got me to give them bl—oral sex—in the boys' bathroom near Mr. Wilson's classroom."

Mr. Case closes his eyes for a second. "Do you know the names of these other boys?"

"Tyler, Ethan, Kyle, and Trent. I don't know their last names."

He reaches behind him and pulls a yearbook off the shelf. "Point them out to me."

The four of them aren't hard to find. Seeing their smiling faces makes my stomach clench. They seemed like okay guys, before.

Mr. Case slides a pad of paper across the top of his desk toward me. He sets a pen on top. "Write down what happened and the names of all the boys, please."

"Why?"

"Because I would like a record of what happened from you." He adds, "You're not in any trouble, if that's what you're worried about."

It is. I don't want to write about it, but it's better than having to sit there and watch his face while telling him every detail. I pick up the pad. "How much information do you want me to give?"

"Whatever you think I should know," he replies. And, "Did you require medical attention?"

I shake my head.

He's quiet while I write. I keep it brief. Just the facts. I make sure I write down that I felt like I didn't have a choice, because I feel like I need to say that. Dr. Lisa would want me to—for the record and for myself.

I hand him the pad when I'm done.

"Thank you," he says. "I'm going to read this, and after, I'm going to talk to the boys."

My heart gives a thump. "I'm not lying," I insist.

He blinks. "I didn't think you were. I'm just telling you the rules I have to follow. I have to talk to the boys, and I will have to talk to your guardians and to their parents."

"It's not that serious," I say, standing up so fast I almost knock over the chair. "Forget I said anything."

His expression is sympathetic. "I can't do that, Alexa. I have a duty as your principal and I'm going to follow it. On this property you're under my protection, and I take that responsibility very seriously. I want you to know that."

It doesn't make me feel any better.

"Now, I assume Detective Willis will follow up with you and proceed from there as far as charges are concerned. Is there anything you need from me?"

I shake my head. The only thing I want is for him to drop all of this, but I know he won't.

He clears his throat again. "It's none of my business, but you should go to the doctor, or at least see the school nurse and have her examine you."

I look at him, feeling that slight shift of self that means I'm disconnecting. It's like I'm watching myself from outside my body. I have to hang on, get back in. "They didn't rape me."

He winces. "No, but if one of them has something, you could get a throat infection. Also, if there's bruising, it should be documented."

One of the girls at the motel got gonorrhea in her throat. "I'll get my aunt to take me." I don't know if it's a lie or not.

Mr. Case smiles slightly. "Good. Is there anything else you'd like to discuss?"

I raise a brow. "I didn't want to discuss this at all."

"No. I don't imagine you did. I wish you had felt safe enough to come to me in the first place."

"I didn't think you'd believe me."

He doesn't seem offended or even surprised by my honesty. "You're not the one who ought to be ashamed. If anyone ever makes you feel that way again, I want you to come straight to me. Please."

"Can I go back to class?"

I can't get out of there fast enough. I have to force myself to pause long enough to respond when he says goodbye.

I practically run from the office. Everyone is staring at me, I know it. To make matters worse, the bell rings for the last class. Students file out of classrooms, filling the corridor. A lot of them look at me. A lot of them don't. I make it to my locker with my head down, grab my books, and head to class.

When I walk into the room, everyone looks up. I can tell who was talking about me. Word has spread fast. There's only one person who isn't looking at me like I'm something they scraped off the bottom of their shoe, and that's Zack. He's sitting in the desk next to mine.

"Hi," he says when I sit down.

I force myself to meet his gaze. "Hi."

"Everything good?"

I nod. "I'm—"

"The school slut," says a girl behind me. Loudly enough that people laugh, and the teacher looks up with a scowl.

My face flames. I don't know why. I've been called worse.

Zack turns in his seat. "That's very misogynistic of you," he says calmly. "Not to mention, cruel and bitchy. *So* unattractive."

Someone giggles. I don't look. The girl doesn't say a word in response. Zack turns back toward the front of the room.

"You don't have to defend me," I tell him.

"I know, but I'm going to. You got a problem with that?"

I smile at his mock attitude and shake my head.

"Good," he says, and he smiles.

For a second, everything is right in the world.

Detective Willis is at the house when I get home. The sight of her pisses me off. My aunt has that look on her face that she gets when she wants to hug me but doesn't know if she should. Can't I just be left alone?

"You could have come to me first," I tell her. "Would have been nice to have a heads-up before getting called to the office."

"I'm sorry about that. We don't always have control over how these things go down once they've been reported."

"I didn't want it reported. I wanted it to go away."

"I need to take your statement," Detective Willis tells me. She's got her cop face on.

"I wrote it down for Principal Case. Can't you get it from him?"

"He emailed me a copy of what you gave him, but I have a few questions I want to ask you as well."

I shrug. "Whatever." I've already opened that door once today, so it's easy to start slipping away from them, to shut myself off.

Detective Willis isn't Mr. Case, though. She sees it. "That's not really why I'm here, though."

I hesitate. It's a trick to keep me present, but it works. "What is?"

"We found a girl this morning. I'd like your help identifying her."

"So?" Then it hits me why they both looked so sad when I came in. "You found her body."

Detective Willis nods. "Yes. She had the same brand on her hip as you. We're in the process of IDing her, but we don't have all the names of the girls from the hospital and none of the other girls who were under Mitch's control will tell me if they knew her."

"They won't?" No, of course they wouldn't.

She shakes her head. Her hair waves around her face.

"Alexa, you're the only one who has managed to reintegrate into society."

Meaning, I'm the only one of the motel girls who hasn't gone back to the life. Have they all gone back to Mitch? If it weren't for Krys, who knows where I'd be. Maybe I'd be on my back again too.

"So, what? You want me to look at the body?" Not like I haven't seen a dead person before. Lily #1 OD'ed in front of me.

"I have a photo." She slides a folder across the table. "Honey, I think it's Ivy. She doesn't look good, just so you know."

Ivy. My heart stops for one chest-crushing second.

Krys reaches over and grabs my hand. "You don't have to look if you don't want to."

"Yeah," I say. "I do." I open the folder with shaking fingers.

It's terrible. I've never seen anything like it. It's obvious she'd been dead for a while.

"What happened to her?" I ask. My voice is a whisper. I don't want to know this girl, but I recognize the scars and the birthmark on her hip. They dumped her naked. The motherfuckers couldn't even give her that much dignity.

"She was beaten to death," Detective Willis replies. "Is it her?"

I wish I had tears for her, but there's nothing but a strange burning in the pit of my stomach. After all she and I went through together, and I can't even give her tears. The last time I saw her, I let her walk away.

I nod, my throat closing up like invisible fingers are wrapped around it. "Her name was Jaime."

We'd only been at the motel a few days. Before that, we'd been in an apartment, but the landlord found out how many of us Mitch had living there and threatened to call the cops, so we moved at two in the morning.

It was a Thursday night. Aubrey, one of my regulars, had already been in, and he always came by on Thursday. He did the long haul from Boston to Florida. He always used my shower before getting into my bed. Some guys weren't so considerate, and there were those who let you know they were going to shower *after* they were done with you—because while we were good enough to use, they didn't want the smell of shame to linger.

Anyway, it was Thursday and my only visitor had been Aubrey. I watched through a haze of indifference as Daisy stared at the TV while "entertaining" a trucker from Idaho. She never missed an episode of *Friends,* even one she'd already watched a hundred times. That world was her happy place. We all had one—the place we went to. Mine was a little spot in my head where I did normal things, like puzzles and crafts. I'd been there while the heels of Aubrey's big hands dug into my collarbones, pinning me to the mattress.

The sheet beneath me was sticky. I could change it, but it wasn't like it mattered. The men that came here didn't care about that.

So, I was still on this sheet, watching *Friends* as Daisy did her thing, when the door opened and Mitch walked in. He had a new girl with him. She was about my age. Blond. Terrified. Her eyes were brown. They were the biggest eyes I'd ever seen.

"Move over," Mitch growled at me. The guy with Daisy

watched us with interest, his man boobs jiggling with the motion of his hips. *Jabba the Hut,* I thought, sliding toward the side of the bed.

Mitch shoved the girl onto the mattress where I had been. It would have been kinder to put her on the clean section, but Mitch wasn't about kindness. He pretended to be, at first, but it was part of the act. He was about to take care of this girl's "breaking in." It was his favorite part of the job, I'd once heard him say.

"Please help me," the girl whispered, her voice little more than a sob.

The muscles in my face were too lax to make any sort of expression. "I can't," I said. Even if I weren't stoned. Even if I were big enough to tackle Mitch, he had a gun and a buddy parked in a half-ton out in the lot with a rifle.

"Shut up." Mitch shoved her face into a pillow with one hand and undid his pants with the other.

I reached over and took her hand. Her fingers gripped mine tight enough to cut off circulation—not that I could really feel it. I laid my head on the pillow beside hers. I couldn't see her face, but I knew she could hear me. "It's going to be okay," I told her.

We both knew I was lying. Nothing would ever be okay again.

She was one of us now. One of Mitch's flowers. And flowers never bloomed for long.

chapter twelve

Detective Willis really likes tea. She drinks three cups while we talk.

After I tell her about Jaime, I tell her the story of what happened in the bathroom. It's almost easier to say it aloud than it was to write it because I don't have to be entirely present when I talk. I can treat it like a story I read, or something I saw on TV. What is hard is having Krys there as I repeat all the details.

"There will be charges brought against the boys," Detective Willis tells me, stirring sugar into her cup. "How do you feel about that?"

"Honestly?" I pick at a hangnail on my thumb. "I don't feel much of anything." And I don't—not really. I have no say over what happens, even though it directly impacts me, so why even try?

She nods, like that's a normal reaction when we both know it's not. "Your principal seems like a pretty good guy."

"Yeah."

"He's on your side in all of this."

"That's nice." What else am I supposed to say? It doesn't really matter if he's on my side or not. I did what those boys said I did. Mr. Case can't change that. Everybody acting like I was forced to my knees at gunpoint is being fucking ridiculous. The whole thing is ridiculous, really. But . . . I don't know. I'm starting to think maybe I really don't deserve to be treated like crap.

And Ivy didn't deserve to die. I look at the folder that sits closed on the table. I don't think I'll ever forget the photos inside it. I still don't cry, though. I can't. Not yet.

"We're going to get him," Detective Willis tells me, looking me dead in the eye. Her eyes are the prettiest shade of green I've ever seen. Ringed with black, they stand out sharply in the darkness of her face. "I promise you."

She means Mitch. The thought of him makes the scar on my back itch. The one from his belt. I hope that someday he won't matter as much. Won't scare me as much.

"I don't think you will," I tell her. "He's tricky."

"I'm still trying to figure out how he knew we were coming that night at the motel," she confides. The night he happened not to be there. I'm not sure she and I should be talking about it this, honestly, but I don't really have a good gauge of what's acceptable and what's not anymore. "You said he left right before we arrived?"

I told her and the other cops at least half a dozen times already. "I only remember because he gave us all some pills—more than usual—and I thought it was weird. He seemed nervous. Jumpy. He told us he loved us."

She frowns. "He knew we were coming."

I shrug. "I guess so."

"How could he have known?"

Her voice is so low, I barely hear her. I don't think she's talking to me, but I answer her anyway. "He's got cop friends." Another shrug.

Detective Willis's head snaps up. Her gaze is hard and angry. "How do you know that?"

I look at her. How come she doesn't know? And does she really want me to tell her? I shift in my chair. "A couple came to the motel."

The detective's face tightens. "Fuck."

It's weird, hearing her swear. "I'm sorry." I hate upsetting her. "I thought you knew." I thought everyone knew.

I watch tension melt out of her as she reaches across the table and puts her hand on mine. Her fingers are warm from her tea cup. "Sweetie, you don't apologize to me, okay? You've done nothing wrong."

I still feel like crap though. "You really didn't know."

"Of course I didn't! If I had, I'd report their asses. No way would I stand by and let something like that happen."

She wouldn't either. I believe her. The realization makes me a little sad. She's a really good person, but she's stupid as shit if she thinks she could have stopped those men from doing exactly what they wanted.

I have one souvenir from the motel. I was wearing it when the cops showed up. When I showed the item to Dr. Lisa, she thought it was okay for me to keep it, that sometimes reminders aren't bad things. I guess she was right, because whenever I look at it, I don't feel bad.

I keep it in the jewelry box that Krys got me. There's

not much in it, but according to her: "Every woman needs a place to keep her shinies." I'll take her word for it.

It's a bracelet. Nothing really special about it, except it was handmade for me by the one girl who refused to be just a flower—Jaime/Ivy. When Mitch wasn't around, she made sure at least one person called her by her real name—or she would herself. She never fully gave in like the rest of us.

Until that day in the park with Frank. I knew she was lost then, because she tried to play me. She wasn't Jaime anymore. Mitch had broken her.

The bracelet is made out of an old necklace chain, a couple of charms, and several strands of yarn and fabric strips. Some of the fabric is from a pair of stockings I had—a lot of the johns liked it when we wore schoolgirl socks or thigh-highs. There's some of the lace trim from a pair of panties in the weave. The yarn is from Jaime's sweater that Mitch ripped when he took it from her. He bought all of our clothes—we didn't get to keep our own things. There's a bit of a pair of her socks in there too, knotted tassels from the cheap curtains and bedspreads. It's all intertwined with the chain, fastened by its delicate clasp.

I love it, but I never wear it anymore. It's all I have left of her. She was the one good thing in the motel. The only one of us who stayed strong and positive, even though Mitch did his best to break her. He must be so smug now. So pleased with himself for breaking her.

She was my friend, though I didn't appreciate her at the time. She was the only thing that kept me from breaking a mirror and slitting my wrists. Her and all her damn questions: *Who are you? Where are you from? What's your old school like? Who was your best friend?* Most of the girls hated her for reminding us of what we'd lost, but now . . .

She made us all remember we were more than fucking flowers. And now she's dead. Someone ended her and tossed her away. She'd be put in a box and stuck in the ground—planted, just like the flower she refused to be. I will never call her Ivy again. From now on, I will use her real name.

I close the lid of the jewelry box and wrap the bracelet around my wrist twice before fastening it. The chain is cool on my skin, the bits of fabric soft and warm. It's funky and pretty and one of a kind. Like Jaime.

There are some things I don't want to ever forget.

Elsa meets me to walk the dogs that night. Isis is happy to see her brother, who Elsa named Willoughby Clarence Trillby the Third and calls Trill for short. She's got Cleo and Caesar as well. She hands me Cleo's leash as soon as my pup and I join her on the step. This is our routine—I walk the girls and she walks the boys. The young ones are growing fast.

"You okay?" she asks once we hit the sidewalk.

I shrug. "No worse than I was."

"I don't know what that means."

I give her a slight smile. "It means I'm okay." I'm not looking forward to the fallout, but I don't much care what happens to Mike and his friends. No, that's a lie. I want them to pay for what they did—what I did. What Mitch did. I want to burn down the world, but I'm too afraid to strike the match.

I think of Ivy's dead, battered face and it makes me sad.

Sick. I'll never forget those photos. Doesn't matter that she was clean and on a medical table; dead is dead, and she didn't deserve to go out like that. What they did to her face . . .

She didn't deserve a lot of things that happened to her. None of us did.

"I heard Mike's afraid you might knife him."

I smile a little. "I doubt that's true."

"He's also afraid of Zack."

"That I believe. Zack's a pretty big guy."

"Mm," my friend says, glancing at me. "How big do you think?"

Shit, I actually blush. Elsa starts cackling like an old witch. "Don't talk about him like that," I say.

"Why not? This is how straight girls talk about hot boys, isn't it?"

"Yeah, but Zack's a friend."

"*Right.*" There's something in her voice I can't identify. "Wanna go for a coffee?"

I shoot her a sideways glance. "Bean Queen?"

Now she's the one turning pink. "Maybe."

The Bean Queen is where Maisie Kaye works. She's a first-year Wesleyan student who refers to herself as "Jew-nesian" because she's Jewish Chinese American. She's also been flirting with Elsa for the last month.

Not long after she came out to me, Elsa wanted me to know that she wasn't being a creeper. She wasn't in love with me and trying to woo me to the "dark side." She didn't have hopes of us being "fuck buddies."

"Okay," I said.

"Just in case you were worried," she added.

I wasn't, but that was why she got so angry when Mike

suggested she have sex with me. We've never really talked about my experiences at the motel with women. I've never been attracted to another girl, though if I had to choose to have forced sex with a guy or a girl, I'd take the girl. No girl ever hurt me. Sometimes there was a little kink, but they never left me sore or bleeding. One time, it was even kind of nice.

Sometimes a few of the girls would pair off and do things to each other. It was never my thing, but if it made them feel better about the situation we were in, whatever. I had my pills. Regardless, I've got no problem with people who are gay, lesbian, trans—any of it. Just don't hurt me, and we'll get along fine.

I don't really want to go to BQ because I find it a little pretentious. Plus Mike likes to go there. But I do want a coffee, and I'd do anything for Elsa, so I start heading in the direction of downtown. Okay, if I'm being 100 percent honest, I don't want to go because of Elsa and Maisie. I'm a bitter, vicious bitch who doesn't want to see other people flirt. It's another reminder of something I'll never be able to have.

I liked Mike because he was cute, but that was all he had going for him. I don't know how to be attracted to someone anymore. I don't trust myself when I think a guy looks good. It doesn't mean he *is* good. I don't know if I'll ever have "normal" sex again. And for me, normal means sex that feels nice and is invited. I mean, how can I have normal sex when the idea of being with anyone is enough to make me dissociate? I just open a door in my head and run away by habit.

Still, I'm not broken enough that I don't want it, that I don't have any sex drive at all. There's only so much a girl can do on her own, though. Sometimes, I think it would be nice to have someone to curl up against—someone to kiss. That's why I get angry when I see other people who seem to take such things for granted. I can't kiss someone without wondering if he's going to hurt me.

Or worse—do something I might like. That happened a couple of times at the motel, and it made me feel dirtier than anything else. Once, I actually came—and I cried for hours afterward . . .

I push the memory back in its box. I don't want that one to go any further. I turn my attention to Elsa. "You going to ask her out?"

"If I can get the guts up, yeah."

"Okay then, let's go."

Downtown Middletown has an old-timey feel to it, that quaint small town thing you see on TV. Bean Queen is off the main drag, on a narrow side street. The front is almost entirely glass, making it easy to see how busy it is inside. It's always busy, but the main area is big enough that you can usually get a seat. It's a big hangout with the artsy crowd, so it usually smells of patchouli and aspirations.

When we walk in, Maisie is behind the counter. She looks up, sees El, and grins. Elsa grins back. I sigh. She's even got treats ready for the dogs, and they stare at her adoringly as well. She really seems great, but I'm selfish enough to wonder what I'm going to do when Elsa wants to spend all her time with a girlfriend instead of me. Maybe hang out with Zack, but that's been a little awkward since the day in my room. And what happens when he finds a girl? Because a guy like Zack is going to find a girl.

Maisie knows our orders—another point in her favor—and makes my chai perfectly.

"You could join us when you get a break," Elsa suggests. Her voice is a little shaky. God, she's so cute when she's nervous.

Maisie's grin gets bigger. She's cute too—with her choppy dark hair, wide eyes, and pierced nose. The two of them together look like some kind of manga wet dream. "Sure."

I glance around the shop so I don't have to watch them make eyes at each other. Sitting by the back wall is Zack. He's bent over a textbook, scribbling notes, so he doesn't notice me.

I stare at him. I like his face and the tan of his skin. Next to me, everyone is tan, but his won't fade in the winter. His hair is practically black and shines under the shaded lights. He has it tucked behind his ears so it doesn't hang in his face. I *really* like his face.

He looks up. "Hello, gorgeous."

It takes me a second to realize he's talking to Isis, not me.

The female pittie pulls at her lead, trying to get closer to him. I arch a brow, a little jealous. Then Cleo gets curious. Both girls walk straight up to Zack and shove their faces into him.

He grins. I hesitate. He's kind of beautiful. When his gaze lifts to mine, I can't bring myself to smile. He doesn't seem to notice—or maybe he doesn't care. "Hi," he says.

"Hi."

He glances over my shoulder to where Elsa and Maisie stand, still talking. "Are they dating?" he asks, curious.

"Not yet," I reply. "Listen, thanks for what you did for me at school."

He nods. "That girl's an asshole. You want to sit?"

I don't, but Isis has curled up on his boot. "What are you studying?"

"Middle Eastern history."

"Mr. Randall?"

He raises a brow. "You take it too?"

I nod. "Are you guys talking about Jesus?"

"Yeah. I like that he doesn't bring any religious stuff in—just talks about him as a man."

"Me too. You know, people think he actually married Mary Magdalene." Score one for the whores.

"I think that makes sense. They were definitely more than friends. Have you ever seen *Jesus Christ Superstar*?"

I shake my head. "That's a musical, right?"

"Yeah. You should watch it. I think you might like it. There's this great song where Mary talks about how she feels about Jesus."

I like musicals, or at least I've liked the ones I've seen. "I'll check it out."

Elsa and Maisie join us, forcing me to move closer to Zack in order to keep the dogs' leads from getting tangled.

"Hey," Elsa says to Zack.

"What are you guys talking about?" Maisie asks.

"*Jesus Christ Superstar*," I reply.

Maisie brightens. "Oh! I love that movie." She starts singing something about a buzz and what's a-happening. It's all very weird. I stare at her as she sings and chair-dances a bit to a song I've never heard before.

"Lex hasn't seen it," Zack informs her. "I was just telling her that I think she might like it."

Maisie smiles at me. "I hope you do. It's awesome."

Elsa straightens. "I haven't seen it either. Maybe we should have a watch party at my place. Next Friday night.

What do you think?" She turns to Maisie. "You want to come?"

I might not be really smart when it comes to love and romance, but I know when I'm expected to play a part in getting my friend more time with the person she likes, so I don't protest. Besides, a lot can happen in a week.

"Sure," Maisie replies, her expression almost coy. Seriously, the two of them are so transparent, it's pathetic and cute at the same time. I hate them even though they give me hope. I'm jealous and petty, but Mitch didn't kill all the romance in my soul. Sometimes, I wish he had.

A huge smile curves Elsa's little lips. She surprises me by turning to Zack. "How about you? Want to join us?"

He glances at me. I shrug. "I'll check," he says. "Can I let you know Monday?"

"Sure," Elsa replies. "You've got my number."

We sit for a little while longer, but Maisie has to get back to work, and I remind Elsa that I need to get home. There's a show on Netflix that Krys, Jamal, and I have been watching every night this week.

"You guys want a lift?" Zack offers. "It's pretty dark out. I'm parked on Main Street."

It's maybe a half-hour walk home, so nothing crazy. "We're good," I say before Elsa can. I don't want to owe him more than I already do.

Elsa says goodbye to Maisie, and the seven of us walk outside. The dogs are eager to get home too. We make it to Main Street when I hear someone yell at me.

"Lex! Hey, Lex!"

I turn my head in time to get slapped upside it. I feel the impact through my jaw and ear, down into my neck and shoulder. I hear both Elsa and Zack shout. The dogs go nuts. Cleo bares her teeth.

Blinking through tears, I look into the enraged gaze of Amanda Fischer—Mike's sister. She's got two friends with her, but both of them are behind her, looking a little timid with Cleo and Caesar growling at them. My sweet little Isis is right in front of me, snarling at the girl who hit me. Amanda looks like she wants to kick her.

"Hurt my dog, and I'll mess you up," I tell her softly. I survived for months with a bunch of scared, fucked-up, stoned girls. If you think girls can't fight, you've never been on the wrong side of one of us.

"I'm going to mess *you* up," she tells me. "You got my brother arrested, you fucking slut!"

I feel nothing at this news. I'm not happy or satisfied. I don't feel ashamed or guilty. I'm just blank.

"Your brother committed sexual assault, you stupid bitch," Elsa fires back. Caesar and Trill strain at their leads, but she holds them close. "And shared child porn. He should be locked up."

"You better watch your back," one of Amanda's friends tells me, lips curled in a sneer. "Mike has a lot of a friends. A lot more than a little skank like you."

"You won't always have your dogs to protect you," Amanda adds. She gives both Zack and Elsa dirty looks. "You know, dogs get hit by cars all the time."

Elsa gives Caesar some slack. He lunges for Amanda, but she manages to jump back just in time. His teeth are wet as his muzzle peels back. There's part of me that would love to see what he might do if she let him go.

Amanda and her friends turn and stomp off. They're

talking loud and tough—like I need to be afraid of them. I'm not afraid for me. I'd have Amanda on the ground and bleeding from three different places before she could do any damage to me.

"What kind of psycho threatens a dog?" Zack asks.

"The kind that stands up for her rapist brother," Elsa answers. She turns to me. "You okay?"

I nod. I'm fine, but if Amanda hurts my dog, I won't be. I turn to Zack. "I think maybe we'll take that lift home after all."

"Yeah." He jangles his keys. "That's a good idea."

chapter thirteen

"What's your name?" the new girl whispered in the dark. Mitch told us her name was Ivy. It was early morning and we could finally go to sleep. Sleep was escape, and I looked forward to it every day. I only wanted to slip away.

She had stopped crying. Daisy threatened to kick her ass if she didn't. Maybe she'd stop talking next.

"Poppy," I replied.

"No. Your real name."

I hesitated. "Alexa."

She took my hand, her fingers soft and cool. She was still in my bed, and probably would be until Mitch got her a room. "I'm Jaime."

"New girl," came Daisy's voice like a blade in the dark, "your damn name is Ivy. Ain't nobody here cares who you were before. You don't exist no more, understand?"

Something hot and wet fell on my shoulder. She was crying again. "Shut up, Daze," I said. I'd taken some pills before bed and my voice sounded faraway to my own ears.

She grunted. I squeezed Jaime's—Ivy's—hand. For a second, I thought about touching her. Maybe if I showed her kindness, made her come, she'd settle down and accept her fate. And maybe she'd give me something in return, make me forget.

But I didn't really like girls, and I was so damn tired.

"Jaime's a nice name." Maybe I liked it because it was sort of like mine—unisex. People used to call me Alex all the time, leaving off the final *a*.

The mellow I was feeling took the thought further. What would it be like to be a guy? To never have to worry about someone fucking you? Someone hurting you? What would it be like to know you could walk somewhere late at night? To not have to flinch from the breath of the guy panting in your face? There were guys in the life, I wasn't so naive that I didn't know this, but there weren't as many of them. And guys could still put up a decent fight.

Fingertips tickled my palm. "How long have you been here?"

"New girl—"

"Jesus Christ, Daze!" I yelled. "Put your fucking headphones on and shut the fuck up! The girl needs to talk, let her talk."

Daisy was the closest Mitch had to a top girl. No one talked back to her when she got pissed, not even Violet. Mitch listened to her, and no one wanted trouble with Mitch. I didn't want trouble either, but Daisy being a cow reminded me of what she'd been like when I'd been the new girl, and I didn't want Jaime to feel alone like I had.

Daisy grunted, but she didn't come at me. Maybe there was some compassion left in her after all.

"I don't know," I replied. "Months." At least six because

I was due for another pap smear soon. Mitch had a "doctor" who came in twice a year to examine us. We were tested for HIV and HPV too. All that good stuff. After, the doc chose which one of us he wanted as payment—usually whoever had the best checkup.

She sniffed. "I'm never going to see my family again, am I?"

"Probably not." Shit, I didn't really miss mine. I was better off by myself.

Yeah, I was so fucking good at taking care of myself. I had an itch between my legs that told me one of the guys I'd been with probably had crabs. Great. I was going to have to get some of that shampoo from Mitch. He was probably going to make me shave too. He was too cheap to take me to get waxed. And too paranoid someone would notice something wasn't right and call the cops.

I wished the pills would hurry up. I groped for the baggy under my pillow. The smooth plastic was comforting under my fingers. I opened the Ziploc top and took out two, then put the bag away. I turned the girl's hand over and pressed the little tablets into her palm. "Take these," I told her. "They'll help."

I shouldn't have given them to her. I shouldn't have made her like me, but it was the only thing I could think to do that might help. I didn't want to hear her cry. I didn't want to hold her hand every time a guy got on top of her. And I sure as hell didn't want her to make me remember what life had been like before Mitch made me little better than a sex doll. Without the pills, those memories would have made me cry, but I just lay there in the dark, the air smelling of perfume, girl BO, and spunk.

She made a noise. "They're bitter."

I closed my eyes. Her voice, the smells, the itch . . . they all began to fade away. I smiled. "You'll get used to it."

Krys and Jamal are making popcorn when I get home. Krys looks at me, then out the window at the headlights leaving our driveway, and asks, "What happened?"

I unclip Isis's leash. "We went for coffee. I ran into Mike's sister, Amanda. I guess the cops arrested Mike earlier. She threatened to kick my ass—and to hurt Isis." I pick up my puppy, even though she's getting heavy, and hold her to my chest. She wiggles and licks my chin.

Krys scowls. "Is the whole family a bunch of sociopaths?"

"I didn't think so," I reply, "but I'm not a very good judge of character."

"I'm going to call Detective Willis. You need to tell her what the girl said."

I shrug. "Okay."

"It's not *okay*," my aunt retorts. I glance up at her sharp tone. She looks so frigging mad, I'm not sure what to do. She swipes a hand across one of her eyes. She's crying. "I don't know why the world can't just let you have a fresh start."

Maybe because I don't deserve one, I think. *Or,* suggests a tiny voice in the back of my brain, *a fresh start isn't what I need. Maybe I need to take what I've got and build from there.*

Jamal rubs a hand down Krys's spine. "Who drove you home?" he asks.

"Zack."

My uncle suddenly looks interested. "Oh, really?" The look he shoots my aunt is obvious.

"Don't be doin' that. We're just friends."

The microwave dings, and Jamal takes the butter out.

"I imagine he's a good friend for you, given his own background."

I frown. "What's his background?" Zack hasn't told me much about himself. I guess I haven't told him much about me either—he sort of fell into finding out. We never talk about it, so I don't even know for sure what he knows.

Jamal pours the butter over the huge mound of popcorn in the bowl. "You should probably ask him. It's not really my place to say."

I roll my eyes as I set Isis on the floor. She scampers after a piece of popcorn that has fallen onto the tile. "Way to leave me hanging, Jamal." He smiles at me and gets salt out of the cupboard.

Krys hands me a can of flavored seltzer. She's been trying to get off soda lately. "I'm glad you still believe a boy might be worth being friends with."

I think about Zack and how he stood up to Mike. He's been so nice to me, even when I was an ass with him. But Mike was nice at first too. So was Mitch.

"We'll see," I say, and head into the living room.

Monday morning, I come downstairs to go to school and find Zack sitting at the kitchen table having coffee with Krys and Jamal.

"What are you doing here?" I demand when they all look at me. Isis lies across his feet like she's his dog, not mine—the traitor.

My uncle raises an eyebrow at my tone. "I called Zack and asked if he'd give you a lift to school this morning."

My frown turns into a scowl. "Why?"

"Because Mike and his friends were arrested Friday

night, but the school has yet to take action. I don't want you going in alone."

"I have Elsa."

Jamal folds his hands on the table. His wedding ring glints in the sunlight coming through the window. "Alexa, in the past few days, you've been assaulted on school property and verbally and physically threatened. We've had calls from the parents of the boys involved that we've not taken, but the voicemails were . . . intense. You'll have to forgive me for being worried about you. I don't even want you going to school until those boys have been dealt with, but your aunt tells me that's your decision to make. So, this one is mine—you either go to school with Zack or I take you, and if I take you, I will not be responsible for what I do or say to anyone who gets in your face." He says this calmly, as though talking about picking up his dry cleaning. It's only when I notice how tight his knuckles are that I realize his hands aren't folded, they're clenched.

The last thing I want is for Jamal to get into trouble because of me. I look at Zack. "Let's go."

Sitting in the driveway is the same silver car he drove me and Elsa home in Friday night. "Is it yours?" I ask.

"Yeah. Mom helped me buy it."

I remember he'd been saving his money all summer. "Must be nice."

"Your aunt and uncle don't let you use theirs?"

"I'd have to get my license first."

He tosses me a surprised look over the top of the car before opening his door. "You can't drive?"

"No." I get in and shut the door.

"Do you want to?"

I hadn't thought about it much since the night Elsa and

I talked about it. Driving seems pretty low on the list of things I need to address. "I guess."

He nods, but doesn't ask any more questions. He starts the car and pulls out into the street.

"You might want to reconsider being friends with me," I tell him. "I'm not going to be very popular."

He frowns. "Fuck off. I don't care about popular."

I look out the window. "You're going to hear things about me."

"Like you were trafficked? Yeah, I figured that out."

No one has ever put it like that. They say "victimized" or "forced." "Coerced" is a favorite. No one ever puts it so simply. Blamelessly. Shamelessly. I glance at him. "I was."

"I'm sorry."

"Thanks." I clear my throat, but I don't have anything else to say.

"Is that how you got those scars?" he asks.

For a second I don't know what he's talking about. "Oh, right. I started stripping in front of you in my room." My cheeks warm. "Not my proudest moment. Yeah. Some people can't get their rocks off without inflicting a little pain."

"It makes them feel powerful to hurt others." There's a bitterness in his voice that makes me think he knows what he's talking about.

"How'd you get that scar?" I'm looking at his left forearm. I haven't had the nerve to ask about it before.

"Broken arm."

"How'd you break it?"

He hesitates. "I didn't." He glances at me. "My father did. He was one of those people. Mom and I were the closest targets."

This is why Jamal thought Zack and I might make good friends.

"It sucks when someone you trust turns on you," I say.

Zack nods. "It does."

Silence falls between us. It's not uncomfortable, but it's . . . heavy.

"I secretly like to listen to Bon Jovi," I blurt out.

He laughs. "Okay. You're telling me this, why?"

Yes, why? "I don't know. I've never told anyone else."

"Your secret's safe with me."

"And yours is safe with me."

He looks confused. "What secret?"

"About your father breaking your arm."

The car turns into the school parking lot. "That's not a secret. I don't care if people know what he did to me."

"You're not a victim," I say.

He puts the car in park and turns to me. "Do I look like a victim to you?"

"No."

"You don't look like one to me either." He opens his door before I can reply. Grabbing my bag, I open my door and get out. Zack grabs his books from the back seat, and we walk toward the school together.

People look at us. I hear them talking as we walk past. I can't hear what they're saying because I'm humming in my head to block them out. *I don't care what they say,* I tell myself. *I don't care.*

But we all care what people think of us, don't we? Even if it's just a little.

Mike's friends are in his usual spot outside on the steps, but he's not there. None of the boys from the bathroom are. The crowd falls silent as Zack and I walk up. I don't trust their silence. I feel their glares burning holes in my back, and I have to force myself not to look at them. Not to hurry past.

Zack opens the door and I go first. The second I'm inside, they start talking again. They say awful, terrible things about me, but nothing I haven't heard before. The words roll off me like drops of water on glass.

"Assholes," Zack mutters.

"They can say what they want," I tell him. "I'm not ashamed."

He glances down at me as I toss his words back at him, and he smiles. We attract stares and whispers in the hall too, but no one approaches me. No one says anything loud enough for me to hear. I'm not sure if they're afraid of me, or afraid I'm contagious.

Zack walks me almost all the way to my locker, where Elsa is waiting. She looks relieved to see us together. When he sees her, he stops. "This is where I leave you, my lady."

"Thanks," I say. "For everything." It sounds silly, but I'm not really sure if you're supposed to thank people for being decent.

He nods and turns to leave.

"See you later?" I ask.

Zack tosses me a grin over his shoulder. "If you're lucky." I watch him go until the crowd swallows him up.

Huh. Maybe my luck's about to change.

chapter fourteen

By lunchtime, it's all over school that Mike and the other boys have been expelled. I expect the glares and sneers I get. I even expect the nasty comments. I don't expect support.

"I'm sorry about what happened to you," a girl says to me in the hall.

"Yo, Mike's an ass," from a boy in the cafeteria.

Mr. Case makes an announcement after lunch reminding everyone of the school's "zero tolerance" policy regarding sexual assault on school property.

"Anyone who commits such acts is in direct violation of school policy and will be immediately expelled," he says. "Anyone caught bullying or harassing someone who has been the victim of said behavior will also face disciplinary action."

I can feel gazes burning into me. God, I hope he stops talking soon.

Eventually, he does, and class resumes. I'm not sure how I feel. I don't like people knowing my business, but I also don't care what they think of me.

Would I feel better if he'd expelled me instead of the boys? Maybe. Yeah. It's what I expected.

After class, I go to the bathroom. I'm standing at the sink washing my hands when a girl I don't know walks in. She stands there, staring at me. I return the stare as I rip off pieces of paper towel.

"I was raped at a college party last year," she blurts out.

"I'm sorry," I say. And I am. I'm not sure what she wants from me, or why she's telling me this.

"You probably already have a therapist and stuff, but there's a small group of us—survivors—that meet on Wednesday nights at the Y. Seven thirty, if you ever want to come by."

I hate the word "survivor" almost as much as I hate "victim," but I don't tell her that. All of us have words that make us feel broken, just like we have words that, like tape, hold the jagged edges of us together in delicate chaos. They're the labels we assign ourselves.

"Thanks," I say.

She looks at me a moment, nods, and spins around. I watch her leave, throwing the paper towel in the garbage and following her out. I should have waited. I walk right into Liane Dunne—Kyle's girlfriend. I remember the things he said to me in the bathroom—the things he told me to do and the names he called me. My scalp still hurts from how he pulled at my hair. Other than Mike, he was the one who seemed to enjoy himself the most.

Lianne's gaze locks with mine. She looks pissed. The last time a girl looked at me like that was when Daisy thought I'd stolen her drugs.

"Did he really do it?" she demands. "Did he make you . . . ?"

When she stops, I nod. I watch as tears fill her eyes. "Asshole."

It takes a second for me to realize she's not talking to me. In fact, I don't realize it until she pushes past me into the bathroom. Her friends follow her. I can hear her crying as I walk away.

I can't take this. It's too weird. Too hard. I can't stand people talking to me like they understand, and I don't want to feel bad for the girlfriend of a guy who thought it was fun to make me go down on him. If I can't have drugs . . .

I go straight to my locker, grab my things, and make a run for it. I'm almost to one of the exits when I see Zack coming out of a classroom. He looks at me and his expression changes. I don't know what it means, and I don't care.

"Take me home?" I ask.

He pulls his keys out. "Let's go."

I keep my head down at school for the rest of the week. With Mike and his friends gone, it's oddly quiet. I know they're all talking about me, but I feel like there's this weird invisible bubble around me that keeps them a few feet away. Only Elsa, Zack, and my teachers talk to me.

I think some of it, though, is that it's not just rumors anymore. The boys have been arrested, and what they did has become more than a joke. It's become real. Serious.

It's been on the TV, internet, radio, and in the paper that a girl was "sexually assaulted by five juveniles" at a Middletown high school—not like there's a lot of those in town. Word gets around.

Jamal has Zack pick me up every morning. He starts picking up Elsa too. He also drives us home, even on the days he has to work after school. We haven't talked any more about his father or what happened to me. With Elsa in the car, the conversation is rapid, light, and full of movie quotes. She's like a walking Red Bull. I don't even want to think about how quiet my life would be without her in it.

I go shopping with Krys on Friday. She thinks I should take some snacks to Elsa's for movie night. I still haven't made up my mind if I want to go.

Watching Elsa and Maisie flirt and get to know each other, it's too much. I don't want to watch them do the stupid things that have been stolen from me. How can I flirt with someone when I know all he wants is to get between my legs? I know how sex ends, and at best, it's disappointing. At worst . . . well, I'm not going to think about it.

We stop by the drugstore first and pick up my prescriptions. Krys takes care of them so I'm not tempted to overindulge. Xanax for when I have panic attacks. Prozac too. It's pretty old school, but it's what works best for me. There was one drug that made me feel like I had bugs under my skin. Another made me feel worse. I've traded in Mitch's lovely pills for new ones that don't make me feel nearly as good, but at least I'm able to function without constantly looking over my shoulder or shaking in a corner, so it's a win.

I get my pills and a new lipstick Krys thinks I *have* to have. I like makeup. We didn't wear much in the motel because Mitch wanted to keep us looking young. He only let us use it when we needed to cover up marks or zits. My stomach lurches thinking how sweet he was at first. How well he fooled me—all of us. At first he was all about how special I was. How beautiful. How sexy.

He also beat me when he got pissed off.

Krys is picking up my birth control too. The woman

behind the counter glances at me. I feel her judgment, even though she may not be thinking it. Some days, I feel like everyone knows and everyone is staring at me. Right now I'm sure everyone in the fucking store knows who I am and what I've done—what was done to me. In a few minutes, I'm going to have to decide if I need to dry swallow a Xanax or if I can calm myself down on my own. Panic comes unexpectedly. It used to come more often, but now it just seems to hit harder the rare times it arrives.

I feel the walls start to close in. Sweat prickles along my hairline and under my arms.

"I have to go," I whisper to Krys. She looks at me and hands me her purse and keys. She has her wallet in her hands.

I make it back to the car and climb in. There's a pillbox in Krys's purse that has a couple of Xanax in it, what she can trust me with. I want to take both, but I make myself take one, chasing it with warm seltzer from the can in the cup holder.

"You okay?" Krys asks when she gets in a few moments later.

I lean back against the passenger seat. "I will be in about twenty minutes." I force a smile. Try to unclench my fists.

She takes my hand in hers and rubs her thumb over my knuckles. It helps. I don't remember the first time she did this, but it's like magic for me. All I have to do is concentrate on her touch and the rest of the world fades away, and I don't have to go with it. I can stay present.

I don't know how long we sit there, her rubbing my knuckles, but eventually, I open my eyes and glance at her. "It's okay. We can go."

She doesn't question me. My hand is cold when she takes hers away. My knuckles tingle, and I shove my hand under my thigh as she starts the car.

The grocery store isn't far. The parking lot is about half-full—mostly middle-class stay-at-home parents that are out shopping for dinner and after-school snacks. My job is to push the cart and scan things with the handheld scanner while Krys does all the picking and choosing, weighing and measuring.

"Do you want bananas?" she asks.

I open my mouth to say sure, but the word never makes it out. Instead, someone behind me says, "You have a lot of nerve."

Krys and I turn. *Mike's mother.* The Xanax has started to kick in, so I smile. The way her face is all knotted up strikes me as hilarious. She always was a bitch to me. "It was on sale," I quip.

She glares at me, but I see Krys's lips twitch. "Go away, Vikki," she says.

"Your niece got my son arrested," Mrs. Fischer continues. "He was expelled because *she* doesn't have a concept of appropriate behavior."

She frowns at the older woman. And *she* is just fed up enough and rational enough to have a little backbone. "I'm sorry, but is asking your girlfriend to blow your friends appropriate?"

I expect Krys to shush me, but she doesn't. Instead, she arches a brow and looks at the older woman. "Is it?"

Mrs. Fischer waves a hand. "You were never his girlfriend."

What's strange is this hurts more anything else she might have said. It's so casually tossed out there—like it was obvious. Why would her precious son waste himself on someone like me?

I suppose if I'd stopped to ask myself the same question, my natural suspicion might have kicked in enough to keep me from dating him. Maybe none of this would have happened.

"What was she, then?" Krys asks. "Because she thought of him as her boyfriend. She thought he liked her." Her back is stiff as a board, and her eyes are so bright they glitter. I feel like someone should warn Mrs. Fischer this means she's about to lose it, but it won't be me.

"You know exactly what she is. You remember Michelle Howard."

I assume this Michelle is someone they both know, and she was known as the town bicycle—everyone had a ride—because my aunt's cheeks flush scarlet. "My niece may have been naive when it came to your son's intentions, but the fact remains that you have raised a young man who believes he has the right to not only objectify women, but to assault them and treat them like dirt. When he's before a judge, you think about the part you played in putting him there. Maybe then you'll feel as ashamed of him—and yourself—as you ought."

I almost clap. Krys is saying all the things I can't articulate. I've been weak and silent so long, I don't know how to stand up for myself—or even if I should—but I take a cruel, twisted joy in the hope that this woman, and her son, are suffering even a fraction of what I have.

Mrs. Fischer takes a step toward me, so she and I are bookended between our shopping carts. "You listen to me, you take back what you said about my boy, or I'll sue your well-used, slutty little ass for slander."

I would laugh if we didn't have an audience. Seriously, people are standing around with their carts, watching like this is a live showing of their favorite soap opera. The whole town will be talking about it tonight. There will be even more gossip at school.

Suddenly, Krys is right in Mrs. Fischer's face. "Don't you fucking talk to her." I blink. I have never seen Krys so angry. "But you had better talk to your lawyer, because we plan to file a civil suit against you and the other parents for what your sons did to Alexa."

Mrs. Fischer recoils as though Krys had punched her. Her face is white. "What?" That's what I want to ask.

Krys puts her hand on my back and pushes me forward, away from Mike's mother. She puts herself between us. "Your son is the one who has no concept of appropriate behavior, and it's easy to see where he got it. If you or he come near my niece again, I'll slap you so hard with a re-straining order, all that surgery you had will come undone. Now, back the fuck off."

I watch in awe as she does just that. Krys gives me another gentle push, and I start walking again. She glares at the people who continue to gawk at us, and one by one, they slink away. I want to hug her so bad, but I don't want to harsh her badass moment. I also feel like crying, so I stare at the handle of the cart and push forward.

"Are we really going to sue?" I ask when we're alone in the cereal aisle.

She's still vibrating with anger as she grabs a box of Kashi. "We are. Someone needs to pay for what happened." She puts her arm around me as she tosses the box into the cart. "And this time it's *not* going to be you."

———

"Oh, grape!" Elsa grabs the bottle of soda from my hands as I walk through her front door. One of the things she and I have in common is our love of sweet, non-fruit fruit sodas.

"And popcorn," I say, closing the door behind me. I let Isis off her leash, and she takes off to find her family. "Anyone else here yet?"

"Nope." She opens the fridge. "You're the first." As the fridge door shuts, she whirls around. "How do I look?"

I give her a once-over. Her hair is cute, her makeup perfect. She's wearing jeans and a faded T-shirt of Disney princesses that she probably picked up in a kids' store years ago. "I'd do you."

She laughs and throws her arms around me, giving me a quick squeeze. "I'm so freaking nervous."

"You'll be fine. She's already half in love with you."

"You think?"

"Bitch, please." I smile. "I don't think she would have said yes otherwise." Then again, what the hell do I know about romance?

She hops up onto the counter and looks at me. "So, what's the story with you and Zack?"

"What do you mean?"

"Come on. Don't tell me you haven't noticed how protective he's being of you."

I blink. "He's being a friend."

"He's being more than a friend."

I stare at her. "Okay." And then, "I hit on him and he turned me down."

She looks surprised. "Why?"

I drape the hoodie I brought with me over the back of a chair. "He said I was better than that. He didn't want to use me."

"Jesus, he really is a *nice* guy."

"And just a friend," I inform her. The doorbell rings, and I'm grateful for an end to the conversation. I lean against the counter and set the popcorn on it as Elsa says hi to Maisie. Then, I hear Zack's voice. My stomach gives a little flop at the sound, and I frown.

He's just a friend.

I force a smile when the three of them come into the kitchen.

"Nice house," Maisie says, glancing about. "Doesn't Amanda Fischer live on this street?"

I cast a startled glance at Elsa, whose attention is focused on the other girl. "Please tell me you're not friends with her," she says, a worried look on her face.

Maisie laughs. The light glints off her tongue piercing. "I can't stand her."

I let out a breath I didn't know I was holding.

Maisie sets a bag of Doritos on the counter next to the popcorn. "She showed up in class yesterday ranting about how her little brother got arrested for rape, and that it's a bogus charge because the girl's a former prostitute—like anyone's sexual history matters when rape's involved. Asshole."

I look at Elsa. She looks at me—horrified. I shake my head. It's fine.

Maisie turns to me. "Am I right?"

I give a little smile. "You are."

She grins. "You know, you have the most beautiful skin. Doesn't she, Zack?"

He looks as though she just hit him with a chair. "Uh, yeah."

My smile gets bigger. Mitch would have known exactly what to say—Mike too. Both of them would have added their own ridiculous compliment, because that's what seducers do.

I'm not sure Zack would know how to seduce anyone, and I like him all the more for it.

We get drinks and snacks and head down to the basement where the big TV is. The dogs are there; Caesar and Cleo watching the puppies play.

"Hello, babies!" Maisie cries, and suddenly the pack is on her, yelping excitedly. As soon as they notice Zack, they turn their attention on him. He doesn't seem to mind, and the grin on his face makes my chest pinch. Dogs are supposed to be good judges of character, I think.

Elsa and Maisie claim the love seat, so that leaves the couch for me and Zack. He sits on one end, and I'm way down at the other. Isis jumps up beside me while Cleo claims the spot beside Zack, right up against him with her enormous head on his lap. Trill comes up with us too, while Caesar and Elsa's brother's dog lie on the carpet.

The movie starts. I make a face as the opening music plays. What's a bus doing in the desert? Isn't this about Jesus? There shouldn't even be a bus. It quickly starts to make sense—it's very meta.

"Jesus is cute," Maisie comments.

"Positively divine," Zack quips. I laugh at his pun, and he shoots me a grin.

Honestly, I don't know what to think of the musical. It's really dated, but the story is a powerful one, and some of the songs are actually pretty good, and the people singing them have incredible voices.

When Mary Magdalene sings "I Don't Know How to Love Him," I feel Zack's gaze on me. It's a beautiful song, and it resonates with me on a few levels. Mary is a woman who has been used by many men and doesn't understand what makes Jesus so special to her own heart. It doesn't matter that she wants him—if he offered himself to her, she'd run away because she's also terrified of what he makes her feel. It's exactly what I think she would have felt.

It's how I would have felt in her place.

After the movie—and its full-circle meta ending—we sit around and discuss it.

"The movie came out in '73," Zack says. "It was controversial because Judas was played by a Black man."

"Would have been more so if he'd played Jesus," I add.

"Or Mary Magdalene," Elsa quips, making us all laugh.

Eventually, Elsa gives me a sneaky "go home" look. She wants to be alone with Maisie. So that's the way it's going to be, huh? When you only have one friend, it's hard not to be possessive of her.

"I should get going," I say. "I'm kind of tired."

Zack smirks, knowing I'm lying. "I'll drive you," he offers.

"You don't have to do that. I'm only a couple of houses down the road."

"Your uncle wouldn't be impressed if I made you walk."

I am about to tell him that my uncle doesn't have to know, when I catch Elsa giving me an almost maniacal look. She jerks her head toward the door like she's got some kind of tic.

"Okay," I say, earning her smile. "I'd love that. Thanks." I can practically feel her sigh, though she doesn't make a sound.

I start to pick up Isis. "I've got her," Zack offers. It's not like she's all that heavy yet, but I shrug and let him gather up my pup. He holds her close to his chest and kisses the top of her head, right where I like to kiss her. In return, she yawns in his face.

Elsa walks us out, shutting the door the second we're through it.

Zack glances back at the house as we walk to his car. "Not exactly subtle, is she?"

I chuckle. "It's not one of her strengths, no."

"So, did you like the movie?"

"I did. Thanks." I climb into the car and hold out my arms for the dog. He sets her on my lap. For a second, his face is really close to mine, and I wonder what he'd do if I kissed him. Would he kiss me back? Get in the car and take me somewhere private? Would he stop if I asked him to? Or would he pull me into the back seat and press my face against the faux leather?

I realize that I really don't want to know what he'd do. I want to keep him clean and nice in my mind.

It's a short drive to my house, so Zack doesn't drive very fast. As we pull up to the drive, I see an old clunker parked not far away on the other side of the street. It's odd to see a car like that on this street. I turn my head to look at the man in the driver's seat.

Mitch.

It's fucking *Mitch*.

A black film oozes around the edges of my mind. The grape soda and Doritos in my stomach churn and revolt at the sight of him, at his too-familiar profile. I will never forget his face. He's the man who took my virginity, my innocence—my life—and rented me out like a car, to be used by whoever had the cash and wanted a ride.

The car's lights come on, and it pulls out into the street as Zack parks the car in front of my house. I sit there, crushing a squirming Isis to my chest, trying to keep from throwing up or passing out. My heart is in my throat, my stomach not far behind. I think I'm about to hyperventilate.

"Are you okay?" Zack asks.

I shake my head. I can't speak. If I open my mouth, I'm afraid of what might come out.

"Lex?" He sounds afraid now. "Lex, what's wrong?"

I suck a deep breath through my nose in an effort to crush the panic that's making my skin sweat and tingle. "Give . . . me . . . a minute," I gasp.

And he does. I hold my dog, who seems to have realized I'm not okay and has gone perfectly still. I feel her warmth, the silkiness of her fur, and the strength of her little body. I bury my face in the back of her neck and breathe her in, letting her calm seep through me.

I'm okay. He can't hurt me here. He can't hurt me ever again.

I lean my head back against the seat. "My pimp," I say. "He was parked across the street."

Zack's expression hardens. He opens the door and jumps out of the car. I don't try to stop him because I know he won't find anything. Mitch is gone.

But he'll be back.

chapter fifteen

"You're my favorite, Poppy. You know that, yeah?" Mitch's breath was hot against my ear. I used to like it, but now I hardly noticed. Still, his words pleased me.

He brushed his hand down my bare back. His thumb found the scar left by his belt and I winced.

"I'm sorry about that, baby," he told me. "But you've been good—haven't given me a reason to do it since, have you?"

I shook my head as he tugged at the edges of the flimsy slip I was wearing, trying to pull the fabric over the scar. "We'll have to get you something new to wear. Can't have that nasty thing putting anyone off."

I took a sip of the cocktail he had the bartender make for me—it was the only thing keeping moisture in my mouth. I'd taken enough pills that my tongue was like a carpet. I was numb, blissfully numb.

It was Friday night and we were all in the back room of

the motel bar—our private little party room. It was where Mitch conducted a lot of his business. He took appointments for us, but new clients sometimes wanted to see what he had to offer before choosing a girl or two. Mitch was paranoid about cops, so he was very careful about letting anyone new into the room. Usually they had to be referred by someone else. Someone he trusted, as much as he trusted anyone.

I watched Daisy walk away with a man in a three-piece suit. He called her "Brown Sugar" as they passed me and Mitch. Daisy's eye twitched.

"She's sweeter," Mitch told him with a grin.

I tried not to snort. Daisy, sweet? Right. If battery acid was sweet, then Daisy could be called the same.

A guy with hair almost as red and skin almost as pale as mine walked up to us and spoke softly to Mitch. I tuned him out. I didn't want to know what he was saying. I listened to the song playing in the background instead and took another drink. There was a mellow feeling that came from mixing booze and pills that I liked, even though it kind of scared me. It was almost like that moment when you woke up from a dream, but weren't fully awake.

"Poppy, this is Owen."

I glanced at the redhead. "Hi, Owen," I said. I didn't even slur that much.

"Take Owen up to your room and treat him nice, Poppy."

I wasn't trusted to do this alone. Tom—a buddy of Mitch's—walked two steps behind us to make sure I didn't bolt and Owen didn't do anything violent. Once we were in the room, Tom shut the door.

I started toward the bed, but Owen grabbed my arm.

He took me into the bathroom and pushed me over the sink. Cool air hit the back of my thighs as he yanked up my slip. I heard the snap of a condom. He didn't touch me, just shoved until he was inside. He called me a "dirty little girl" over and over as my hip bones smacked against the porcelain. I counted the faucet drips and braced one hand against the mirror so my head didn't crack the glass.

Sixty-five drips—that was all it took before he grunted and pulled away.

At least he threw the condom in the garbage. I'd had them land on my feet, my stomach, my back—my face.

"You really look like her," he said, breathing hard as he did up his fly.

I didn't ask who she was. I didn't care.

"I'm going to come see you again."

I leaned against the sink and waited for him to leave. When he did, he paid Tom, who came in to inspect me— make sure I wasn't damaged—and took me back down to the bar. Tom liked his work a little too much. I felt dirtier when he was done than I did with Owen.

My drink was still on the bar, and I needed it because my lips felt like they were stuck together. Ivy was sitting in the chair on Mitch's other side. She was sucking on a lolli-pop, because that was what he'd told her to do.

I climbed up onto the stool, wincing as I tried to get comfortable, and took a sip of my drink.

"You're my favorite, Ivy. You know that, yeah?" I heard Mitch say. I almost laughed.

I didn't tell her how little that meant. She'd figure it out soon enough.

I don't tell Krys and Jamal about Mitch. I know I should, but I can't do it. It's easier to pretend it didn't happen if I keep my mouth shut.

Elsa texts me Sunday night. She wants to get coffee. Of course, I know what she really wants is to see Maisie. I guess Friday night went well after we left. I haven't asked. I think I might be a terrible friend, but I don't want to hear about her crush.

No dogs, Elsa texts. Fine by me. If Mitch is sniffing around, I don't want him to see Isis. I don't know what he'd do to her, and she's not big enough to take him on. I consider asking El to bring Cleo, but I don't want Mitch near her either. Instead, I toss the pepper spray Krys got me into my bag, along with a box cutter I found in the garage.

Elsa comes by a few minutes later, and we leave. Krys smiles and tells me not to stay out too late. She knows I won't. She also knows my homework is done and that I have clothes already picked out. I'm anal like that. And I want to please her.

I want to hug her before I leave, but she'll think that's weird, so I don't.

The walk downtown is mostly Elsa talking about Maisie and me looking over my shoulder, checking for Mitch. My friend doesn't seem to notice; it's not really weird for me to be vigilant when we're out walking, and she's way too infatuated to pay attention to anything outside of that.

"There's something about a girl with a tongue stud," she says dreamily.

"Rose had one," I say, almost absently.

She looks at me, surprised. "Rose was at the motel?"

I nod.

"You don't talk about that very often."

I shrug. I don't talk about it with her, but I do talk to Dr. Lisa about it. I have an appointment with her this week. Last week's visit was spent discussing how pissed I was at her for calling the cops on Mike. I know she is required to do it, but I wish she'd told me first. She apologized— sincerely—for not giving me that consideration, which then made me cry and apologize for being a bitch.

Therapy. It's so much fun.

"Do you miss them?" Elsa asks. "Those other girls?"

Another shrug. "Sometimes I miss Daisy, even though she was a total bitch. I miss Jaime."

"The girl they found?"

"Yeah."

"I'm really sorry, Lex. Really."

"Me too." I don't want her to ever see photos of me looking like Jaime had. "If anything ever happens to me, I want you to know you're the best friend I've ever had."

She stops walking and turns to face me. The sun is sinking behind her, casting her in an orange halo. She looks worried. "Why would anything ever happen to you?"

I look away. Maybe I can lie to Krys, but not to Elsa. She's with me so much . . . I don't want her to get hurt because of me. "Friday night I saw Mitch outside my house."

"What?" Her eyes are wide. "Jesus Christ, Lex! Why didn't you say anything?"

I shrug. "You've been so high on Maisie, I didn't want to harsh it."

She grabs my hand and squeezes it. "My love life is *not* more important than your safety, got it?" She shakes her head. "Did he see you?"

I pull my hand from hers and start walking again.

Sometimes being touched freaks me out, and other times it makes me want to cry. This is one of the cry times, and I don't want to break down. "Yeah. He gave me this smirk. Zack went after him, but he was gone."

She falls into step with me. "I'm glad he was with you. Fuck, Lex, what if you'd walked home? What if you'd been alone?"

"Yeah." It's all I can think to say, because I keep seeing those pictures of Jaime in my mind.

"I'm going to buy Zack a coffee when we get to the Queen," she says.

My heart gives a little thump. "He's going to be there?" I haven't talked to him since Friday. All I can think about is how he sat there with me once he was certain Mitch was gone. Sat with me and made sure I was calm and okay before he left. He even walked me to the door.

"Yeah. He texted me earlier and asked if I had notes from history."

I cast her a sideways glance. "Zack wants *your* notes?"

She nudges me with one of her sharp little elbows. "I'm good at history, I'll have you know."

I smile, despite the smarting in my side where she connected. "I don't doubt it."

"I'm surprised Krys and Jamal let you out with Mitch around."

"They don't know."

"You didn't tell them?"

I shake my head.

"I have never thought of you as stupid, but I'm reconsidering. What the hell, Lex?"

"What if they decide I'm too much trouble?"

"Of course you're trouble! Loving someone *is* trouble.

If you weren't worth it, they wouldn't have taken you in to begin with. You're not being fair to them."

Her words shame me. "I can't help it."

"You've been saying that shit since I met you. Maybe it's time you start helping it."

It's like a smack to the head. I didn't think anyone could hurt me anymore, but she has.

"What the fuck do you know about it? You don't know what it's like not to know who you can trust."

She whirls on me, an angry sprite. "My uncle—*my favorite uncle*—molested me when I was twelve. When I finally got the courage to tell my mother, she cut him off. Had him arrested. His wife stopped speaking to us. I haven't seen my cousins since. I felt like I destroyed Mom's family and thought everyone hated me. I wanted to kill myself." She holds up her arms so I see those pretty tattoos. "I tried."

I stare at her, mouth open, stupefied. "El . . ."

She's scowling at me. "You're not the only person who has had something horrible happen to them. You can stay shut down forever and never let anyone in, and die broken and lonely, or you can live your life and try to let people love you, Lex. It's your fucking decision, but don't tell me you can't help it. You're the only one who can."

She stomps off ahead of me. I stand there staring after her for about a minute before I give chase. Her legs are short, so it doesn't take me long to catch up. I grab her by the arm, and when she turns to face me, I hug her. I hug her like I never want to let her go. Tears trickle down my cheeks.

"I'm so sorry," I whisper.

She nods and pulls away. She's crying too, but she wipes

them away. "It was a long time ago, and I'm okay now. *You're* going to be okay."

I know she believes that, and I want to believe it too. I wipe my face with the backs of my hands, and we keep walking.

"So, tell me more about Maisie," I say.

Elsa smiles.

When we get to the Bean Queen, not only is Zack there, but so is Mike.

"We can leave," Elsa says.

"No," I say. I don't feel anything when I look at him, so I don't care if he's there or not. Technically, I think he's supposed to leave, but whatever. "Let's get drinks and sit with Zack." Mike won't try anything with Zack there.

Wait. I don't need Zack to protect me. I can protect myself against guys like Mike. It's guys like Mitch I need help with.

"Hey, guys," Maisie says when we reach the counter. I notice how she smiles at Elsa, like she's the most amazing thing Maisie's ever seen. She is pretty awesome.

I order a chai latte with a shot of pumpkin spice. I love that it's pumpkin spice season now. It'll be Halloween soon. Elsa gets some caramel cider thing that probably has a gazillion calories in it, and we join Zack at his table. He's sitting there with his history book and a notebook. He thanks Elsa when she gives him her notes.

"You study a lot," I remark, feeling awkward.

He smiles. "I have a part-time job, so I need to cram as much into my free time as I can."

"Where do you work?" Elsa asks. Why have I never asked him that?

"At the Y. With an after-school program for little kids three days a week. I teach sports and stuff."

Elsa melts a little. "Aw. That's so cute."

Behind me, I feel Mike's gaze burning a hole in the back of my head. I don't turn around, even though it's like an itch demanding to be scratched. I hear him and his friends talking, their voices rough and angry, but I can't quite make out what they're saying with Elsa chattering beside me.

Maisie sits down with us. "I'm on my fifteen," she says, and leans over to kiss Elsa quickly on the cheek.

"Slip her the tongue!" one of Mike's friends yells.

Elsa glares at them. "Don't you have a court date to prepare for?" she asks.

That shuts them up, but only for a second.

"Yeah, and your fucking slut friend is to blame for that," one of them says.

I sigh. All I wanted was a quiet night. How long has it been since I had one of those? Lately, it seems like every day brings some new kind of drama with it. Still, when I hear a chair being pushed back, I tense. Elsa and the others look up. One of them is coming over.

I make myself meet his gaze.

"You've ruined my life," Mike says. "You know that, right?"

"I didn't have anything to do with that," I tell him.

"You told Case we raped you."

"I told my therapist what happened. She's the one who called the police, and what would you call what you did, Mike?"

He blinks. "It wasn't fucking rape. You wanted it. You went at us like ice cream cones."

"Hey," Zack says. "Shut the fuck up."

I shake my head. "I didn't want it."

"You didn't say no, did you?" Mike's angry, disgusted expression tells me he thinks it actually matters.

"Do you know what would happen to a girl at the motel if she said no?" I ask. I don't give him time to answer. "The same thing that was going to happen if she said yes—only a lot more violently."

He doesn't get it. His eyes are indignant, showcasing how sheltered and easy his life has been up until now. Until me.

I look at Elsa. Her lips are pursed and her cheeks are red. She'd tear Mike apart if I asked her to. Zack looks close to taking a swing at him. He went after Mitch, even though he had no idea what he might have been running toward.

They like me, these two people. Elsa, I think, even loves me. I love her as much as I let myself, but at that moment, I want to love her like she deserves. I want to appreciate the danger Zack put himself in for me. And I want to feel something beyond sadness and mediocrity.

I want to be okay.

I stand. My knees shake, so I keep one hand on the back of my chair. I turn to Mike. He's taller than me, but at least we're more evenly matched.

"Do you remember those scars you asked me about?"

He nods, frowning.

"That's what saying no got me." I swallow. "Mike, you knew what happened to me, and you took advantage of it. You knew I wouldn't say no—that I couldn't. You planned to get me in that bathroom and let your friends do whatever they wanted to me. How would you feel if Julie's boyfriend made her give blowjobs to his friends?"

Julie is his younger sister. I shouldn't have to mention her, but her name hits him hard.

"I'm glad you got arrested," I continue. "I'm glad you were expelled. You can blame me if you want, but it's your own fault you're in trouble. I am not a thing to be shared with your friends, and you are a fucking terrible person for treating me that way."

Elsa jumps to her feet. "That's right, asshole!"

I turn to the rest of the coffee shop, who are looking at us with curiosity. Most of them are college students, and girls.

"I'm the girl who was assaulted at school last week," I say, my voice loud, but trembling. They all stare at me in surprise. I point at Mike and his friends. "You probably heard about it. These are the guys who did it. They thought they could because I'm"—not a victim, not a survivor—"because I was once forced to have sex with a lot of people. Oh, and because I didn't say no. Who do you think is worse, me or them?"

The onlookers exchange confused and uncomfortable glances.

"Them," says a girl a little older than us. Her face is red and her eyes glitter. "Definitely them, sweetie."

"Yeah," says someone else.

A few more murmur in agreement. A few nod. A couple just sit there and do nothing. Their silence speaks louder than the music playing over the speakers. Their answer is me.

I turn back to Mike. I'm shaking more than ever. In fact, I think I might be sick, but I feel light and almost giddy. I told a room full of people what happened to me, and the world didn't end. Even if some of them think I'm to blame, I know I'm not.

I don't know what to do, so I start walking. I don't stop until I'm outside. I grab the rim of the garbage can on the sidewalk for support because my knees are still shaking. *I'm okay. I'm okay. Just breathe.*

And I throw up.

chapter sixteen

"Wanna go for a drive?"

I glance up from the trash can to see Zack hovering over me. He hands me my latte, and I take a drink to get the taste of vomit out of my mouth. Inside the shop it looks like some of the college girls are confronting Mike and his buddies as they get up from their seats.

"Yeah." I want to be as far away as possible.

"Let's go." He jangles his keys like he always does. "Text Elsa and let her know you're with me. We'll come back for her later if she wants."

I send a brief text, and we cross the street quickly. As I'm getting into the car, the door to the Queen flies open and Mike and his buddies pour out. One of them kicks the garbage can I puked in, toppling it. What would he have done to me if I'd still been standing beside it?

"I shouldn't have done that," I say once we're a few blocks away.

I feel him glance at me. "I don't know about that. I think you might have gotten through to him—Mike, I mean."

I shrug. "Maybe."

We turn onto Washington Street and drive past Wesleyan buildings, houses, businesses. Finally, we take another turn, and I realize where we're headed. "Wadsworth?"

"Yeah. I like it. Do you mind?"

I shake my head. "I like it too."

Krys took me to Wadsworth Park when I first got Isis. It's got some great hiking trails and it's perfect for dogs. It's usually pretty quiet unless the LARPers are out.

We park in the gravel lot. "Do you want to walk or sit?" he asks.

"Sit," I say. My legs are still weak. I stare through the windshield at the dark sky. "I can't believe how short the days are getting."

Zack laughs. "Seriously?"

I smile a little. "It's true."

He takes a drink of his coffee and shakes his head. "You just did one of the bravest things I've ever seen, and you want to talk about the earth's eternal dance around the sun?"

Dance. That's a nice way to phrase it. "You think that was brave? I was shaking the entire time. I puked."

"Yeah, but you did it."

"Doesn't change anything."

"It might have changed Mike."

I'm not sure what to say. I'm tempted to tell him people don't change, but that's a lie. I changed. Mitch changed me.

I unbuckle my seat belt. "Do you hope your dad will change?"

"Nah." He sets his cup in one of the holders between us. "I used to when I was a kid, but I gave up on that. He doesn't think he's the one with the problem."

"You and your mother are."

"Bingo."

"Bingo? What are you, ninety?" The second I say it, I feel bad. What if he doesn't take it as a joke?

"You found me out. I'm a centuries-old vampire trapped in an eighteen-year-old body, damned to an eternity of senior year."

"Wow," I say. "Sucks to be you."

Zack laughs, and I smile. I feel like I should thank him for being so nice to me when he really doesn't know me that well yet.

"Do you ever feel sorry for yourself?" he asks me. "When you think about what you've been through?"

Is he joking? "Yeah." And, because I'm not sure I want our conversation to turn heavy, "If I don't, who will?"

He chuckles again and takes another drink of his coffee. The shaking in my legs has almost stopped.

"You said something to Mike about scars. Do you have more than the ones I saw?" He's never mentioned the night I took my shirt off in front of him.

"Yeah," I say softly. "Do you have any others?"

He nods but doesn't elaborate. "You didn't tell your aunt and uncle about the guy watching the house, did you?"

"Sure I did," I lie, but when he looks at me, I know he can see right through me. "No."

"You should tell the cops."

"You should mind your own business."

One of Zack's eyebrows lifts. "Getting defensive only tells me you know I'm right. What are you afraid of?"

I consider changing the subject. But it's dark and safe in his car, and he makes me feel the same way Dr. Lisa does—that I can say anything. I don't know if I can trust it, but my tongue doesn't care. "That they'll decide I'm not worth the trouble anymore. That they don't want me."

"Do you really believe that?"

I shrug. "They wouldn't be the first people to kick me to the curb."

"I don't think they would have taken you in if they didn't want you."

Another shrug.

"You must have incredibly developed shoulder muscles," he says dryly. "All that shrugging."

I look at him. In the dark I can barely tell he's smiling. "I was starting to like you," I say. "But you're making me rethink it."

He laughs. "You want me to take you home?"

"No." I lean my head against the back of the seat as I look at him. "I'll tell them."

"Hey, you're right, it's really none of my business. I just want you to be safe."

"You don't even know me," I scoff.

"I know you and Elsa were the first people to make me feel welcome here. I know you hate being called a victim as much as I do. I know that despite everything that's happened, you want to be okay." He takes a drink. "And I know you don't completely trust me, but I think we might be friends."

I want to ask him why he would even want that—but I don't. "Okay," I say.

Zack laughs again. "The verbal equivalent of a shrug."

Heat fills my cheeks. "What do you want me to say?"

The words thicken as they come out of my mouth. How many times had I asked that same question of a stranger?

"Nothing," Zack replies. "You can say or not say whatever you want. It's all good."

He can't be this good. This nice. Not really. "What if I said I wanted to fuck you? Right here, right now?"

He goes perfectly still, a little frown pinching the skin between his eyebrows. When he finally looks at me, his shadowed face looks sad. "I'd think you were lying."

I move closer. "Still think it?"

"Yes." His gaze meets mine. "Why are you doing this?"

"Because no guy turns down free sex, even if he says he's nice."

Zack turns away, sets his cup down, and turns the key. "This guy does," he says as the car roars to life. "Put your seat belt on, Lex. I'm taking you home."

The next morning, Krys drives me to school because I finally told her and Jamal about seeing Mitch. She called Detective Willis and now we're going to have regular patrols outside our house at night.

That won't freak the neighbors out.

"The boys are going to court on Wednesday for their plea hearing," she tells me.

"Do I have to be there?" I ask, glancing out the window. The leaves are rapidly turning red and gold as the weather cools. It's pretty.

"No. You won't have to give testimony until it goes to trial."

"Okay."

My aunt clears her throat. "Detective Willis also wanted me to tell you there's a service for the girl they found—Jaime?—on Friday if you want to go."

Do I want to go to a church and see Jaime in a box? See that box put into the ground and covered over like she never existed? No. But do I want the chance to say good-bye? "I'd like to, yeah."

Krys smiles. This is what she hoped I would say. "Good."

She drops me off at the front of the school a little before the first bell. I ignore the looks I get as I walk to my locker. When I get there, I sigh. The small group of students gathered in front of it disperses when they see me. I hear their laughter echo as they walk away.

The entire door of my locker is wallpapered in my Stall313.com ad. Pictures of me in my underwear—thin and stoned—posing for Mitch and his camera. My hair is in pigtails in a couple of them, the underwear white and frilly. He really liked the "little girl" aesthetic.

"You think that's funny, asshole?"

I smile at the sound of Elsa's voice, followed by a sharp "Ow!" I can only imagine what she did to the "asshole." Kicked him, probably. She likes to wear clunky boots sometimes.

"All right, fuckwad," joins Zack's voice. "You're done."

I turn my head to see both Zack and Elsa approach. Zack has a kid by the collar of his jacket and shoves him toward me. "Tell her you're sorry."

The kid can't be much more than a freshman. His cheeks are red, his chin dotted with little whiteheads. He can't even look at me.

"Domanski is the one who thought it would be funny to decorate your locker," Elsa tells me. "Didn't you, dickless?"

The kid nods.

I reach up and tear one of the pages off the locker. "This is an ad selling a girl for rape. Is that funny to you?"

The red blotches in his cheeks get bigger, but he doesn't say anything.

"If this were your sister in this picture, would you think it was funny?" I ask him. I'm calm, so incredibly calm. My voice sounds strong, almost foreign to my ears. I can be indignant for the girl in this ad, "Sweet Little Poppy" she's called. I can even pity her and the glassy look in her eyes.

The kid finally shakes his head. "I'm sorry," he says. I'm not sure he means it. He'd have to understand it to mean it, and there's no way he could possibly understand what it was like.

"Take them down," Zack says, giving him a push. His dark eyes look at him coldly and his jaw is clenched.

The kid rips the remaining pages from the locker, balling them up in his hands. I take them from him. "Go away," I say.

He doesn't need me to say it twice, and walks away at a pace slightly under a run.

"Turd," Elsa says. She grabs the crumpled ball of paper from me and buries it in a nearby trash can.

I look up at Zack. I feel awkward after last night. He drove me home from the park, said good night, and drove away. I didn't think he was going to talk to me again. "Thank you."

He reaches up and peels a stray piece of tape off the top of my locker door. "Elsa's right. The kid's a shit."

"He doesn't get it," I say.

"Yeah, well maybe it's time someone made them get it,"

Elsa comments as she joins us. The first bell rings, and I hurry to put the books I don't need inside my locker.

"There's no way to make them get it if they don't want to."

"We'll make them want to," she insists. I don't argue anymore. Mostly, because when she's like this, there's no telling her she's wrong, and also because I don't have the heart to tell her.

When we reach homeroom, Elsa goes in first. Zack's class is down the hall. He says goodbye to us and starts to walk away.

"Hey," I say.

He turns back. A guy and girl walk between us to get into class. I move closer so only he can hear me. "Are we okay?" I ask.

He nods. "Yeah, sure."

"Honest?"

Zack smiles a little. "Yeah. Just try not to make any more assumptions about me, okay? Especially when you're assuming I'm a shit like Mike or Domanski."

"You're not a shit. You're the anti-shit."

He laughs. "Yeah, okay. I'll see you later."

I smile as he walks away. He's the real thing. A nice guy. A nice guy who knows my baggage and still wants to be my friend.

I erase the smile as I walk into class. People are watching me, and the smile that lingers inside me isn't any of their business.

I get home a little earlier than normal after school. It's raining and Zack offered to take Elsa and me home before he had to go to work. He dropped her off first.

As Zack pulls into our drive, a cop car drives by. It slows down as it passes. "You got protection now?" he asks.

"Something like that, I guess. They want to make sure Mitch doesn't come back."

"Mitch. That's his name, huh?"

"Yeah."

"That's a pretty lame fucking name." He grins. "Who names their kid Mitch? Now, Zack is an awesome name. Like a spy or a superhero."

My lips twitch, but I try not to smile. "Or an IT guy."

"Ouch. This coming from a girl with the same name as the voice of an AI."

"Yeah, but Lex is a pretty cool name."

He nods. "It is. Really cool." His grin fades. "See you tomorrow?"

I tell him yes, say goodbye, and get out of the car. When I walk into the house, it's fairly quiet, even though Krys's car is in the drive. She must be in her workshop.

I kick off my shoes and head to the kitchen for something to eat.

"What the fuck were you thinking, Char?"

I jump at the anger in Krys's voice. Heart pounding, I look toward the living room where she's pacing with the phone to her ear. She obviously didn't hear me come in because she doesn't even look in my direction.

Char is what everyone calls my mother.

"You told that monster where we live . . . It's more than a stupid mistake. I should have taken her from you years ago . . . No, you shut up. Just shut up. You let him take your daughter and you let him do horrible things to her. She's got scars, Char. *Scars.* Some of them are from him.

He hurt her and you let it happen. You live with that. If he comes near her again, I'll put a bullet between his eyes myself, you hear me? You tell him that the next time you see him." She laughs harshly. "Yeah, right. Sure you're not going to see him again. Fuck you, Char. Do me a favor and forget my number. Next time you need money, go begging somewhere else."

She hangs up and throws the cordless across the room. It lands on the sofa, bounces off the cushions, and clatters across the top of the coffee table before finally landing on the floor.

That's when she turns and sees me standing there, staring at her with my mouth and the fridge door wide open.

"Lexi-bug." She runs her hand through her copper hair. "I'm sorry you heard that."

I shut the fridge, my appetite gone. "She's been asking you for money?"

Krys closes her eyes—looks like I punched her. "I'm even sorrier you heard that part."

"She thinks you owe her for taking me, doesn't she?"

My aunt sighs, all of the anger draining out of her. She walks over to me and puts her arms around me. "She's an addict, sweetie. It's not that she doesn't love you, it's that booze is her life."

My eyes burn, but I don't want to cry—not for my mother. I open a little door inside my head and tuck those tears away. "Can we get pizza?" I ask, pulling away.

Krys blinks at me. Then, she gives a decisive nod that tells me she gets it—or at least she's trying to. "You bet."

"Hawaiian?" I ask hopefully.

She smiles and brushes some hair back from my face. "Anything you want, sweetie."

And I love her even more. She's not just talking about pizza.

chapter seventeen

Dr. Lisa's office is in Rocky Hill, in the back of her house. It's nice and comfortable—like sitting in someone's den or living room, only it's small. There's a waiting area outside, so Krys can sit out there and watch TV or read while I'm in session.

"Hello, Alexa," Dr. Lisa says when I walk in. She's tall and thin, with long, dark hair and green eyes. Her eyes say a lot about her. They are hard and appraising. She's had a tough life too.

"Hi," I say as I sit in my usual spot—an overstuffed arm-chair that's super comfortable.

"How are you?"

"It's been crazy," I tell her, before filling her in on what's been going on—all of it.

"Tell me more about Zack," she says when I'm done.

"Seriously? I told you Mitch was outside my house, and you want to know about my friend?"

Dr. Lisa smiles slightly. "I'm not surprised by Mitch's

actions, but whenever there's a new male person in your life, I want to know about him, especially one you seem to respect and like."

"I don't have to like him to respect him," I counter. I don't appreciate the emphasis she put on "like."

"Yes, but you do have to respect him in order to like him."

I shrug. "I don't want to talk about Zack."

"Why not?"

"Because he's not part of the problem. He's just a guy." In that second, I think of Mary Magdalene singing about how she's had so many men and Jesus is just one more.

There's a glint in Dr. Lisa's eye and I know I've given something away, but I'm not sure what. I'm annoyed—at myself and at her.

"Mike and his buddies go to court tomorrow," I tell her, changing the subject. "Can we talk about that?"

"We can talk about whatever you want," she reminds me.

I don't know what I want to say. I like it better when she asks me questions and I spew answers.

"Are you nervous?" she asks—*finally*.

I shrug. "I figure they're going to get away with it."

She tilts her head to one side. "Why?"

"You know why."

"No, I really don't."

"The judge will figure it was my fault. Everyone at school thinks it was my fault."

"Mr. Case doesn't think it was your fault. And regardless of what happens at court, those boys have been expelled—they won't be back to school."

I stare at her. "So, I'm going to get blamed for that too."

"You'll be safe from them."

"During the day. They were at the coffee shop the other night. We live in the same town. It's not like I can avoid them."

"Are you afraid of them?"

"No. They can't hurt me."

"Then why does it matter if you see them or not?"

"Because every time I see them, I'm reminded of what I am, right when I'm starting to—" I tighten my lips, keep the words in.

"Starting to what, Lex?"

I hold the words, hold my breath, but eventually the need to let both out wins. "Forget," I blurt, and suck in a lungful of air. "Just when I'm starting to forget, they remind me of what I am."

"What are you?"

"Broken."

Her expression changes—softens. "You are not broken. If you were broken, you wouldn't be here. You wouldn't be doing everything you can to heal."

Maybe not. "What if it never happens?" I ask. "What if I never feel whole again?"

She smiles sympathetically. "Then maybe—like a lot of us—you'll have to find strength in being a little cracked."

Ivy had a fever and was bleeding. Her hair was sweaty and stuck to her forehead.

Rose's john had complained about the noises Ivy was making and wanted some of his money back. Mitch wasn't happy and moved Rose to another room. Then, he called me and Daisy in.

Daisy took one look at Ivy and shrugged. "Prenatal sui-cide," she said to Mitch.

His frown deepened. "How did the bitch get pregnant?"

"She had a UTI," I said. "Antibiotics." They looked at me funny for knowing penicillin could interfere with birth control.

"Fuck," Mitch said. He looked at Ivy like he wanted to kill her. Or maybe dump her off the interstate somewhere and let nature do the job for him.

"She needs a doctor," I told him.

He glared at me. I took a step back, but I didn't look away. "Please, Mitch."

It was the "please" that got him. The understanding that I owed him if he did what I asked.

He pulled out his cell phone and made a call. When he hung up, he turned to Daisy. "Back to your room. And you—" He pointed at me. "You stay here with her. Doc'll be by in a few."

I nodded. "Thanks."

Daisy shook her head at me like she pitied me before she left, but I didn't care. I went to the bathroom and found a face cloth that smelled reasonably clean and wet it with cold water. I brought it back and laid it on Ivy's forehead.

"What's wrong with me?" she asked.

"Miscarriage," I told her. We didn't lie to each other at the motel, not unless it was necessary. "The doctor's coming."

"Shit," she groaned, writhing in pain. "I hate that ass-hole."

"Don't worry about it. It's going to be okay."

She looked at me. "You always say that."

I tried to smile. "And I'm always right."

She snorted, closing her eyes as she suddenly cried out.

She grabbed for my hand and I let her squeeze it, even though I thought she was going to break my fingers.

How could Mitch not know? This wouldn't have happened if he made the johns all use condoms. If he took care of us with as much attention as he did his pretty face. His "money maker" as he called it. There were times when I remembered to hate him.

This was one of them.

Ivy was quiet except for little moans of pain. The doctor—that slimy bastard—arrived about fifteen minutes later. I stood out of the way as he examined Ivy, wincing every time I saw more than I wanted. They were going to need to put new sheets on the bed—probably a new mattress. Ivy cried until he gave her a shot of something that put her to sleep.

When he was done, he stripped off his gloves and tossed them in the garbage. He winked at me. "Better her than you, huh, red?"

I didn't say anything.

Mitch came in. Doc gave him more antibiotics for her and something for any pain. I listened with half an ear as he told him everything that needed to be done.

"No pussy action for two weeks," he said. Mitch swore. "Oral or anal only. I mean it. She'll be real messed up if you don't make sure all that stuff's come out. Start using that spermicide I gave you."

My gaze jumped to Mitch. He was still frowning. "Didn't think they needed it when they're on the fucking pill."

"Yeah, well, surprise," Doc said.

He could have prevented this. Could have saved Ivy all this pain. I could have shoved those discarded bloody gloves down his throat until he choked on them.

"Now, about my fee?"

I braced myself. I knew Mitch was going to point at me before he even raised his hand. It was my punishment for asking him to help Ivy. At least I wouldn't have being in his debt hanging over my head.

Doc grinned. "Red. It's been a while."

I stepped forward—a little unsteady because the pills I'd taken before he came were kicking in. I knew it would be me he got, and I'd prepared. Doc was not known for being gentle. He never left marks you'd notice—he left them in places most people don't see.

He gestured to the bed that usually belonged to Rose, but was going to belong to me for the next few days. Mitch would make me look after Ivy. He thought that was punishment too. He wasn't as smart as he thought.

"Hands on the bed, sweetheart," Doc said.

I did what he said, but in my head I was already leaving. When the door closed behind Mitch, I heard the familiar unzipping of a fly, and I opened one of the many doors in my head. Fingers grabbed at me as I crossed the threshold and . . .

. . . escaped.

Detective Willis is at the house when I arrive home after school on Wednesday. Elsa comes in behind me. I told her it was okay, but she insisted on coming with me to hear about the plea hearing.

Isis runs to meet me and I scoop her up in my arms, holding her wiggling body close. Detective Willis looks apprehensive, and Krys looks upset.

"There's not going to be a trial, is there?" I ask. I'm not surprised.

"What?" Elsa cries before anyone else can speak. She looks at me, indignant—like I made it happen.

Detective Willis clears her throat. "No, but they aren't getting away with what they did, Alexa."

"What did they get?" Elsa demands. "A slap on the wrist?"

The detective draws a heavy breath. "They entered a plea agreement. Each of them got probation and is not allowed to come anywhere near you. Mike has also been ordered to attend regular sex offender meetings. They're being punished."

Punished. Ha. Mitch could teach the justice system a little about punishment.

"No," I say. "They're getting away with it. Next year they'll be eighteen, and it will be like it never even happened."

"It's still on their academic record," she counters. "It will affect them getting into college. And you can go forward with the civil suit."

"Oh, we will," Krys promises. There's a vicious gleam in her eyes I've never seen before.

Detective Willis nods. "Each of the boys has also been ordered to apologize to you, either in person or in writing—whichever you're more comfortable with."

I frown. "I don't want their apologies. You think they're going to mean it?"

"It's been court-ordered. They have to do it," she tells me.

"I don't care. It doesn't change what they did. Saying the words isn't going to make them actually sorry. They're only sorry they got caught—and now they get to laugh about getting away with it." Isis whines, like she can feel my anger. I kiss the top of her head. "It's okay, baby girl," I tell her softly.

But it's not. So far, the only person that has paid for anything that's been done to me is me.

"The whole bunch of them are probably going to go to college next year," Elsa says, voice shaking. "And now they know how to get away with rape."

"A lot of colleges have a zero-tolerance policy for sexual assault. They'll be lucky if anyone accepts them, and at eighteen, they will be tried as adults," Detective Willis reminds her.

"Well, I'm sure that will make it all better for the girls they rape after their birthdays," she fires back. She seems ten feet tall in that moment, and I love her so much.

Detective Willis slumps back in her chair. "Look, I know this sucks. No, really, I can't imagine how you must feel. It's not what I hoped for, but it *is* something. The first thing those colleges they apply to are going to see is that each one of them was expelled from school for sexual assault. It's going to limit their choices severely."

But not completely. They'll go on. Mitch has gone on. Stall 313 has gone on. Their lives have not been ruined. I'm the only one who is ruined.

"I'm going for a walk," I say, setting Isis on the floor.

Elsa nods. "I'll come with you."

"No." I give her a look I hope she'll understand. "Thanks, El, but I need to be alone."

"Okay."

"I don't think that's a good idea," Krys says, a worried frown on her face.

"I'll be fine," I tell her. "I won't be long."

"But . . ."

I don't give her time to finish; I turn on my heel and walk out of the kitchen and out the front door. My pace quickens as I head toward the street until I'm running. I run as hard and fast as I can for as long as I can, until my lungs are burning and my legs feel like they're going to give out. I stumble over a crack in the sidewalk, but I don't fall. I stop running. Bent at the waist, I gasp for breath and don't stand up until I feel half-normal.

I glance at my surroundings. I've crossed into the next neighborhood. One block up I see a house I recognize as Zack's. His car is in the driveway.

Still breathing hard, I walk the rest of the way until I'm on his doorstep, ringing the bell. He looks surprised to see me when he opens the door.

"You okay?" he asks, stepping back to let me inside.

"They got probation," I say, moving around him. "Is it okay that I'm here?"

"Yeah, of course. Mom's at work, so we can talk."

He leads me into the living room. His books are laid out on the coffee table. Who starts homework as soon as they get home from school? Zack, apparently.

We sit on the couch. "Do you want a drink?" he asks.

I shake my head. "No."

"Do you want to talk about it?"

Another shake. "No."

"Okay." There's a silent question—what do I want?

I look at him. He's so perfect—his hair, his bones, his skin. Everything about him is exactly as it ought to be. I admire and hate it. I admire and hate *him*.

What do I want?

Suddenly, I launch myself at him. Zack gasps in shock as I straddle him, using my body weight to push him back against the couch. I press my mouth against his as I yank at his shirt. I shove my tongue between his lips and grind against him.

He pushes at me, pulls away. "Lex, what the hell?"

"Fuck me," I whisper, still rubbing against him. "Please."

"What? No." He shoves my hands away, but I keep coming back.

"Fuck me," I beg. "Hurt me. You can do whatever you want, I don't care, just make me feel something. Please. Please!" There's a loud ripping sound, and I realize I've torn his shirt.

I'm airborne as he pushes me off him. I hit the back of the sofa hard, and I welcome the pain in my shoulder blades. It feels so good.

Zack jumps up off the couch, puts a few feet between us. "Lex, stop."

I lurch forward, falling to my knees before him, like I was for Mike last week. I don't smell urinal cakes this time, just Zack. I grab at his jeans, try to unzip them.

"Lex, stop!" He grabs me by the shoulders and pushes me back. Then, he's on his knees too, and he's got my face in his hands. He's looking at me like he's scared, worried.

"I'm *never* going to hurt you," he tells me. "And I'll never, *ever* use you. Not even when you ask me to. Especially not when you ask me to."

I stare at him, at his perfect face and his perfect eyes. I see a girl reflected in his gaze—a pale and scared little girl who looks like she needs a hug, and I know that's how he sees me.

I wish I could hug her. I would hug her so hard. I want it

to be okay for her. I want her to have the life that someone took from her a long time ago—a life full of hope.

Tears burn my cheeks. Zack and the girl blur until I can't see either one of them. I'm sobbing now—a great, wet, snotty mess. I don't resist when Zack's arms close around me. I don't freak out and try to break free. I lean into his chest, into the ruined fabric of his shirt, and let the tears flow. He holds me so tight, a breath couldn't even slip between us. I wrap my arms around his waist and clasp my hands in case he tries to push me away. But he doesn't push, not Zack. That's not who he is. I'm the one who is always pushing and pulling. He's just . . . still. Grounded.

Warm lips press against my forehead as he strokes my hair. "It's going to be okay," he whispers. "It's okay."

And even though it's a lie I've told many times, I let myself believe it.

Because when he says it, I almost do.

chapter eighteen

Thursday morning, I'm tempted to stay home from school. I don't want to face the people who will throw Mike's win in my face. Mostly, I don't want to see Zack. I'm not sure I ever want to see him again.

Also, I'm pretty sure he doesn't want to see me. Why would he? I'm the girl who went absolutely crazy on him. I tore his favorite T-shirt. Which was why I asked Krys to drive me to West Farms last night—so I could get him a new one.

My aunt asked who the gift was for.

"It's not a gift," I told her. "It's an apology."

She didn't ask any more questions, except if I wanted to pick up "apology" wrapping paper for it.

So, even though I don't want to see Zack, I am going to school and I'm going to walk up to him and give him the new shirt. I'm going to tell him I'm sorry.

He's on my doorstep when I open the door.

"Oh," I say. "Hi."

He runs a hand through his hair. "Hey. I thought you might want a lift."

I glance at his car. Elsa waves at me from the back seat. "Yeah. Sure. Thanks." I pull the shirt out of my bag and hand it to him.

He frowns at the sloppy wrapping. "What's this?"

"A new T-shirt."

He goes very still. Slowly he raises his head and his gaze meets mine.

My heart skips a beat. What's he thinking?

"Thank you," he says.

"I'm sorry." I take a step forward and hesitate. "For all of it."

"It's okay." He's looking at the shirt, not me.

"No, it's really not. Thank you for not . . ."

Zack nods as if he knows exactly what I'm going to say. "C'mon. Elsa will be wondering what we're talking about."

He's right. I have no intention of telling my friend what happened when I walked out on her yesterday. She called last night to make sure I was okay and I didn't say anything about Zack. It's not even that I'm too ashamed to tell her—I mean, I've told her stuff about the motel—it's just . . . it's private. It's something no one but Zack and me needs to know.

"Ooh," Elsa says when we get in the car. "Presents! Where's mine?"

As luck would have it, I have something for her as well. Out of my bag I pull a plastic container and pass it between the seats to her. "Krys thought you might like a pumpkin muffin."

She snatches the container from me like she's starving. "Oh my God. Tell her I love her. Because, I do, you know—love her."

I smile. "She loves you too."

"I'd like a little love," Zack jokes. "Did she send me food?"

"Of course." I pull another container from my bag and hand it over. "Here you go."

His smile lets me know everything is okay.

The feeling goes away when I'm at school and in a class without Elsa or Zack. I sit there, in my history class, listening with only half my brain to Mr. Randall talk. The other half has gone somewhere else. There's a heaviness in my chest that hasn't been there in a while. When it shows up, it comes back and tries to crush me.

I'm never going to be normal. I know that. I look at the kids around me and wonder if they have any idea of the horrors that are out there. The worst thing most of them will ever have to face is having their phones taken away. I envy them so much for that, and I hate them for it too.

"What do you think, Alexa?"

I glance up. Mr. Randall is looking at me expectantly. Of course he asked me a question, today of all days. "I'm sorry," I say, voice rough. "Could you repeat the question?"

"Get on your knees," someone suggests. "Maybe you'll hear him better."

People laugh—only a few. Whatever. These people can't hurt me.

Mr. Randall turns bright red. "Get out," he says to the girl who made the remark.

It's Keyleigh Holmes. I think she used to date Mike a couple of years ago. It's not a really big school—everyone knows each other. Her eyes widen. "What?"

"Office," Mr. Randall tells her. "Now. *Now.*"

"Okay, don't have a stroke." I don't look at her, but I can

hear her gathering her things. The entire class has gone eerily quiet. Mr. Randall hardly ever loses his temper. It's him I look at, with his thick gray hair and kind blue eyes. He looks like he'd be a good grandfather, or host of a children's show.

Keyleigh takes her time getting to the door, strutting like she's on a catwalk.

"I won't tolerate any of you speaking to a classmate with such disrespect," he tells us before she leaves. "I have no time for ignorance and bullying. If you want to display your stupidity and narrow-mindedness, you do it on your own time, not mine. Got it?"

There is a low murmur of: "Yes, Mr. Randall." The door slams shut behind Keyleigh. Mr. Randall doesn't even glance at it.

"Now, Alexa, I asked you—why do you suppose the Romans crucified Jesus—and other Jews who dared oppose them?"

I swallow. "Because it was the most shameful of deaths." At least that's what it said in my textbook when I read it last night. "They wanted to put them in their place."

"Yes," he says with a smile. "Very good."

As he returns to his lecture, I stare at my book, acutely aware of the gazes burning into my back. If this were ancient Rome, I have no doubt they'd all try to crucify me.

"Did you know there's a lawsuit against Stall 313?" Jamal asks.

We're at the dinner table. Krys has made fried chicken and mashed potatoes. It's been months since I left the motel, but I'm still getting used to eating home-cooked meals. I can't get enough of it. I've gone up almost two sizes since moving in with Krys and Jamal. My doctor is finally happy with my weight. Me, I don't care. I just want another biscuit.

"Yeah. I don't know much about it though."

"It was started by a couple of women whose daughters were trafficked on their site. The lawyers attached to it represent at least six other girls. They're looking to help more." He gives me a pointed look.

I swallow a bite of chicken and glance at Krys and back to Jamal. "You want to sue Stall 313? I thought you wanted to sue the Fischers?"

"I want to do both," Krys says, spooning more potatoes onto her plate.

"Do you guys need money?" I ask, stomach dropping. "I can get a job—"

"No," Jamal interrupts. "We're not doing it for the money, Lex. We're fine financially, believe me. No, we want to do this for you—for the principle of it."

I don't get it. "How's making parents pay for what their kids do fixing anything?"

My aunt and uncle exchange glances. "They made Mike what he is. Maybe having to pay something will make them—and him—consider that," Jamal explains.

"As for Stall 313," Krys picks up, "they make millions off their ads every year. They're enabling traffickers and protecting them behind every loophole they can find. If we win a settlement, it won't buy back your past, but it will make some of the bastards who took it pay. And it will ensure your future."

I set down my fork. "If we take money from them, won't

it be like they're paying me for services rendered? That will really make me a whore."

Krys looks like I punched her. "It will not."

Jamal clears his throat. "In 1973, my aunt Tissa was raped by a man who called her a 'nigger whore' and said it was no different than raping a dog."

"Shit," I whisper. Sometimes I forget how Black people have been—and are—treated in this country.

"The guy was friends with the judge—they were both rich white men—so the charges got tossed out. But her lawyer decided to launch a civil case and that judge was not friends with her rapist. He had to pay her a lot of money. When she died, she left some of that money to me so I could go to college without loans and have a better life. Is she a whore, Lex? Am I?"

I shake my head dumbly. There's no anger in Jamal's deep voice; he's making a point—it hits home, just like in class earlier. Maybe the universe is trying to send me a very pointed message.

Krys reaches over and puts her hand on mine. We're both so pale and freckled. "If you don't want to do this, we won't. But, sweetie, I want to take on this fight with you. I want to make them pay. The lawyer wants us to come to New York and meet the other parents and girls involved in the case. Do you want to go?"

Other parents. My throat grows tight. Does she even realize what's she's said? If she feels like that about me, like I'm hers and she's mine . . .

"Other girls," I say. "Like me?"

She nods. "You could talk to them."

Other girls who have been through what I have. Who

understand. Who have decided to take back something for themselves.

"I don't know," I say. "Can I think about it?"

The two of them exchange another look. "Sure, sweetie," Krys says.

I've disappointed them. What is so hard about saying yes? Why is it so fucking hard for me to stand up for myself? For me to make up my damn mind about anything? Why do I always seem to make the wrong choices?

I push back my chair. "I'm not feeling great. I'm going to lie down." I jump up and leave the room before either of them can say anything. They'd probably tell me it's all right, and I don't want their understanding.

It makes everything worse.

Friday comes. I put on the one black dress I own, along with some tights and a pair of low heels Krys thought I needed. I wear my hair down and a little wavy. I even put on some makeup, winging my eyeliner in the way Jaime begged me to teach her how to duplicate.

I don't know why she attached herself to me. I don't know why she liked me, but she did, and I liked her. I knew better than to make friends with the other girls at the motel, but I couldn't help it when it came to Jaime.

"Why did she go back?" I wonder out loud. "I should have stopped her."

"You can't take responsibility for the actions of others," Krys replies.

"But that's what you want Mike's parents to do. And the rest of them—to take responsibility for what their sons did."

"That's different."

"It doesn't feel different."

"You are not responsible for Jaime. Her parents are—just as the parents of those boys are responsible for them." She frowns. "Do you want to drop the civil suit? Is that it?"

I stare out the window. "Does it matter?"

"Of course it does!" She's looking down at me. "It's all for you, Lexi-bug."

I don't think it is. Some of it is for Krys and how helpless she feels where I'm concerned. She can't fix me, but she can fight for me. Like she fought for me in the grocery store the day Mike's mother said all those horrible things.

My eyes narrow.

His sister threatened my dog.

"No. I don't want to drop the lawsuit. I want a say in what happens to me." For once, I want to have a say in my life.

She pulls the car into a gas station parking lot without even signaling. She parks half-assed across two spots, puts the car in park, unbuckles her seat belt, and grabs me in a fierce hug. It takes me a second to realize she's crying.

"I'm sorry," she says. "I thought I was protecting you, but I'm not, am I?"

I hug her back. "No one's ever stood up for me like you do."

She pulls back. "I want to make the world better for you, sweetie. I'm sorry that you feel like I'm not listening to what you want. I promise from now on we'll talk about everything. Whatever we do, it's your decision."

I nod, throat tight and hot. My aunt wipes her eyes, buckles up, and resumes driving. Within a few minutes, we're on I-91 North. We stop only to use the bathroom and for me to take half a Xanax. I'm freaking out. But going to the funeral of a girl my age, who was killed by a john, or maybe our pimp, is a valid excuse for anxiety.

We arrive at the church shortly after two. The service is supposed to begin at two thirty, so we check our makeup, gather up our things, and make our way inside.

"Not many people here," I remark, looking at the few cars in the lot.

"We have a while yet," Krys says. "More could come."

But they don't. Only three people wander in after we do. The church isn't even half-full. Only a couple of mourners are my age. Where are her friends? Classmates? There should be more people here to say goodbye to the girl in the cream-colored casket at the front of the pulpit.

When the family comes in, I'm surprised. They're not what I expected. Her mother is a heavy woman with bright eye shadow and dark roots. Her father is wearing work boots covered in a thick layer of dirt. They have seven kids with them, ranging from a little younger than me to a toddler. Their clothes look faded from years of hand-me-downs and her parents look exhausted. It's no wonder Jaime ran off with Mitch. He probably looked like a knight in shining armor. He probably told her she'd be helping her family.

The minister is old, but he obviously knew Jaime. He says nice things about her as a child, and about the family. We pray and the choir sings. The minster reads something from the Bible. I'm not really listening. I'm staring at the box that Jaime's in. It's closed. I remember the photos Detective Willis showed me, and I'm glad it's not open.

"Would anyone like to say a few words about Jaime?" the minister asks.

No one moves. I look at the adults. They're staring at

their shoes. Even her family looks uncomfortable. The kids that are my age are on their phones. What are they doing, live-tweeting the funeral?

No one is there for Jaime. No one will speak for her. What a sad way to go.

It could have been me.

I stand up. Krys glances at me, surprised. "I'll speak," I say. My voice echoes in the nearly empty space.

Everyone turns and stares at me as I make my way toward the smiling minister. He leads me up to the pulpit and positions me in front of the microphone.

My palms are itchy and damp as I look out into those blank faces. One of Jaime's younger sisters is crying. She looks so much like her sister. Her mother looks at me with curiosity and sadness. She's obviously taken a few Xanax herself.

"My name's Alexa," I say—too close to the mic. I step back. "I only knew Iv—Jaime for a short period of time, but she was a good friend." My mouth is dry, tongue like carpet. "She was always kind and nice to everyone. She was always asking questions." I laugh awkwardly. "A lot of questions."

Jaime's father smiles at me, and I look at him as I continue, "She was one of the sweetest people I've ever known. I loved her like a sister, and she didn't deserve to die like she did." My voice breaks, and I step back again, this time turning and rushing down the steps to the main floor. I practically run back to my seat next to Krys.

The minister thanks me.

No one else speaks.

Afterward, there's a line to give condolences to the family. I want to leave, but Krys thinks it might be good for me to speak to them. She goes first, shaking hands and telling everyone how sorry she is.

I make my way through the siblings, finally reaching her parents, the toddler, and the sister who's not much younger than me.

The father grabs my hand. "Thank you," he says, his eyes wet with tears. "Thank you for being such a good friend to our little girl."

I nod because I can't speak—my throat is too tight. There are a couple of people behind me, so I have an excuse to walk away. Krys leaves a sympathy card on the pile by the door. The actual burial is family only, so there's nothing left to do but go home.

We're in the car with the engine running when I realize I left my purse inside.

"Do you want me to get it?" Krys asks.

Jaime's brothers and sisters are outside, around the side of the church, and most of the cars are gone. "No, it's okay. I'll be right back."

I run in and grab my purse off the polished wood bench. As I'm heading back out, I see Jaime's parents in the lobby.

"I'm almost glad Jaime didn't come back," her mother says. "Did you see that girl?"

The father looks surprised. "The one who spoke about her? I thought she was nice."

"Her eyes. I looked in her eyes and saw her pain and suffering, Joe. It was the same look Jaime had. She was broken. That's worse than death."

"I'm not broken," I hear myself say.

Jaime's mother jumps, looking at me in horror.

"I'm not broken," I repeat. "You're right that I'm messed up, but I'm going to be okay."

Jaime's father looks apologetic. "I bet you are, sweet-heart."

"I'm sorry I couldn't stop her from going back. I tried."

"She could be stubborn when she wanted," the mother tells me. "It wasn't your fault."

"I don't think she felt like she belonged with us any-more," the father adds. "I don't think she felt like she be-longed much anywhere."

The mother offers me her hand. God, I don't even know their names, or Jaime's last name. I've never asked because I didn't think it was important. "I'm sorry I said those things about you. You ain't broken at all, just hurting."

"I saw her once. I couldn't get her to stay with me. I should have tried harder."

"Don't," the father says, with such force that I shut my mouth. "Nothing good comes from should haves. Lord knows we've said enough of those over the past year."

His wife nods. "The only people to blame are that despicable man and the people he works with. Do you know that horrible website wanted a copy of her death certificate before they'd take down that awful, shameful ad?" A tear trickles down her cheek.

I wonder if she realizes how close she is to being broken herself.

"I'm so sorry," I tell them, and I hug them both.

"You go have a good, long life," her father whispers near my ear, and pats me on the back. Her mom's embrace is soft and limp, like she's going through the motions.

They don't ask me to keep in touch, and I don't offer. I walk out of the church into the cool October air and head straight for the car.

"You okay?" Krys asks when I get in.

. . . that horrible website wanted a copy of her death certificate before they'd take down that awful, shameful ad.

"I want to do it," I tell her.

She looks at me blankly. "Do what?"

"Meet that lawyer and the girls like me. Take on Stall 313. I want to do it."

Krys's grin could light up our entire town. "I'll call him now." She hugs me, fast and hard. "I'm proud of you, Lex."

Nobody's ever said those words to me before—not that I remember. They echo in my head as though trying to make me hear them as deeply as possible. As we pull out onto the street, I glance at the hearse and I see Jaime's casket in it.

I hope she's proud of me.

chapter nineteen

Dr. Lisa once asked me where I went when I dissociated. When I opened that door and ran through, what waited for me on the other side?

Sometimes there was nothing. At least, I think there was nothing. I remember it as being nothing but warm, enveloping darkness. The kind that only happened when I was stoned enough to zone out.

Other times I'd be on the playground at my old elementary school. It had the best climbing equipment ever.

But my favorite—and this sounds dorky—was the puzzle room. When I needed to not be in my body, I'd go into this room that had a low table in the middle of it and cushions all around. I'd sit on a pile of cushions at the table and start working on a jigsaw puzzle that had endless pieces. I wouldn't stop until the guy on top of me was done.

I haven't put a puzzle together since before Mitch got me, so when I call Zack to see what he's up to Friday night and he tells me he's doing a puzzle with his mother, I ask if I can help. It seems almost too good to be true. Like an omen, or something. Not that I believe in that crap.

"Seriously?" he asks. "I told you how lame I am, and you not only want to come over, but you want to participate?"

Since the stuff with Mike, I haven't been invited to any parties—not that I got invited to many before. People always seem to think high school is nothing but parties, but not in my experience. I'm one of those fringe kids, and I'm okay with it. Parties offer up too many temptations I'm not ready to face.

"If you and your mom don't mind."

There's silence. My stomach begins to knot. Has he decided I'm not worth the trouble after all? I finally get to the point where I'm almost confident I can trust him as a friend, and this is how I find out I'm wrong? Via puzzle rejection?

"I'll come get you."

I let out a breath. "I can walk." I really need to get off my ass and get my license.

"Not with that asshole out there. I'll be over in a sec." He hangs up.

I grab my bag and go downstairs. "Is it okay if I go over to Zack's?" I ask Krys and Jamal, who are about to watch a movie. "He's said he'd pick me up."

They exchange a glance I can't quite read. Either they're happy I'm hanging out with a guy, or they're terrified.

"Will you be late?" Krys asks.

"I don't think so," I tell her. "We're doing a jigsaw puzzle with his mom."

They both stare at me. I'm tempted to take their picture. "And then we're going to smoke some pot and rob a liquor store."

Jamal actually laughs. "Call if you need one of us to pick you up. Do you need money for snacks or pot?"

I grin at him. "I'm good." Headlights pull into the drive. "There he is. I'll see you later."

As I walk away, I hear Krys say, "Did you see that? She was *smiling*."

I shove my feet into my sneakers and grab my hoodie before heading outside. It's a cool night, which is kind of nice because it's been really warm lately—too warm for almost Halloween.

Elsa wants to go to Lake Compounce for their Haunted Graveyard next weekend. She wants to do the Trail of Terror too. I've never been really big on haunts, but it might be fun. I kind of want to do a ghost tour of a town, go to Salem and see all the actual historical stuff or something.

"Hey," Zack says when I get in the car. "How do you feel about pizza?"

"Oh, I already had dinner."

He looks at me blankly. "What's that got to do with getting pizza?"

Teenage boys have unfair metabolisms. What the hell, I can eat. "Sounds great."

"Good, because Mom ordered it before I left the house." He backs the car down the drive. "By the way, she's excited to chat with you."

"She is?"

"Yeah, apparently Jamal's been bragging you up."

Right. Jamal. "Did you tell her I'm actually a crazy bitch?"

He flashes me a smile. "I left out the bitch part. Hey, did you go to your friend's funeral today?"

"Yeah."

"You okay?"

I shrug. But it hits me that Jaime deserves more than my indifference. "It was sad and weird. Hardly anyone there. I heard her mother say she was glad Jaime was dead rather than like me."

"*What?*" His expression is part shock, part anger. "I hope you told her to fuck off."

I give a small smile. "No. She apologized. She's just looking for something to make herself feel better."

"Your therapist must have gone to the same school as mine," he quips.

"Ha."

When we go inside his house, his mother is at the table with a glass of water. There's a prescription bottle beside the glass.

I hesitate behind Zack, staring at it. I shake my head, forcing my feet to move.

"Stuff hurting?" Zack asks her.

She gives him a tired smile. "Little bit, babe." She pushes herself to her feet, wincing with the effort. "You must be Alexa. I'm so glad to finally have a chance to get to know you."

I take the hand she offers. Her knuckles are large and warm, her fingers slightly twisted.

She catches me looking. "This sudden turn in the weather has me stiffened up. Zack treats me like I'm glass. Imagine any other eighteen-year-old staying home with his mama on a Friday night."

I meet her gaze. "Some moms are worth staying home for."

Dr. Bradley flashes her son a bright grin. "I like this girl."

"She's okay," he replies with a glance to let me know he's teasing. "You want a drink, Lex?"

"Uh, soda if you've got it," I say. "Krys is still on her seltzer kick."

He asks his mother if she wants anything and gets a glass out of the cupboard.

Dr. Bradley points to the chair to the right of hers. "Have a seat. Pizza should be here soon. I hope you like Hawaiian."

I'm surprised and don't bother to hide it. "It's my favorite."

Zack sets a glass of soda in front of me. "Maybe you're more than okay." He winks.

The older woman tilts her head as she looks at me. "Lex, I hear you've had some bad things happen to you."

"Mom!" Zack looks horrified.

Five minutes. That's all it's been since the last time I thought about my past. Oddly enough, I'm not bothered by it. Dr. Bradley isn't looking at me like I'm a freak, she's looking at me like I'm just another woman. Another woman who has suffered and survived. It reminds me of a conversation I once had with Detective Willis. I'd asked her why all those things had happened to me. What I had done to deserve them, and she said, "You're not special, Alexa. You weren't singled out to suffer. Bad things happen to good people all the time." At the time, it felt mean, but it's comforting now.

"Yeah," I tell her. "I have."

"She didn't hear it from me," Zack informs me, looking worried.

"It's okay," I say. "I figured it was Jamal."

"He wasn't loose-lipped," she insists. "He wanted me

to know how glad he was that you and Zack have become friends, because trust is difficult for you."

Zack sits to my right. "Mom teaches Feminist, Gender, and Sexuality Studies." He takes a drink of soda. "She thinks of herself as something of an expert on 'the feminine experience as it pertains to patriarchal violence in society.'"

His mother looks at him fondly. "Someone's been reading my course descriptions again." She turns to me. "My husband was abusive. If Zack weren't here, I'd tell you how much."

"Yeah, please don't." He looks embarrassed. "Can we just work on the puzzle?"

"Of course," she replies, picking up a piece and studying it. "I've been thinking about putting together a panel on human trafficking for my class. Would you be interested in taking part?"

"*Mom.*" Zack's expression is desperate now.

I shake my head. "Oh, I don't know. You mean, talk about what happened to me in front of people?"

"Exactly, yes. I already have a lawyer lined up, and a young woman by the name of Lonnie may join her."

I freeze, fingers poised over the puzzle. "Lonnie?" It's been a while since I've heard that name.

"Yes. Apparently she was not only trafficked by also worked as a 'top girl'?"

"That means she recruited other girls," I say, "helped her pimp break them in."

Dr. Bradley looks appalled. "Hard to think of a woman participating in the breaking of her own sex."

"Actually, it's pathetically easy," I tell her. "It happens a lot."

"That's what I'm told. Horrifying." She rolls a puzzle

piece in her gnarled fingers with surprising ease. "I'd like to have another panelist who was in the life, and perhaps a therapist on board as well. Maybe even a police officer—all female."

I instantly think of Detective Willis. "I know a detective who might be interested." When she brightens, I say, "But let me think about it."

The doorbell rings. I hear Zack mutter, "Thank God," as he gets out of his seat.

His mother smiles kindly at me. "I apologize if I upset you with my bluntness."

I shake my head. "You didn't. I kind of appreciate you not talking to me like I'm on the edge of a breakdown."

"Ah, yes. Fragile Woman Syndrome. Because how can anyone with ovaries be strong enough to come out of a bad situation with her mind still intact? Thank God I've raised my son not to think such foolishness."

"Everything I am I owe to you," Zack retorts as he returns with the pizza. His tone is light, but there's enough truth to it that I smile. I wish I had this kind of relationship with my mother, but if I had, I wouldn't be sitting here, and I'd be missing out on some good people and some good pizza.

I watch Zack get plates out of the cupboard. His shirt lifts up on the side, revealing a glimpse of the tanned, smooth skin on his back. I wonder, for a second, what it would feel like beneath my fingers.

Then I see it—the tail end of a scar. It's thin and pale. I want to go and pull his shirt up, see the damage his father did. I want to see all of his scars, and show him mine. I want to. I want . . .

To touch him.

Shocked, I quickly look away. I'm shaking—the tremble all the way down in my bones. If I were normal, I'd probably be giddy right now. Instead, I want to puke. I take a sip of soda, and the feeling subsides, but not the need to feel Zack's skin against mine.

I keep sneaking glances at him as we eat pizza and work on the puzzle. He and his mother tease each other, and he openly praises her when she finds the piece we've all been searching for, for like, fifteen minutes. When her fingers fumble with the pieces, he places them for her. When she grimaces, he asks if she needs anything. He opens her bottle of pills without her having to ask.

He's a good son. A good guy. That's what is scary about him.

We finish the puzzle—and most of the pizza—by nine thirty. Dr. Bradley gets up slowly from the table and says she might go read for a bit.

"Thank you for a lovely evening, Lex," she tells me with a smile. "I hope to see you again soon."

"Me too," I say. I watch her leave the room, every step looking like it takes all her strength.

"I'm sorry she came on strong," Zack says. "She does that sometimes."

"I liked it," I admit. "It's kind of nice having someone be matter-of-fact about it, y'know? How long has she had arthritis?"

"She got it in her early thirties. My father was pissed—said she was faking it to get out of doing housework."

"Did he hit her after that?"

His face darkens. "It got worse. First time I ever hit him was because he hurt her."

"How old were you?"

"Twelve. I hit him with a hockey stick. Surprised the hell out of him."

"Good for you."

Zack shrugs. "He beat the snot out of me after, but I left a mark. I think Mom figured one of us was going to kill the other, so she finally stopped trying to make it work."

He didn't have to justify anything he or his mother did to me. "I should probably get going. I still have to walk Isis."

He nods. "I'll come with you."

I don't argue. He seems surprised when I don't. We drive back to my place. He comes inside while I get the leash and my dog. Isis goes nuts when she sees him. Jamal and Krys come out of the living room to say hi and thank him for bringing me home.

"We can just go around the block," I say, as we head back out. "I'll take her to the park tomorrow."

Zack seems vigilant as we walk. "Have you seen him again?" he asks.

"No. He probably knows the cops are watching." As if on cue, a police car drives by. The officer in the passenger seat nods at me and takes a good look at Zack.

"I'm glad they're watching you. Do you think he'd try something?"

"Depends on the mood he's in," I reply. "Do you think your mom was serious about having me speak to her class?"

"Oh, yeah," he says with a laugh. "She'd put you in front of them in a minute. She wouldn't take advantage of you, though. It's not like that. She just wants to build a better world, and she sees you as part of the Lego set."

I smile at the reference. "Maybe I'll do it. Think she'd let me check out one of her classes before that?"

"Are you kidding? She'd probably want you to sit up front."

I laugh.

He glances at me. "There's something different about you the last few days. You seem . . . happier."

I give him a vaguely amused look. "I attacked you."

"You were upset."

"No excuse, but thanks." I look up at the dark sky. There are a few stars out. "Now that everyone knows about me, it's like I don't have to hide anymore. I can just be me—whoever that is."

"Makes sense. When Mom finally called the cops on Dad, it was a relief. It wasn't all on me anymore."

"Yeah," I agree. "That's it. A relief."

We walk around the block. It takes longer than it should because Isis has to stop and pee every two seconds, marking territory. I also let her take a dump on Tyler's front lawn. He probably won't even notice, but it gives me great satisfaction to walk away and leave it there. A little payback for the way he held my head in the bathroom that day.

When we finally get back to my place, Zack doesn't come inside. "I'd better get home," he says.

"Thanks for letting me come over tonight," I say.

He frowns. "You don't need to thank me. You can come over whenever you want. Friends are allowed to hang out."

Friends. Right. Now is the moment when I decide if I want to keep things the way they are or not. I mean, we've only known each other a short time, what could it hurt to see how things go?

But life can change so fast. I don't want to die knowing I didn't at least try to be brave.

"What are you doing tomorrow night?" I ask.

He opens his car door. "Nothing, why?"

"That new horror movie *Uninvited* is playing at the theater on Main Street. Do you want to go?"

"Is that the one based on that online short story?"

"I think so." I have no clue; I saw the trailer and thought it looked good.

"Sure," he says with a lift of his shoulders. "Who else is going?"

I swallow. "No one. You and me."

He stares at me. "Are you asking me out?"

Oh, shit. I take a breath. "Yeah. So, do you want to go or not?" Oh, that doesn't sound childish at all.

A slow grin curves his lips and brightens his face. It almost hurts to look at him. He's the most beautiful thing I've ever seen. It's like every day I've known him he's gotten prettier and prettier. "Yeah," he says. "Call you tomorrow about the time?"

I nod, tongue too tied to speak.

Still grinning, he gets in his car, starts the engine, and drives away.

As I climb the steps to the house, a car drives by. I glance up at the familiar sound. Mitch's car. He must know the times of the patrols. Guess he still has a few cop friends. I'm tempted to run down the driveway and scream at his taillights. I rush inside and text Detective Willis. Maybe she can do something to make sure Mitch gets his ass in jail soon. Because if he ruins tomorrow night, they won't have to arrest him. I'll freaking kill him myself.

chapter twenty

When Zack arrives to pick me up for the movie Saturday night, I'm wearing jeans and a sweater with a new pair of boots. I put on a little makeup and clip up my hair.

"God, you look so grown up," Krys says when I come downstairs.

Jamal beams. "She looks a lot like you did the night we met."

"That's reason right there to go change," I say. I'm only half joking. But Zack is at the door and it's too late.

He's taller than Jamal—taller than anyone I know. He's wearing a leather jacket that makes his shoulders look broader, and his hair is swept back from his face.

Maybe this isn't such a good idea, I think. I can change my mind. I'm allowed. But then Zack smiles. "You look nice," he says. And he obviously doesn't care that other people heard him say it.

A lot of men have told me I was "hot" or "gorgeous"

or even "sexy," but none of them ever said I looked nice. "Thanks," I say. "So do you."

And now we're awkward. We weren't awkward yesterday.

"You want to get going?" he asks. "We're going to need popcorn."

"You have money?" Jamal asks, taking out his wallet.

Zack holds up his hand. "I've got it, Dr. Morgan, thanks." He looks back at me. And waits.

"Have fun," Krys says. "Let us know if you're going to be late."

I tell her I will, and Zack and I leave the house. I'm buckling my seat belt when he says, "I feel a little weird. Do you?"

"Yeah," I admit. "Do you want to bail?"

"No. Do you?"

"No."

He starts the car. "Okay, we'll have to get over it."

By the time we get to the theater, we're almost back to normal. I'm still very aware that it's only the two of us, but not like I was.

"You don't have to pay for me," I say when he buys both of our tickets. "I asked you out, remember?"

He looks at me. "You have money?"

"I do."

He nods. "Okay. You can buy popcorn and soda."

I buy us a jumbo popcorn and a huge soda. I also have a big bag of Twizzlers in my purse, because I'm not paying theater prices for their pathetic little candy portions.

The theater is fairly full, but we get seats in the middle. Zack holds the popcorn bucket, and I manage the Twizzlers. The soda is between us.

Zack has a comment for every trailer they play before the movie. I'm almost disappointed to see the coming attractions end.

The movie itself is super scary. It is about a group of teens who decide to spend the night in an old house because it's a place where they can hang out, party, and have sex. One by one, they're picked off by an angry ghost until only two of them are left. I jump at least three or four times. Zack jumps once—and swears.

"That was so good," he says afterward as we're leaving. "I didn't see that ending coming at all."

"I know, right?" I shove what's left of the Twizzlers back into my bag. "I thought it was going to be another 'punish the promiscuous kids' kind of thing, but it wasn't at all."

"And there wasn't a virgin saving the day."

I glance at him. "Are you a virgin?"

He chokes on a drink of soda, coughs for a few seconds, and takes another drink. His eyes are watering when he looks at me. "Seriously? I pick you up. I pay for tickets. I even wore clean jeans, and *this* is what I get in return?"

"Dude," I say. "Do you have any idea what I'd give to still be a virgin?" I mean it as a joke, but it's clear from how fast the color drains from his face that he doesn't take it that way.

"I'm sorry," he says.

"You didn't do anything," I remind him. "It was a stupid thing for me to say."

He unlocks the car and opens my door. "Do you mean it?"

I pause. Shrug. "Yeah. I'd love to go back to thinking sex is something special."

"I'm sorry it got ruined for you."

I try a smile. "It's not ruined—it's just going to take something awesome to fix it."

He smiles too, but it doesn't quite reach his eyes. Once again, I'm left kicking myself for saying something I shouldn't have. He probably can't wait for this night to be over.

Neither one of us says much on the drive home. By the time we pull into the drive, I'm feeling slightly nauseous. I'm not sure if it's all the butter and sugar, or regret. I unfasten my seat belt to relieve some of the pressure.

"I had a good time tonight," Zack says.

"Me too," I say. "When I wasn't saying stupid shit."

He frowns. "When did you say anything stupid?"

Seriously? "The virgin thing."

"That wasn't stupid. Sad, but not stupid."

"I feel kinda stupid for saying it."

He leans back against the seat and sighs. "You know, I'd like to know what it's like to be one of those kids who has an awesome dad. I can't imagine what it must be like not to be afraid of my own father. Not to hate him with every frigging bone in my body. Do you think that's stupid?"

"Of course not."

"So cut yourself the same slack you give everyone else."

"You ever get tired of being right all the fucking time?" I ask. I'm only a little annoyed.

"Ha! *Now* you're being stupid." He grins.

God, he's gorgeous. Impulsively, I lean across the distance between us and kiss his cheek. His skin is warm beneath my lips, and the contact feels like an electrical shock. I pull back fast.

"Was that stupid?" I ask.

He's not grinning anymore. "No," he says. "That was the least stupid thing ever."

I smile and grab my bag. "Good night, Zack. Thanks."

"Hey," he says, stopping me as I step out of the car. When I lean down to peer in at him, he continues, "You want to do homework with me at the Bean Tuesday night?"

I smile. "Pick us up?"

"Us?"

"Me and Isis."

A slow grin curves his lips. "It's a date."

I'm upstairs in my room working on a paper when the doorbell rings Sunday afternoon. I peek out my window to see if it's Elsa because we're supposed to get together to work on a math assignment sometime today, and instead, see Detective Willis's car parked out front.

Have they figured out how it's going to work getting apologies from Mike and his friends? I admit—but only to myself—I've started looking forward to them.

When I walk into the kitchen, Detective Willis is standing in the middle of the room, talking to Krys, a leather portfolio under her arm. I hope it isn't pictures of more dead girls.

"Sorry to bother you on a Sunday," the detective says, "but we've made an arrest in the murder of Jaime Phillips, aka Ivy, and I'd like Alexa to look at some mug shots."

Aka—like she was a conman or something.

Detective Willis opens the portfolio and sets a sheet of paper on the table. On it are six grainy photos. "Is the man who abducted and trafficked you on this paper? If so, please point to him and say out loud that it's him."

I look at the sheet. Five of them are strangers—all pretty sad-looking guys. One of them is all too familiar. His face is vivid in my memory. At one time, I thought it was the most gorgeous face I'd ever seen because it belonged to the man who I thought loved me. Now, the sight of him makes my stomach roll and my palms sweat.

"That's him." I point to his photo. "That's Mitch."

"You're certain?"

"Fifty years from now, I'll still know his face," I tell her.

Detective Willis smiles. "Excellent. Thank you."

"Wait," Krys says. "Does this mean you've arrested him? When? Where?"

She looks uncomfortable. "We have. We picked him up last night. Not far from here."

Krys goes pale, which is something, considering how white she is to begin with. "How far, Marianne?"

Detective Willis closes the portfolio. "He was turning onto this street when the patrol got him. Right around nine thirty."

Zack and I were still at the movie.

"Is there any chance he's going to get out and come here?" my aunt asks.

"No. We've got him on trafficking, drug charges, and suspicion of murder. He's not going anywhere except prison."

I stare at her. "Really?"

She nods, that little smile pulling at her lips again. "Really. I told you I'd get him."

I wrap my arms around her waist. She hugs me back, and when I pull away, I catch her wiping at her eyes.

"Thank you," I say.

"It's not over yet," she says. "But this is the beginning

of the end. With your help, Lex, he's going to go away for a long time."

With my help. There's part of me that doesn't want to testify. But Jaime was so scared when Mitch brought her to the motel. She tried so hard to please him, and he killed her. He drove by this house. *My* house. He still thinks he owns me.

"Could he get life?" I ask.

Detective Willis nods. "Yes. We'll push for no chance of parole. It will depend on how the jury responds to our case."

I meet her gaze, now familiar rage starting to gnaw at my insides, hot and indignant. It feels good. Strong. "What do I need to do?"

Krys wants to celebrate, so we plan to do just that.

I refuse to think about what might happen. Mitch has been arrested and he's going to jail. I have to believe that. He'll pay for what he did to me. To the other girls. To Jaime.

My aunt invited Detective Willis to come back that night after work. She also told me to invite Elsa and Zack and his mother over if I want. Do I? If I call him, I will have seen him three nights in a row. Is that normal? Is it too much?

I take the chance, because I don't know what's normal and it doesn't matter—I'm not normal. When I tell him Mitch has been arrested and we're celebrating, he tells me he'll be over as soon as he can.

Elsa arrives first. She comes up to my room where I'm finishing up some homework.

She pounces on me. "I'm so happy, I could spit," she says. "How are you doing?"

"I can't believe it. I keep waiting for them to tell me he escaped or something."

She tilts her head and gives me a sympathetic look. "He's not going anywhere, buddy. You're going to put him away for the rest of his life."

"I hope so." Are there any special punishments for pimps in prison?

"So?" Elsa asks.

I look at her. "So what?"

"You and Zack."

"What about me and Zack?"

"You went to the movies last night."

I frown. "How did you know?"

She grins and stretches out on my bed. "I called the house last night. Krys said you were on a date. You have been holding out on me!"

I roll my eyes, but my stomach is all butterflies. "We saw *Uninvited*. It was awesome."

Her gaze searches my face. "Did he try something?"

I scowl. "No."

"Did you want him to?"

"I . . . I don't know."

She nods, like she understands. I guess she does. "Sucks when you feel guilty for wanting something normal, doesn't it? I finally got up the guts to kiss Maisie Friday night, and for a second, I felt bad for wanting her—like I don't deserve it after what happened to me."

"Like there's something wrong with you for still being able to want to be touched."

She looks me in the eye. "Exactly." She gives a sly grin. "Do you want Zack to touch your lady bits with his big hands?"

I flush as she waggles her eyebrows. "I want to touch him," I admit.

Elsa sits up, swinging her legs over the side of the bed and planting her hands on either side of her thighs. "You like him."

"I do. He's . . ." I turn my head when I hear a noise. Zack leans against the doorframe, arms crossed over his chest.

"He's what?" he asks, smirking.

I should be mortified, but I'm only mildly embarrassed. So many girls act like it's the worst thing ever for a boy to know they like him. I want to tell them there are so many things that are worse.

"Stealthy," I reply.

"Silent, but deadly," he says with a nod. "Your aunt sent me up to get the two of you. Apparently she wants to have a toast since everyone's here."

Elsa jumps to her feet. "Booze!" As she brushes past Zack, she slaps the back of her hand against his stomach— she only comes up to his armpit. "You're lucky you heard something good, eavesdropper."

He smiles down at her. "Like you could think of anything bad to say about me. You love me, admit it."

My heart rate spikes a bit watching him. He's like something exotic to me. Once, when I was little, we went to a zoo and I saw a lion. I remember standing there, staring at it. I'd never seen anything so amazing before. I feel that same kind of wonder when I look at Zack.

Elsa gives him a grin. "Ours is a love that can never be." She walks away as he laughs.

I get up from the desk and walk to the door. He hasn't

moved. When I hesitate at the threshold, he holds out his hand.

"He likes you too," he says.

"No one's ever held my hand before," I tell him. I feel stupid for admitting it.

"I've never wanted to hold anyone's hand before," he replies.

I reach out my hand, lowering it so our palms touch and our fingers entwine. My heart clenches. I look up at him. "I don't think you're like other guys."

He smiles. "You're the first person to ever make me glad for that."

I smile back, and we walk downstairs together.

chapter twenty-one

"Have you ever had a boyfriend?" Ivy asked. Her fever had broken, but she was still pretty weak after the miscarriage. We were sitting on her bed and I was French-braiding her hair. Mitch had given me time off to look after her, but that also meant that if he came around looking for a little loving, I had to give it to him.

Mitch expected us all to act like we wanted it. Like he was the best we'd ever had.

"Other than Mitch? No."

"Mitch was never your boyfriend." She said this like it was a fact, not like I was stupid.

I shook my head. "So, no. I've never had a boyfriend. You?"

She nodded. "His name was Cal. He lived down the street from me. Well, from my parents."

My hands paused. I waited to see if she would start crying.

She didn't. Something had changed in her. She was starting to shut down. She was becoming one of us.

"Did you love him?" I asked, resuming my work. Her hair was soft and fine, slipping through my fingers.

"I thought I did. He broke up with me for another girl. I cried for days."

"Jerk."

She shrugged. "Just a guy." She was quiet for a moment. "Do you think the miscarriage was God's way of punishing me?"

"I don't know much about God, but no. If anything, it was a favor."

She turned her head. "Didn't feel like one."

"Would you want to have a baby, knowing the father was a guy who comes here?"

Ivy shuddered. "No."

"So, there. Maybe God was looking out for you." Honestly, I didn't think God saw any of us. If he did, he was an asshole.

She patted my leg. "Someday you'll have a boyfriend."

I snorted. "I'd have to get out of here first."

"You will. I know it."

I wanted to tell her we were going to die in this place, or some place like it. But if she wanted to believe there was hope, I wouldn't stop her. It would get beaten out of her soon enough.

"I don't want a boyfriend," I said. "Men are all bastards."

"Not all of them. My father's not."

I wondered if her mother would have agreed. "My father walked out when I was a kid."

"I'm sorry."

I shrugged. "I don't really remember him."

"You're probably better off without him."

"Maybe." Or maybe if he'd stuck around, I wouldn't have been sitting on a saggy mattress with crusty sheets, wondering if I'd live to see eighteen.

I finished her braid and wrapped a battered old elastic around the tail. She looked about twelve.

The door to the room opened and Mitch came in. He looked at Ivy and smiled. "You feeling better, darlin'?"

She nodded. "A little, Mitch."

"She's still bleeding," I told him, reminding him the doc said she wasn't supposed to work.

"She'll be better in no time," he said. He pointed at me. "You, come with me."

I glanced at Ivy. "But . . ."

"You can come back when you're done, but get off your fucking fat ass and come with me now."

I got off the bed and walked toward him. I wasn't wearing the stuff we wore during business hours. I looked like a regular girl.

I glanced over my shoulder at Ivy as Mitch opened the door. "I'll be back," I promised her.

She nodded.

Outside on the walkway, it was chilly. There was snow on the ground, and I shivered in my T-shirt and jeans. Both had gotten too big for me since I came to the motel. I sucked in great big breaths of fresh air as Mitch guided me to another room.

"You do whatever he wants, you hear?" I was told as he knocked on the door. "I don't want to find out you were a disappointment. He's paying good money for what's between your legs, so you better make it worth it."

Yeah, yeah. Whatever.

"You shower this morning?" Mitch asked.

I nodded.

"Good. You won't smell like spunk."

The door opened and I looked up. Standing in the doorway of the motel room was Frank, my mother's boyfriend. He was wearing a button-down shirt and dark jeans—the outfit he wore when they went out.

"Alexa," he said, his tongue darting over his lips. "It's good to see you."

I looked past him into the room. "Is Mom here?"

He and Mitch both laughed. "No, sweetie," Frank said. "It's just you and me."

I stared at him, his meaning finally sinking in past the haze of shock and pills. I didn't think I was capable of surprise, or even disappointment anymore, but I was wrong. Bile rose in my throat.

He was going to use me. And then he was going to go home to my mother and leave me here.

"I've been waiting a long time to be alone with you," he told me, drawing me into the room with a hand on my arm.

I glanced back at Mitch, hoping he'd stop this. I wanted to beg him not to let this happen, but he only smiled. "She's worth the wait, aren't you, sweetheart?"

The door shut and he was gone.

On Monday, we find out the apologies from Mike and his friends will be published in the town newspaper and its website on Thursday. We're going to get our copies on Tuesday to make sure we're okay with them.

"I feel like this is another win for you, don't you?" Krys says.

Another win? I know what she means, but I'm not sure I've been winning at all. Maybe it's a tie?

I start to shrug but catch myself. "Ask me once I've read what they've said."

She nods, strands of hair bobbing around her freckled face. I love her face. It's so open and honest. Everything she feels is right there and she doesn't care who sees it.

"Krys?"

She raises her gaze to mine. "Yeah, Lexi-bug?"

I swallow. "Thank you. For everything."

Her gaze softens, dampens. "Oh, sweetie. You don't need to thank me."

"I want you to know I appreciate what you've done for me."

"I know you do."

"I haven't made it easy."

"Sure you have. You're my girl." She gives me a hug and a kiss on the forehead. "I love you."

"I love you too," I say, and blink back the tears that threaten.

"So," she says after a few minutes. "You and Zack, huh?"

"Maybe," I say. There's no point in playing dumb with her.

"I like him better than Mike."

"You never met Mike."

"Exactly, the little bastard."

I smile. "I like Zack too. He's . . . different."

"I don't care if he's from Mars, so long as he treats you right."

"I threw myself at him. A few times," I confide. "When we first found out Mike and the others got probation. I was so upset, I went over to Zack's house and tried to have sex with him."

My aunt's eyes are wide as she stares at me. "Okay. And?"

"He said no. He said he wasn't going to let me use him, and he wasn't going to take advantage of me. Then he brought me home. He could have taken advantage of me at any time and he hasn't."

Krys's shoulders sag in relief. "Good boy." She looks at me. "We've never really talked about sex."

I hold up my hands. "And we're not going to now. Seriously, I do not need that kind of image of you and Jamal in my head."

She laughs. "I don't want that either, but for the record, I want you to be able to have physical relationships—healthy ones—during your life."

"I know—I have all those books you bought me upstairs in my room." Books on getting over sexual trauma, on building trust, on reclaiming my sexuality. "I have read some of them, you know."

"Good." She looks a little uncomfortable. "Have you ever had an orgasm?"

My eyebrows shoot up to my forehead. "Uh, wow. Yes. Can we stop talking about this now?"

She nods. "Yeah. We can." And, "You're taking your birth control pills?"

"Yes. And I'm super anal about making sure I take them exactly like I'm supposed to."

"Okay, good. Do you have any questions? Anything you want to know?"

I thought we were going to stop discussing this. But, as I look at her, I realize there *is* something I want to ask her. "What's it like to have sex with someone you care about—who cares about you?"

She looks at me like I've broken her heart. She looks at me that way a lot. "It's wonderful," she says. "So much better than with a stranger."

"Been with many strangers?" I ask with a smirk.

She gives me a pointed look. "You really want to know about my sex life?"

"Nope." With that, I gather up my stuff. "I'm going to do my homework. Do you need help with dinner?"

"Nah, but thanks." I'm almost out of the room when she calls after me, "Lex?"

I stop and look at her over my shoulder.

"Do you care about Zack?" she asks.

I smile at her. I know what she's really asking me. "I'm not sure yet, but I think I could." I turn without waiting for her reaction and leave the kitchen.

Alexa—

When the police arrested me, I blamed you. When I got expelled, I blamed you. When you told me how you felt that night at the coffee shop, I realized you were not the one to blame. I was. And when the judge gave me probation, I realized how lucky I am because what I did to you can't be taken back.

I stop reading. The paper trembles in my fingers. "Someone must have written this for him," I tell Elsa.

I'm on my bed, reading her the letters while we Face-

Time. The ones from the other guys are half-assed like I expected, but at least they admitted to what they'd done and people will see it.

Of course, when the letters are published, no names will be attached, so maybe none of it matters anyway.

"Yeah, no way he knows half those words," she agrees. "I'm sorry I ever introduced you to him."

I shrug. "It's fine. Not like he did any lasting damage."

"You realize something like this would traumatize most people."

"Yeah, well . . . I like to pick my traumas and my dramas."

She laughs. "You're a freak, and I love you. I just wish you could find someone like Maisie."

I roll my eyes. "Sorry, I'm not a taco lover."

"Yeah, well, sausage gives me heartburn. Speaking of sausage . . ."

Oh, God. Here it comes.

". . . Are you seeing Zack tonight?"

She's terrible. "Yeah. He's coming over to work on some homework." We were going to meet for coffee, but Jamal and Krys went into New York this morning to meet with the lawyers handling the case against Stall 313 and are staying in for dinner. I don't really feel like leaving the house. Sometimes I don't want to be around a lot of people.

"Be gentle with him," she says.

If it were anyone else, I'd probably be uncomfortable, but not with El. "I promise not to break him."

"I don't think you could," she responds. "He seems pretty tough."

He does, but he's also really sweet. I don't tell her that because she'll only torture me more. And . . . well, it's private.

I spent almost a full year being used in front of an audience. My body wasn't my own. I had no privacy at all. I ate with other people, slept in a room with others. I didn't really even have privacy when I needed to use the bathroom. So, I don't feel I need to share every thought I have with my friend.

Elsa frowns a little as she looks into the camera. "You're not going to ask about me and Maisie, are you?"

I roll over onto my stomach on the bed. "Do you want me to?"

"Well, it would be nice if you pretended to be interested." There's an edge of hurt in her tone, and a twist to her mouth I'm not used to seeing.

"Hey, I'm interested. I figured you'd tell me what you want me to know."

"I have. But, haven't you noticed that I'm always the one asking about your life?"

My first instinct is to get defensive. It's not my fault she's fucking nosy. I could get upset, but it wouldn't change the fact that she's right. "I'm sorry you think I don't care. Honestly? I'm jealous."

Her already wide eyes widen even more. "Of what?"

"Of you and Maisie. Of the fact that you can have a normal relationship."

"Normal? Have you met me?" She laughs. "I feel like such an ass. I never thought me dating might be a trigger for you."

"Trigger might be too strong, but it's definitely a reminder of the things that make me different."

"Hey, you asked Zack out. That counts for something. You're able to be alone with him and not freak out. That's awesome, right?"

I guess so. But I've never freaked out around a guy—or guys. I'm not afraid of being raped or beaten. I mean, I'd fight it, but I've already survived it; I could survive it again.

"Sure," I say. "He's pretty nonthreatening though."

Her expression turns incredulous. "Dude, he's a frigging giant. He looks like he could crush my head with one hand."

I laugh. "Not a skull as hard as yours."

I glance at the clock. Zack will be here soon, and I have a little prep work to do before he arrives. I tell Elsa I need to get going, and we make plans to hang out tomorrow. I hang up and head for the shower.

When Zack arrives, I'm clean—I like to be clean—and dressed in a long sweater and leggings. I thought that was Krys's style, but it's grown on me. I've brushed my hair out and put on a little mascara and lip gloss.

He smiles when I open the door, and a weird warm feeling blossoms in my stomach. "Hi," he says.

I blush. "Hi." I stand back so he can step inside. God, he has to duck. I've never noticed before.

We do our homework at the kitchen table where we can spread out our books. Mostly we quiz each other for the upcoming history test.

He knows this stuff *way* better than I do.

"Do you have a photographic memory or something?" I ask when he answers one of my questions almost word for word with what's in our text.

"No. I like history. I remember dates and names easily— like you remember book and movie quotes."

I give him a dubious look. "I think it's more than that."

He raises an eyebrow. "I'm not going to apologize for being smart."

"You shouldn't," I tell him. "It's just not fair that you're smart *and* pretty."

Both brows go up this time. "Pretty?"

I shrug. "Handsome?" He makes a face that's anything but. I laugh. "Cute, then?"

He leans his elbow on the table and props his chin on his palm. "Of the three, I think I prefer pretty. Thank you."

I have a hard time holding his gaze. I'm not sure exactly what I see in his eyes. I do know that it's now or never. "Zack, we're friends, yeah?"

He frowns a little. "Yeah. Why?"

"If I asked you to help me with something, you would, right?"

"Sure. What do you need?"

I make myself look him in the eye. "I want to have sex with you."

chapter twenty-two

Zack stares at me. I don't know what to do, so I stare back. "You what?" he asks.

This is going to be harder than I thought. "I've never had sex with a nice guy. You're nice."

He closes his history book and shoves it in his backpack. "That's not a good enough reason to sleep with someone."

"What do you mean?" It seems like a pretty good one to me.

His eyes are almost black when he looks up. "I'm not going to be your experiment, Lex. I like you, but I won't let you use me to make yourself feel whatever it is you need to feel."

Why can't he be like other guys a tiny little bit? "You like me?"

His eyes narrow. "You know I do. I told you. Don't pretend you don't know. You wouldn't try to play me like this if you didn't know."

He's right. "Okay."

"Okay? That's all you've got to say? Want to at least throw in a shrug with that?" He zips up the backpack and stands. He's going to leave, and I don't know how to make him stay. If he were anyone else, I'd know what to do.

"I like you too!" I cry, jumping to my feet. My chair scrapes the floor. "And I don't know what to do! I want . . . I want . . ."

"What?" he demands. "What do you want?"

He looks so intense, a little voice inside me says I should back off—run. But there's a louder voice, and that's the one I listen to.

"I want to feel what it's like to be loved." As soon as I say the words, I want to take them back. "I know you don't love me, and I'm not asking you to. I mean, I don't love you—I don't know if I can love anybody, but . . ."

"Lex? Shut up." He takes a step closer. "You don't know anything." Zack lifts his hand. "Can I touch you?" he asks.

Throat tight, I nod. But he doesn't grab for one of the usual places. Instead, he touches my cheek, moves his hand back so his fingers can thread through my hair. "I don't know how love feels," he tells me. "But when I look at you, all I can think about is kissing you."

The breath I've been holding escapes in a laugh, even though none of this is funny.

"I want to have sex with you," he tells me and something warm unravels deep inside me—a little throb between my legs that I haven't felt in long time. "But I think we should take this slowly."

"I'm so tired of people thinking for me," I tell him, jaw clenching.

"I'm not thinking for you." He looks into my eyes. "I'm telling you what *I* think. We haven't even kissed yet. Not really. We haven't made out—that's one of the best parts about being a teenager, you know. So I'm told."

Is this not-so-experienced thing of his real or an act? He doesn't seem to be faking it, but I can't believe girls don't throw themselves at him.

"Kiss me," I command.

He tilts his head. "I don't want to be one of the many guys who has kissed you, Lex." My heart drops. I try to pull away, but he stops me. "I want to be the one you chose to kiss first."

I freeze. My heart is pounding so hard, I can feel it in my head. "What do you mean?"

"Do you want to kiss me?" he asks.

"Yes." It comes out a whisper.

"Then kiss me."

I'm not sure what to do. This isn't like when I shoved my tongue in his mouth before, or when I took off my shirt. This is . . . intimate. I take a step closer—my knees tremble. We're almost touching. I lift my hand, place my palm over his heart—it's beating almost as fast as mine. Slowly, I slide my hand up, over his shoulder, behind his neck, and tug his head down. He doesn't resist.

I press my mouth to his. His lips are warm and soft. I slide my other hand up his arm—so I can push him away if I need to.

"Kiss me back," I whisper. And he does, but he lets me lead. It makes me want him more. "Touch me."

Zack's arms close around me, his hands warm and solid against my back. He's so strong. He could force me to do whatever he wanted, and I couldn't stop him. But he's not forcing me to do anything. He's making me do it all and that's . . . frustrating.

I pull away.

"Are you okay?" he asks, looking alarmed.

I try not to glare at him. "Don't treat me like I'm fragile. I want you to kiss me, Zack. Do what you'd do with any other girl and I'll let you know if I don't like it."

He hesitates. "I don't want to do anything that might freak you out. I don't want to be one of those guys, Lex."

I sigh. "I don't think you could be one of them if you tried. Just, don't treat me like I'm broken."

"You're not broken," he says, and he brings both of his hands to my face, holding me still as he lowers his head. When he kisses me, it's like firecrackers going off in my chest.

I've had guys shove their tongues in my mouth, slobber on me, act like they're trying to devour me in one gulp, but I've never felt *this*.

When he pulls back, I open my eyes. They're wet at the corners. "Now what?" I ask. My voice is hoarse.

He smiles. "Now, we sit on the couch and watch a movie. And the whole time we watch the movie, we think about that kiss, and what it will be like when we get to do it again. And maybe, if you're lucky, I'll let you hold my hand."

"I've changed my mind," I say. "You're not nice, you're actually evil."

He laughs and puts his arm around me. "Come on."

We get some snacks and go into the living room. I find a movie on Netflix that we've both seen but like and start it up.

Halfway through, I realize Zack might be on to something. I've been sitting there beside him, thinking about that kiss and holding his hand. His fingers stroke mine in a soft, lazy pattern that almost tickles. Makes me think what that pattern would feel like traced on other parts of me.

I've had enough—the movie's boring compared to him. I shift on the couch and kiss the side of his neck. His skin is warm and he smells slightly spicy, but sweet. His body wash, maybe? I don't know, but I like it. I let my lips and tongue trail over his jaw.

"What are you doing?" he asks, his voice a whisper.

"What teenagers do," I reply, before softly biting his neck. I reach up and turn his face toward me so I can kiss him. This time, I use some of the things I learned in the motel. It's amazing to me how different something can feel when you *want* to do it.

"Lex," he groans, but I lower my body down onto the couch and bring him with me. He braces one hand on the cushions, the other is high on my ribs, just below my breast. If he just moved his thumb . . .

I bring my leg up, hook it around his and pull him down on top of me. He's solid and warm. He's kissing me now— we're kissing each other, and I can hear the shallow rasp of our combined breath. He moves his thumb and I gasp, raise my hips.

My body moves on its own—hands, hips, legs. I can't seem to get close enough to him even though we're as close as ocean and sand.

I open my eyes and look at him—slightly blurry, he's so close. His eyes are shut, his eyelashes long and thick on his cheeks.

How terrifying. There's that urge to run away, to open a door and dive through. Zack deserves someone who's present. He deserves my full attention—no running away to one of my mind rooms. No hiding. I have to experience it all with Zack, and I'm not sure I'm ready for that.

I'm pretty sure I'm not.

"Stop," I whisper.

Zack instantly goes still. His hand leaves my chest and his body lifts off mine. He raises himself above me, and I'm suddenly cold. "Are you okay?" he asks.

I nod.

"Then why do you look like you're about to cry?"

He looks so concerned, it hurts my heart. "Because I asked you to stop, and you did." I don't think he understands the significance of that.

Or, maybe he does, because the expression that comes over his face begins as anger and ends as something soft and sweet.

He sits back on the couch and offers me his hand, pulling me up beside him. He shifts me close against his side and puts his arm around me. "Is this okay?"

I snuggle closer, leaning my head on his shoulder. "Yeah. Thank you."

When he offers me his free hand, I take it. His lips brush my forehead. I close my eyes and listen to the beating of his heart.

That's how Krys and Jamal find us when they get home—curled together, asleep with the TV on and credits rolling. And me, one step closer to knowing what it's like to be a normal girl.

Mitch's arraignment is scheduled for Friday.

Detective Willis tells me I shouldn't go—that it's a long wait only to hear him say he's not guilty. But I want to see him. More importantly, I want him to see me.

"I don't know," Krys says when I tell her I want to go.

"It could be really hard for you, Lex. What if his friends are there?"

I shove my hands in my pockets. "I don't care. I'll take Zack with me, or Elsa. I need to do this."

She sighs and runs a hand through her hair. "Okay."

I hug her. "Thank you."

My aunt doesn't immediately let me go. "I'm proud of how far you've come, Lex. You're not the same girl I saw in that hospital bed eight months ago."

"I still feel like her sometimes."

"But not all the time," she says. "And that's what matters." She gives me another squeeze before letting me go.

I start to walk away, but stop. I turn back to her. "Krys?"

"Yeah, sweetie?"

I swallow hard against the lump in my throat. "I wouldn't even be here if it weren't for you."

"Oh." Her face falls. "Honey, that's not true."

"It is," I insist. "If you hadn't come for me, I'd be dead, just like Jaime."

She blinks and a tear trickles down her cheek. "Then I'm even more grateful they found me so I could bring you home."

Friday morning, Zack picks Elsa and me up to go to Mitch's arraignment. I have no idea how long it's going to take, but I hope we're done before Zack has to go to work that afternoon. I don't need him there beside me, but he makes it a lot more bearable.

Detective Willis meets us there. "You're sure you want to do this?" she asks.

"Definitely."

"Okay. Come with me."

I don't know exactly how long we've been sitting in the courtroom when I catch a glimpse of familiar red hair. I shouldn't be surprised that she's here. They're friends, after all.

My mother's eyes widen when she sees me. She looks old. Old and wasted. Her skin has a yellowish cast to it; so do the whites of her eyes. I guess her liver's probably giving out.

Frank's with her. I'm more surprised they're still together than anything else. They've been together three or four years now, a record for Mom. Frank gives me a little smirk when he looks over. All I can think about is how hot his breath was on the back of my neck. Sour and hot.

"Is that who I think it is?" Elsa asks, eying my mother.

I nod.

"Who's that greaseball with her?"

"Her boyfriend," I tell her, turning my head so I don't have to look at Frank anymore. I can smell him; the memory is that strong. I don't want to puke in the courtroom. Of all the things I experienced in that motel, I think he was the worst. He should have taken me home. He should have been good.

"Do you think she'll come over?"

"She's not here for me," I say.

Zack gives me a nudge. "You don't need her. You have us."

"Damn skippy," Elsa adds. She grabs my left hand. "You traded up."

We wait maybe another half hour before Mitch's name is finally read. My heart jumps at the sound of it. Instinctively, the fingers of my right hand tighten around Zack's.

Mitch wears a prison jumpsuit. He's handcuffed and looks like hammered shit. His vanity must hate that his hair is greasy and he needs a shave. He looks like a pathetic old man. How could I have ever thought he was beautiful? Next to Zack, he's about as beautiful as a bucket of worms.

As he's led toward the front of the courtroom, he glances around. I see him nod at Frank—watch my mother wave in return. As if pulled by invisible strings, Mitch turns his head just enough.

And looks right at me.

He didn't expect to see me, I can tell. A smile tugs on my lips as I stare at his surprised face. Did he think I'd fade away? Did he think he could kill Jaime and I'd let it go?

Did he think he'd broken me so far down that I'd be afraid to look him in the eyes? That I would think I owed him silence?

He thought wrong.

The charges against him are read—trafficking, kidnapping, wrongful imprisonment, attempted murder, actual murder. I look around. I'm the only girl from the motel there. Detective Willis told me I was the only one to make it back to some degree of a normal life. Where are the others? Are they still out there? How many more of them will end up like Jaime?

He enters a plea of not guilty. The judge is an older man who doesn't look the least bit impressed with the bit of humanity standing before him. He denies Mitch bail. He's going to be locked up until his trial.

We waited almost three hours for what amounted to about three minutes of court time, but they are three minutes I will treasure for the rest of my life.

"I'll be right back," Zack says when we step outside the

courtroom. Detective Willis appears as he walks away. Behind her, I see my mother waiting for Frank. She doesn't even glance in my direction. She's digging in her purse for her flask. I can see her shaking from withdrawal twenty feet away.

"You okay?" Detective Willis asks.

"I'm good," I tell her.

She looks pleased. "The prosecution will start putting their case together soon. We're going to crucify the son of a bitch."

"Crucifixion's too good for him," I say. "But it's a place to start."

Suddenly Zack is back. His cheeks are flushed and his eyes are unnaturally bright. If I didn't know better, I'd think he is hopped up on something.

"We should get going," he says.

I say goodbye to Detective Willis, and we head out.

"What's wrong with you?" Elsa asks Zack as we reach the door.

Then I hear my mother's voice. "Oh my God!"

I glance back and see Frank stagger out of the men's room with his head tilted back. The front of his shirt is soaked with blood.

"You beautiful bastard," Elsa says, giving Zack a look so intense, it makes me thankful she doesn't like guys.

"Let's get out of here." He pushes one of the doors open, and we step out into the chilly sunshine.

"Why did you hit him?" I ask when we're in his car.

Zack glances at me as he turns the key in the ignition. "I saw how he looked at you." That's all the explanation he offers. It's all I need.

Elsa leans up from the back seat and kisses his cheek.

"Find a drive-thru, Zack-adoo. I'm buying you lunch, you big luscious brute."

I smile at her glossy lip prints on his cheek, and I add my own. He looks at me in surprise but quickly turns his attention back to the road.

"I could go back and hit him some more," he offers. Elsa and I laugh. Inside, I'm shaking. I didn't even have to tell him what Frank had done. He knew.

I was wrong when I told Zack I didn't know how to love someone.

chapter twenty-three

Neither the apologies nor Mitch's arraignment make any huge changes in my life. I still go to school and get stared at—or avoided like I'm contagious. People still talk about me, but not to me. I still want to get numb every once in a while, like after a particularly vivid nightmare or a rough day at school.

I'm still going to meetings, though not like I did fresh out of rehab. We talk about shame a lot because it's something we all have in common in addition to our involvement in the sex trade.

When I talk to Zack about it, he tells me he used to drink a lot when he was younger. He says he was almost a foot shorter and fifty pounds heavier. I don't believe him until he shows me photos.

"This is why I didn't have a girlfriend," he says.

The picture doesn't even look like him. Not because of the extra weight, but because his face looks tired and puffy—his eyes unfocused and glazed. It's a look I've seen my mother wear for days at a time.

"What made you stop?" I ask one night when he comes with me to walk Isis.

He doesn't look at me. "I realized how much I'm like my father when I drink."

I slip my free hand into his. "Whenever I miss being numb, I remember my mother at the courthouse."

"She's pretty hard looking," Zack reflects. "Sad looking."

"The walking dead." Krys will never look like that.

We hang out a lot—me and Zack. Sometimes we "double date" with Elsa and Maisie, like going to Lake Compounce's Haunted Graveyard. It's fun and campy, but there are parts of it that make me hold Zack's hand so tight, I'm afraid I might hurt him. Those are the places where it's so dark, I can't see my own hand in front of my face, and I know there are bodies around me. I get a little panicky. But Zack leads me through it and buys me a funnel cake when we're done.

We spend a lot of time kissing too. Just kissing. Sometimes it goes a little further, but he always stops when I ask. He stops when I don't ask too, which is starting to become an issue for me, but I don't say anything because I'm trying to come to terms with not wanting him to stop.

I don't want to freak out in the middle of sex with Zack. That would be terrible. Even more terrible would be to dissociate and go into one of my "rooms." He deserves better than that. So do I.

But I also know there's only one way to find out if my mind is as ready as my body seems to be. The human body's a resilient thing. It heals with very little memory of what's been done to it. Maybe a scar, something tender. It's the mind that carries all the damage, that remembers all the pain. The mind that gets twisted and broken.

The funny thing about minds, though? They only get so messed up because they also remember what it was like to be happy, to not have that pain. Even if you think you've forgotten, there's a part of you that remembers.

I'm not sure if I'm trying to remember or trying to forget.

The end of October is a lot of meetings with the people prosecuting Mitch's case and the lawyers suing Stall 313. I've told my story to so many people that it doesn't really feel like mine anymore. Every time I tell it, I feel a little more removed, a little less ownership. It's okay—it's not like any of it was something I wanted.

Halloween night, the four of us—me, Zack, Elsa, and Maisie—go out for Thai at a place on Main Street. Maisie and El are going to a party later on campus. Zack and I are going to have a horror movie marathon at his place. He's decided I haven't watched enough del Toro. I don't care what we watch—I just love hanging out with him.

We drop Maisie and Elsa off at Maisie's apartment to get ready for the party and drive to Zack's house. Along the way, we see a ton of little kids in costumes trick-or-treating.

"I used to love that," I tell him. "All that candy."

"Yeah," he agrees. "It was the one night of the year I could be someone else."

"I like who you are."

He shoots me a smile, and we drive the rest of the way in silence.

When we get to his house, his mother is handing out candy to three little girls all dressed like Wonder Woman.

She laughs as they thank her and scamper back to their parents.

"I told them that I was Wonder Woman one Halloween, and one of them told me I was too old," she says, still chuckling. "Tell that to Lynda Carter."

I don't ask who Lynda Carter is.

"Want to watch the movie with us?" Zack asks. Even though we already ate, he grabs a big bag of chips out of the cupboard and two cans of soda from the fridge.

"No," she says with a wave of her hand. "But do you mind watching it in your room? There's a documentary on Netflix I want to watch."

Zack looks surprised. "My room?"

His mother rolls her eyes. "Yes, Zachary. I trust you to have your girlfriend in your bedroom while I'm down here watching TV." She shakes her head as the doorbell rings. "Unless you want to hand out candy instead?"

We practically run from the room and upstairs.

His room is exactly what I thought it would be. It's neat and nerdy. I know he likes things to be orderly and in their place, so I'm prepared for how organized everything is. His walls are decorated in posters advertising books and movies. I recognize most of them.

There's a desk with a computer, two large bookshelves, a TV, gaming console, and a king-size bed. I guess a guy his size needs a lot of room.

"Yeah," he says. "This is where I sleep and stuff."

"I like it."

"So, the bed is really the only place to watch the TV. Is that okay?"

"Yeah, sure."

He props up a bunch of pillows along the headboard for us to lean against, and we sit side by side, the bag of chips between us.

"I'm going to turn off the lights," he says.

"Okay. I'm not going to freak out, Zack." Maybe he's the one I should worry about. "Am I the first girl you've ever had in your room?"

The lights go out, leaving us with only the glow of the television. I can see the screen reflected in his eyes. "Yeah," he says. "You are."

"Are you uncomfortable?"

"No." He pops the top of his soda can. "It's nice. Really."

"But weird?"

He laughs. "Yeah. Nice weird."

"Well, hey, you're the only guy I've ever had in my room."

"Elsa was there too."

"Next time you come over, we can hang out in my room. Just us."

"You've never had a guy in your room before? Not even before you moved in with your aunt?"

I look down at first, but make myself meet his gaze. "You'd be the first that was by choice."

"Shit." He looks mortified. "I'm sorry. I forgot."

I stare at him. He forgot that I'd been trafficked? Forgot all my baggage? Forgot that I wasn't like any other girl?

My throat is tight as I lean over and kiss his cheek. "Thank you," I say.

"For what?"

I smile. "Forgetting."

When Ivy recovered, I got sent back to my old room with Daisy. I didn't know why Mitch didn't let me stay where I was. Maybe he realized Ivy and I had become friends and he didn't like that. We might have plotted against him or something.

Or maybe I was the only one who would put up with Daisy's shit.

I walked into the room to find Daisy on her bed in her underwear, painting her toenails a dark pink. My bed was unmade. "What the fuck is this?" I demanded. There was blood and . . . other stuff on the sheets.

Daisy glanced at the bed and shrugged. "New girl."

I made a face. "I'm not sleeping in that." *Gross.* I picked up the phone and hit *0* for the front desk—it was the only button that worked on our phone. We couldn't make outgoing calls. We couldn't even call room to room. Only the front desk.

It rang three times before someone picked up. "What?"

It was a guy. It was always a guy. I didn't think any women worked here except to maybe clean the other rooms. And honestly—they didn't really clean.

"I need clean sheets," I told him.

"Gotta charge ya."

Yeah, and I knew how he'd want to collect too, the asshole. I wasn't in the mood. "Either bring me clean sheets, or I'll throw these out the window."

"Fine." I heard him mutter, "Fucking bitch." He hung up.

"Listen to you bein' all dominant," Daisy commented, setting aside her polish. Her toes glistened wetly against her dark skin. "You looking to take my job, pretty little Poppy? You got a plan?"

"I just want clean sheets, Daisy, and a fucking nap." I started yanking the soiled sheets off my bed.

"Don't let me stop you," she muttered—always had to get the last word.

When the door opened—no knock—I had the old sheets balled up and I thrust them at him after he tossed the new ones onto the bed.

"Whoa!" he said. He was young and skinny. Tattooed and missing a tooth. But shove some sheets with girl blood on them—and God knew what else—at him, and he was suddenly not so tough. "I ain't touching those."

I threw them on the walkway. "So call housekeeping. I don't care. They're not staying here."

He whirled on me. We were in the doorway to the room and I could see the parking lot below. "Cleaning up this shit is not part of our agreement," he argued. "This is gonna cost you."

"Take it up with Mitch," I told him, turning to go back inside.

He grabbed my arm. "I'm takin' it up with you, red."

Slowly, I turned my head to look at him. A few rooms down there was a man about to unlock the door. It wasn't one of our rooms. I didn't know this place got legitimate guests. He looked at me—and at the sheets and the guy holding my arm. I held his gaze for a second, then gave my attention back to the scrawny addict about to lose it on me.

"Leave a mark and Mitch will have your balls," I reminded him. He reluctantly let me go.

"You and me ain't done," he said. There was sweat on

his upper lip. "You gonna pay me back for them sheets. I'm thinking a little BJ."

I forced myself to meet his gaze. "If you ever take your dick out in front of me, I'll bite it off." I gave him a shove and shut the door. I didn't know what I was trying to prove—he could just open it again.

Daisy laughed maniacally. "The look on his face! Girl, what's gotten into you?"

I ignored her as I started making the bed. I didn't tell her about Ivy or Doc, or that I'd been forced to let my mother's boyfriend have sex with me. And I certainly didn't tell her about the man down the hall who looked at me like he wanted to help.

And then looked away.

chapter twenty-four

On Veterans Day, Zack and I hang out at his place. His mother is at the college, so we have the place to ourselves. We're on his bed, kissing. We lie facing each other because that's more comfortable for me. I also like to be on the outside of the bed because it gives me an escape route.

We haven't progressed that far—at least I don't think so. We've touched each other, but there's been very little nakedness involved.

"This has got to be driving you crazy," I say to him during a break in the action. I've noticed I only allow myself to get so involved in what we're doing before I back off. I'm frustrated that I haven't let myself come. I can do it by myself, and I have when I think of Zack, but I stop when I'm close with him.

That I know of, he hasn't gotten there either.

"I don't mind," he says.

I raise a brow. "Seriously? Because I feel like I'm about to explode."

"It'll happen when you're ready." He sounds so certain that I feel panicked. What if I'm never ready?

"I know where your crazy brain just went," he says. "Stop it. If you want to have sex, you'll have sex."

I snuggle up next to him. "A few weeks ago, I practically tried to rape you, and now that I have you on a bed, I can't do it."

"You didn't try to rape me."

I don't correct him, even though we both know I tried to force the issue. And if it had been possible for me to over-power him, I might have done it. I'm not proud. His phone rings and he checks it. "It's Mom." He answers it.

I roll away from him and get off the bed to go to the bathroom. When I come back, he's leaving his room. "Mom wants me to bring her a book she forgot this morning. Want to come with me?"

"Sure." I don't have any other plans until later when Elsa and I have a girls' night scheduled. She's going to spend the night, and we're going to do facials and pedicures and watch rom-coms while eating too much.

Zack grabs the book from his mother's office, and we make the short drive to the college. It's gotten cold, and the damp cuts through me like a knife, straight to the bone.

He parks and we walk into the building. I love the Wesleyan campus. It's so pretty. Since Jamal works there, it's pretty much understood it's the school I'll attend next year—if they accept me. Krys, Jamal, and I have talked about them legally adopting me because it will drastically help with tuition costs. It will also prevent my mother from having any claim to me.

She called the house last week and wanted to talk to me. Krys lost her shit. She didn't tell me what the conversation was about, but I can guess. Mom wants to convince me not to testify against Mitch. My mother has known where I am since the day I moved in. She never called to talk to me until after Mitch got busted. Doesn't take a genius to make the jump.

It was probably Frank's idea. Asshole.

We walk into Dr. Bradley's classroom right as her students start coming in. She smiles when she sees us and comes around her desk. Her movements are stiff and slow, and I notice she's got a cane by the podium.

I watch students fill up the seats as Zack talks to his mom. No one seems the least bit interested in me, until . . .

"Lex?"

I turn my head. Standing in the aisle is a girl a little older than me. It takes me a second to recognize her because she doesn't look the same. Her dark hair is shoulder length now, and her blue eyes are brighter than I remember. The first time I saw her, I wanted to punch her in the mouth. The last time I saw her, I cried because it was goodbye.

"Lonnie."

I move toward her, so she doesn't have to come to me— she still has a limp. When she immediately comes in for a hug, I give her one.

"You look fabulous," she tells me before letting me go.

"So do you."

"What are you doing here?"

I point at Zack.

Her eyes widen. "Are . . . are you dating Dr. Bradley's son?" She sounds impressed.

I nod, surprised to be admitting something so personal. "We haven't been seeing each other that long, but yeah."

She looks so genuinely happy for me, it hurts. "That's amazing."

"Are you seeing anyone?"

She shakes her head. "Not ready yet."

That makes me hurt for her even more. And makes me feel better for myself.

"You're going to be on the panel, aren't you?"

She nods, glancing around. "I haven't told anyone in class yet. How did you know about it?"

"Dr. Bradley asked me to be on it."

Lonnie's pretty face brightens. "Oh! You should be. It would be fantastic to have you next to me. Maybe we could get a coffee after and catch up? Here, let me give you my number."

I punch her number into my phone and text her so she'll have mine. When she goes to sit down at the table, I recognize someone else right next to her.

Amanda Fischer.

"What are you doing here?" Mike's sister demands, glaring at me as though I purposefully invaded her territory.

Lonnie looks surprised. "You two know each other?"

"I went to school with Amanda's brother," I say, before Amanda can say something rude. Hopefully she'll take the hint and not say anything. I won't if she doesn't.

"Oh, cool."

"How do you know Lex?" Amanda asks her.

"Oh, we knew each other a long time ago," Lonnie replies. I watch for Amanda's reaction. I want to see the moment when she realizes her classmate was trafficked. I wonder if she'll call Lonnie a whore too.

But all Amanda does is shrug. It's that disconnected gesture—one I've been guilty of so many times—that makes me say goodbye to Lonnie and return to Zack and his mother.

"I'd like to be on the panel if you still want me," I tell her.

She practically beams. "Wonderful! I'll send you all the details. Now, do the two of you want to stay for the lecture?"

"Nope," Zack says before I can say anything. "See ya later, Mom." Once we're outside, he turns to me. "What do you want to do now?"

Standing there, the sunlight glinting off his dark hair, he's the most beautiful thing I've ever seen. He deserves to be happy. He deserves to know exactly what he's getting with me. And I deserve to know whether or not he can handle it.

"Can we go for a drive?" I ask. "There's someplace I want to show you."

He looks interested. "You know how to get there?"

I force a tight smile. "Yep." I haven't been there since the night Detective Willis rescued me.

Some people think trafficking means you're taken far away from your home and your family. It's not true. The motel Mitch kept us in was only thirty minutes away from Mom's apartment. It's closer to an hour's drive from Middletown, but still in the state. Still very close to home.

"Take the next left," I tell Zack. He does without question. It's not far from the highway—that was why Mitch chose it.

When it was operating, it was called The China Flower motel. I'm pretty sure the owners knew nothing about

China, or flowers, but that was where Mitch got his self-proclaimed genius idea of renaming us all.

It wasn't ever a nice place. Maybe when it first opened a million years ago. It certainly wasn't now. It had been shut down after the raid, but it hadn't taken long for it to become a place for homeless squatters and drug addicts. There'd been a fire shortly after we left—probably set by Mitch to get rid of evidence. The main office was still standing, but the door was boarded up.

Zack puts the car in park. "Is this what I think it is?" he asks.

"Yeah," I say, taking a deep breath. I open the door and get out. No turning back.

I hear him follow me. I'm slow as I approach the motel. I can see where the fire started, the room right below Iv . . . Jaime's. It was usually empty. I think the manager kept it for himself if he wanted a girl or had a friend come by. Or if a girl happened to come by looking for a room . . .

Cinder blocks, black with soot, make up the walls. I climb the concrete staircase to the second floor. Dirty strands of yellow police tape rustle against the balcony, but no longer block the way. There is half of a NO TRESPASSING sign on the wall, but I ignore it.

They didn't bother to board up all the windows and doors. Or, if they did, someone has decided to "unboard" them. I stop in front of a large broken window. The glass has shattered inward. On the floor by the bed is a red high heel I recognize.

Zack comes to stand beside me.

"This was Jaime's," I tell him.

"The girl whose funeral you went to?" I'm glad he doesn't call her the girl who was murdered.

"She and I lived here for a while. That's her shoe." I turn and walk farther down. The whole place smells like when my grandfather used to dump lighter fluid on charcoal briquettes and drop a lit match in. He was too cheap to buy a gas grill.

I stop in front of my old room—the one I shared with Daisy when I first came to the motel. The room where I became Poppy. The door is open, as though it's been waiting for me. I hesitate, reach back for Zack's hand. His fingers are right there, closing around mine.

I step inside.

The mattresses are still on the beds—naked and grimy. The drawers of the nightstands hang as though someone yanked them open and couldn't be bothered to close them again.

I turn to the dresser. It's been ransacked as well, drawers dumped on the floor, clothes reduced to rags strewn across the filthy carpet. There's a boot print on the pink slip I sometimes wore. I put my own foot on that print to keep myself from picking it up.

The closet is practically empty—only Daisy's old bathrobe and a pair of ratty pumps remain.

"Do you think people came here to take souvenirs?" I ask. "Steal a little something from the trafficking motel?"

"Maybe," Zack says. "People might have taken anything that was in good shape and donated it."

Sometimes I worry he thinks too highly of people. If Poppy had walked into this place after the fire, she would have stolen every fucking thing she could carry.

The bathroom is filthy, the toilet seat completely off the bowl, lying broken against the tub. The sink is ringed with black mold, but there, on the edge, is a pink toothbrush.

I make a noise when I see it. I'm not sure if it's a laugh or a sob, but it makes me look up.

The girl looking at me doesn't belong here. For a second, I don't recognize my own face because it's not the face I should see. Not here.

"Are you okay?" Zack asks.

"I don't know." I leave the bathroom. He's right there with me as I return to the main room. I need him to see this place like I do—like I did. I need him to know.

"That was my bed. The other one belonged to Daisy. She watched TV all the time. Sitcoms mostly. Drove me crazy. Even when some guy was shoving himself in her, she'd be focused on the screen." I walk closer, bringing him with me. I point at the bed. "I had sex with hundreds of men on that bed. Maybe over a thousand." I look at Zack. I need to see his reaction.

His expression doesn't change. He's looking at me the same way he always does. "You were *raped* on that bed," he corrects me. "What happened there was not your choice."

My throat tightens. "They did everything you can do to a person, Zack. There's nothing I haven't had done to me."

He lets go of my hand, and I think, *This is it. This is when he decides I'm too damaged.* But he doesn't walk away. He bends down, grabs the side of the bed, and flips it. The mattress and box spring fly off. The wooden frame splinters.

"That's what I think of the fucking bed," he says, face flushed. I stand there, gaping at him. "Wait here."

He could be planning to leave me here for all I know, but I wait all the same. He returns a minute later, a hatchet in his hand.

"What's that for?" I ask.

He hands it to me. "Mom makes me carry one for emergencies. Didn't think I'd ever need it."

My fingers close around the handle. I look from it to the bed and back. The next thing I know, I'm attacking the wooden frame like a Viking at battle. Splinters fly as I swing over and over again. Sweat starts at my hairline and builds until it's running into my eyes. When my shoulders start to ache, I finally stop.

I have blisters on my fingers.

There's a pile of wood at my feet. I'm covered in tiny slivers. I'm warm and sticky and thirsty. Oh my God, that felt good.

Zack takes the hatchet from my stiff fingers, tossing it aside. He pulls me against his chest and hugs me. I wrap my arms around his waist and press my cheek against his sweater. I blink. Frown. I pull away.

"What is it?" he asks.

I walk over to the toppled box spring on legs that tremble with spent adrenaline and move it so I can see the markings better. Zack joins me.

"Alexa and Jaime are girls, not flowers," he reads. It's written in black marker. The words have blended into the fabric, but they're still readable. There's a date beside them. I remember that night.

That tightness I felt earlier in my throat returns, only this time it brings tears with it.

"Did you write that?" he asks.

"No," I whisper. "Jaime did. That's the night Mitch brought her here. She asked me my name. My real name." I run my fingers along her words, as though somehow tracing the letters will make me feel closer to her.

"You looked after her," Zack says.

A tear trickles down my cheek, hot and stinging. "We looked after each other."

She never let me forget who I was. I can't take care of her anymore, but maybe I can make sure other people know who she was.

He reaches down and takes my hand. "Ready?" he asks.

I wipe my eyes with the heel of my hand. "I'm ready." As we get in the car and pull out onto the road, I take one last look at the motel. Finally, I'm ready to leave it behind.

chapter twenty-five

The panel for Dr. Bradley's class is the day before Thanksgiving break. I figure this means not too many people will show up.

I'm wrong. The lecture hall isn't completely full, but it's close. Lonnie tells me it's because a lot of people are finally cluing in to what a problem human trafficking is in this country. The only criminal enterprise that's bigger is drugs, and that's only because the pimps give girls drugs. You can sell a pill once. You can sell a girl many times before she's all used up.

Lonnie and I are the only people on the panel that have been trafficked. Detective Willis is there, and a woman named Tina from DCF. There are also people from different antitrafficking organizations, a state prosecutor, and Noreen Williams, a documentary filmmaker working on a new project.

Dr. Bradley introduces us all and speaks briefly about trafficking, giving statistics. After, she starts directing questions our way. I'm twisting my fingers together under the table as my heart threatens to tear through my ribs. I thought having Zack and Elsa here would make me braver, but it's not. Krys and Jamal are here too, and feeling their gazes on me only adds to my anxiety. I wish I'd taken a Xanax.

It's going to be okay. It's fine. No one here wants to hurt me, and the people I love already know my story—or most of it. They know the important parts. Anything I say today isn't going to change what they think of me.

And if it does, they aren't the people I think they are.

"Let's talk about trafficking as an industry," Dr. Bradley begins. "Detective Willis, can you give us some perspective?"

Detective Willis repeats a lot of information I've heard before and the statistics Lonnie shared with me earlier. The prosecutor joins in with her experiences and opinions.

It's interesting to me, because the lawyer talks about everything from a criminal perspective, while Detective Willis talks about the girls more than the pimps.

"Lonnie and Lex, we hear about traffickers luring girls away from their families and the different types of coercion they use. Would you mind telling a little bit about how you were forced into this terrible industry?"

Lonnie goes first. She talks about how she was brought in by a guy she met at a new school.

"He was a student?" Dr. Bradley asks.

Lonnie nods. Everyone seems surprised. Well, not the panel. "He was a senior. I was a sophomore when we met."

"And he was actively recruiting at school?"

"Yes," Lonnie replies. "A couple of girls warned me about him, but I didn't listen. He invited me to a party at his place, drugged me, and took pictures of himself and a couple of his friends having sex with me. He threatened to show my parents if I didn't do what he wanted. I thought I could get myself out of the situation, but I was wrong. I found out he was connected to a gang, and I was handed over to them once it was determined I was broken in. It's a fairly common practice for gangs to use underage 're-cruiters' to bring girls in. If they're juveniles they can't be charged to the same degree."

I hear gasps and murmurs in the audience. I look out at their disturbed expressions with a sense of wonder. I wish I were that ignorant. It must be nice to live in a world where you don't see the darkness in people. I envy them.

When it's my turn, I tell them how Mitch was friends with my mother's boyfriend, and how he seduced me. It's hard to make eye contact with the audience. I spend a lot of time looking at the wall, or at people's mouths.

"Your mother allowed you to date a man twenty years older than you?" This was from the filmmaker.

"Yes."

"Did she know he was trafficking you?"

"I don't know. Her boyfriend did."

"How do you know?"

"He came by the motel I was at," I explain. I can't be-lieve I said it.

Detective Willis turns her head and looks at me. I can see the question in her eyes. I tilt my head and let her know that no, he didn't come to save me.

"My pimp put ads for all of us on Stall313.com," I tell them when asked how we were trafficked. "My ad was still up until a month ago. In fact, someone got a hold of it and shared it with most of my school."

"I'm so sorry," Lonnie whispers.

I almost shrug, but I'm trying not to treat things so casually. "Thanks."

Detective Willis takes the mic. "I want to add that with Lex's help, we have arrested her pimp, and he is currently in jail awaiting trial for trafficking, murder, kidnapping, and other charges."

"Murder?" Dr. Bradley asks.

"Yes. We've found the bodies of two girls whom we know were trafficked by this man."

I stare at her. "Two?"

She nods, her expression sad. "Daisy," I say softly. I turn back to the mic in front of me. "My pimp called us all by flower names. He thought it was clever."

"It's also a dehumanizing technique," the prosecutor chimes in.

I glance at her. I don't need a reminder that I've been dehumanized, but I guess she didn't say it for my benefit.

We talk about drugs and how the men who bought us often seemed like normal guys. It was only a few of them that were violent or weird. Some were young; some were old. Some were handsome; some were ugly. Some were nicer than others—but none were ever our choice.

This leads to Tina discussing dissociation and how many of us use it to survive the horror of our lives. She says it like someone who's been there.

"What got you through it?" a girl asks when we start taking questions from the audience.

"I had a friend," I tell her. "Her name—her real name—was Jaime. She never let me forget who I was."

"Where is she now?"

I swallow. "She's dead." The girl looks horrified.

"A lot of us go back," Lonnie says, leaning into the mic. "The conditioning the pimps do is like brainwashing, even Stockholm Syndrome. It's all we know. Plus, they've gotten us addicted to drugs, so we go back to them because they can get us high."

"You didn't go back."

Lonnie smiles at her. "He tried to kill me. I might be an addict, but I'm not stupid." Hesitant laughter follows.

My turn. "I was very lucky. I had family—my aunt—who wanted to take me in. I wouldn't be sober or in school if it weren't for her. I wouldn't be here at all, I don't think." I look up at Aunt Krys and smile. She makes a heart with her hands.

"What about dating?" someone else asks. "Have either of you been able to have relationships?"

No one has used the word "normal" yet, and I appreciate that. Lonnie tells them that she hasn't. And it's back to me.

I sigh. "My last boyfriend is who spread my Stall 313 ad all over school." The epic groan from the audience almost makes me smile. "So, yeah, we broke up." This is followed by laughter.

I glance up at Zack and take a deep breath before looking away. I can't watch him and speak. "I'm actually dating a really great guy right now. He's been very patient with me, even though I'm totally crazy at times. I also have an amazing best friend who has supported me and always has my back."

"Support is a huge component of helping these girls heal," Tina continues. "Just the simple act of being there makes a remarkable difference in the life of a girl who has been trafficked." She goes on to talk about a girl she worked with. When she's done, I reach for the mic Lonnie and I have been sharing.

"The thing that has helped me the most has been acceptance," I tell them. "My friends, my family, my boyfriend, they accept me for who I am. They give me a lot of slack, but they don't let me get away with being a jerk. When I'm with them, I'm not a victim, I'm just me. I know if something triggers me, I'm safe."

"How have your experiences altered how you look at sex?" This question comes from a guy. I arch a brow and he continues, "I'm interested in a girl who has been through something similar, and I don't want to upset her by doing something unintentionally triggering."

Lonnie answers first. "That's great of you, but what you need to understand is that we all have different triggers. The best thing you can do is let her know you're willing to take things at her pace. For me, I'm just starting to trust guys again. I have yet to meet one I want to get to know better, let alone date." She looks to me.

"Before I was trafficked," I begin, "I thought sex was some kind of magical thing that would make me an adult and unlock the secrets of the universe, kind of like the Force." Laughter. My smile fades fast. "That was taken from me, until I knew sex wasn't magical at all. It became something . . . well, bad. Shameful. Neither of those views are realistic."

"What do you think is realistic?" he asks.

I have to think about this—fight the urge to raise my shoulders and avoid it. "I'm not sure. What I want it to be is something special. I think it should mean something, you know? Everyone wants to be treated like they're worthy of love."

"This guy you're dating. What did he do to convince you?"

I laugh. "Well, for one thing, he's here, so thanks for asking." Everyone laughs a little. I glance up at Zack. I don't care who sees. "He gives me the same respect he gives himself."

Zack crosses his arm over his chest and nods at me. This seems to be getting to him, so I'm glad when the next question is for Detective Willis.

The panel question period lasts a total of an hour and a half. Afterward, almost everyone who was there comes up to thank us for speaking. A few of them tell me how brave they think I am—that I'm inspirational. I don't scoff or play it down. I thank them.

Noreen offers me her card. "Are you by any chance involved in the lawsuit against Stall 313?" she asks.

I nod. I'm not sure how much I'm allowed to say.

"I'm currently working on a project about their involvement in trafficking and how difficult it's been to hold them accountable. You speak really well, and I'd be honored to have you involved. Maybe you or your aunt could give me a call and we could meet? I'm based out of Greenwich."

"I'll talk to her about it," I say. She shakes my hand and wishes me the best.

And suddenly, I'm not a victim. I'm not even a survivor. I'm an activist. That's a label I can wear. By being part of this panel, I've morphed from someone who wants to change herself to someone who wants to change the world. I feel like I'm part of a movement—something bigger than myself.

Me against the world is frightening. *Us* against the world is comforting.

Dr. Bradley thanks me for taking part and gives me a

big hug. Lonnie and I make plans to get together soon, and Detective Willis walks outside with the rest of us.

"I'm sorry I didn't tell you about Daisy," she says. "We only IDed her yesterday. We . . . we had to use old medical records. I was going to tell you after the panel."

My stomach lurches at the thought of what she must have looked like.

I clear my throat. "It's okay," I tell her. "I'm just . . . I thought Daisy would survive the end of the world."

Detective Willis puts her arm around my shoulders and gives me a squeeze. We say goodbye and she leaves me, Zack, Elsa, and Krys standing there, outside the doors of the college. Jamal had to return to class.

"So," I say. "That wasn't so bad."

Krys hugs me. "You were fabulous, Lexi-bug."

"Like a professional," Elsa chimes in. "Hey, I'm going to meet up with Maisie. You guys want to join?"

I shake my head. "Thanks, but I think I need to unwind."

She hugs me and promises to call me later before walking away.

"I have to run some errands," Krys tells me. "Do you want to come with?" She smiles in such a way that I know she doesn't expect me to say yes.

I turn to Zack. "I can take you home," he offers.

"Okay," I say.

The three of us walk to the parking lot together. Krys hugs me again before she leaves.

"Tell me the truth," I say when she's gone. "Did I do all right?"

He looks at me. "You did great. Really great."

There's something off about him and I don't like it. "Are you okay?" I ask as we reach his car.

He stops as he's about to unlock it and turns to me. Tears run down his face. I don't know what to say. He puts his arms around me and hugs me tight. I hug him back.

"I'm so sorry," he says. "I'm so sorry." That's when I realize he's not crying for himself. He's crying for me.

And I love him for it.

When we get back to his house, Zack is still quiet. We go up to his room.

"Are you okay?" I ask.

"No." He shakes his head. His eyes are wet again. "Fuck, Lex."

I put my arms around him. His close around me. We stand there in the middle of his room holding each other. He sniffs once and squeezes me tight. I squeeze back.

After a few moments, he pulls back. "I gotta take this sweater off."

I watch as he pulls it over his head. The yarn grabs the fabric of the T-shirt he's wearing underneath and pulls it up, revealing his midriff and back.

I see the scars his father gave him—vicious and permanent. They are thin, sharp tears that I can't imagine inflicting upon anyone you're supposed to love, let alone your kid.

I reach out and touch one—gently. Zack stiffens, but he doesn't pull away. I step closer, push his shirt up, and press my lips where my fingers had been, against that warm smooth ridge.

"Lex," he whispers, but he doesn't stop me when I move in front of him and pull his shirt up. He bends slightly and lifts his arms, helping me. I toss his T-shirt over the chair by his desk and close his bedroom door.

He looks confused.

I step back, and he watches me as I grab the hem of my sweater and pull it over my head. Zack's gaze moves from one mark to the next, before lifting to meet mine. "You're beautiful," he says.

I blink against the heat that needles the backs of my eyes. "So are you."

"You don't have to do this," he says.

"I want to," I tell him. "You're the only person I've ever wanted to do this with." Sober, clear-headed, and without expectations.

He swallows. I unfasten my jeans with trembling fingers and step out of them. My underwear follows. I stand there, naked and unashamed in the fading light.

Zack's gaze turns dark and hot. Color flushes high on his cheekbones. He unbuckles his belt and soon he's naked too.

I've seen a lot of naked men. None of them were as beautiful as Zack. I walk toward him, unafraid.

When our bodies meet, I push him backward, until the back of his legs hit the bed. He draws me down onto the comforter with him. We lie facing each other.

"What should I do?" I ask.

His fingers brush my cheek. "Whatever you want."

"I want to touch you."

He lies back, splays his arms out across the bed. He lets me explore him with fingers and lips, from his face to his feet. His skin is warm, the muscle beneath firm and strong. I'm amazed by the textures and tastes that are so perfectly blended into his body. I want to know every inch of him.

When I finally lie down beside him, he's trembling. He kisses me like the bed is the desert and I'm a lake. I give myself up to it. This is what it feels like to be wanted—not as a thing, but as a person.

"Tell me what to do," he says, lips brushing my eyelids, my cheeks, my neck. I sigh. He moves lower.

"Oh," I say, heat flooding my cheeks. "Yeah. Do that."

He does to me what I did to him, his hands and lips tracing every inch of me until my skin tingles and I feel like there's an electrical hum resonating from deep inside me.

"Zack," I say—it's a breath, a plea. "I want . . ."

He grabs a packet from the bedside table, opens it, and puts the condom on. Then he's on his back, lifting me above him, letting me take control. Our gazes lock, and I reach down . . .

His eyelashes flutter. I let out a breath I didn't know I was holding. I put my hands on either side of his head. His palms are warm on my back as his gaze lifts to mine and stays there as our breaths mix, friction warming our skin. We don't speak, barely blink. My fingers dig into the pillow. There's a second when I'm afraid of what I'm feeling in my body and in my mind. I have a choice—open a door and hide, or let go.

One of Zack's hands curves around the back of my thigh. "Lex," he murmurs. His fingers tighten. I decide to let go. *Oh, God.*

"Kiss me," I beg. His other hand slides up to my neck, brings my head down to his. Our mouths meet, lips parted, swallowing up the sounds we make as we fall over the threshold.

Afterward, we lie on our sides, facing each other. He brushes away the tears that leak from my eyes with his thumb.

"I'm sorry," I say, sniffling. I feel like such a virgin.

"Don't," he says. "You don't need to be sorry. Are you okay?"

"Yes . . . I didn't know . . . Is it always like that?"

He makes a sound that's kind of like a laugh, but not. "No. It's never . . . I haven't . . . No, it's not always like that. Maybe that's the way it is when you're with the right person."

My eyes leak some more. "How do you always know the right things to say?"

"I say what I feel." He pushes my hair back, trailing his fingers along my temple. "You sure you're okay?"

"Better than okay." I smile slightly. "Thank you."

"I'm not going to say you're welcome because that just feels weird."

I laugh. Kiss him. We cuddle in silence, and for a few seconds I'm perfectly at peace. And then . . .

"Zack," I whisper, throat tight. "Being my boyfriend is not going to be easy. There might be times when we do this and I freak out, or times when I don't react the way I should to things. I'm not like other girls."

"I don't want any other girls," he tells me with a little smile. "Just you."

God, I hope there are more guys in the world like him. We need them.

"You know what I want?" I ask. "Pizza."

He raises an eyebrow. "Seriously?"

I kiss him. "I want to have after-sex pizza with my boyfriend," I tell him. If we lie there any longer, I'm going to say something stupid, or cry more. I'm feeling really vulnerable. I need to do something normal. I'm not ready to dissolve in front of him.

He rolls over and grabs his phone from his jeans. "Hawaiian?" he asks.

I quickly swipe the backs of my hands over my eyes. "Perfect," I say. I'm not talking about pizza.

chapter twenty-six

The hospital was quiet. It was late, but I was wide awake. I wondered if the other girls were awake too. Probably. None of us were used to going to sleep before dawn.

I could watch TV, but I didn't want the nurses to know I was awake. They'd only tell me to turn it off, anyway. Turned out other patients didn't like being woken up at four in the morning.

If I'd had some decent drugs, I could probably have fallen asleep, but that was not going to happen. Not the way I wanted at any rate.

The door to my room opened. I flinched against the bright light.

"Lex?" a voice whispered.

Only one person who called me that would be awake at this hour. "What are you doing?" I asked.

"Couldn't sleep. This place creeps me out."

"Yeah." I was not used to having a room to myself. It felt . . . unsafe.

"Move over," she commanded. The bed was a lot smaller than we were used to, but both of us fit. She slipped under the sheets with me and lay on her side facing me. "Did they call your mother?"

I made a face. "She won't come for me."

"She might, if Mitch asks her to."

"The cops know she's friends with him. They wouldn't let me go with her even if she did show. My aunt wants to take me."

"My parents were here. Mom cried the entire time. Dad looked like he didn't know what to do with either of us. I wish they hadn't come."

This was a surprise coming from her. All I'd heard since the night we met was how much she missed her family. "You'll feel differently once you go home."

"Will I? Or will I have to watch Dad drive himself nuts thinking of all the things other men might have done to me?"

I didn't really have a father, so I couldn't relate. "It will be okay," I told her.

She made a scoffing noise. "You're so full of shit." She scratched her shoulder. "I could really use a little calm right now."

That was her code word for pills, or alcohol—anything that could make her numb. "Mm," I agreed.

"Are you going to go with your aunt?"

I shrugged. "Where else am I going to go?"

"Wherever we want. Daisy got out."

I frowned. "How? Where'd she go?"

"I don't know."

"Yeah, you do. Did she go back to Mitch?" Why would he take her and not the rest of us?

"Of course she went back. He came and picked her up."

I closed my eyes. "Bitch is probably dead."

She stared at me. "Not Daisy. She's a cockroach."

"Let's run away," I said, grabbing her hand. "We can go anywhere." At that moment I meant it.

She sighed. "I can't. They're treating me for I don't know how many STIs and another UTI. I'm not letting this one get that bad. At least now I don't have to worry about the meds messing with my birth control."

She sounded like that was something to be happy about. I guess it was.

I loosened my grip on her hand, but she didn't pull away. She rolled onto her other side, putting her back to me. She pulled my arm over her and hugged it to her stomach.

"Promise you won't ever forget me," she said, her voice not much more than a whisper.

"Like I could if I wanted," I joked. Having her with me was almost like pills. I started to feel my muscles relax.

"Seriously. Promise me we'll always be friends."

"I promise." The tightness in my throat was proof of how much I meant it.

"Promise me we'll always have each other's backs."

"I promise."

"Promise you won't leave without me."

I was really sleepy now. My eyes wouldn't stay open. I yawned.

"Lex, do you promise you won't leave without me?"

"I promise."

Thanksgiving. This time last year I was in a motel room eating takeout with Daisy and some of the girls. We didn't have anything to be thankful for, not even being alive.

This year I'm in a house that feels like home, and I've got Krys and Jamal with me. They've invited Zack and his mother over because a freak snowstorm prevented them from driving down to Maryland to be with Dr. Bradley's sister. They bring pumpkin pie and green bean casserole.

Isis goes nuts when Zack walks into the house. She runs at him full tilt, sliding into his legs and knocking him backward as she makes noises that sound like someone's trying to kill her. He picks her up—despite the fact that she's getting too big—and cuddles her while she licks his face.

"Oh my God," Krys says. "That dog is crazy." She takes the casserole and pie and puts them on the counter and offers Dr. Bradley a glass of wine.

Zack turns down a glass, and I do too out of solidarity. Not like I need to drink, and I don't really feel the need to be numb at this moment.

Jamal makes us both hot chocolate instead.

"Did you talk to the documentary people?" Dr. Bradley asks.

Jamal nods. "They seem legitimately dedicated to bringing down Stall 313."

"They are," she agrees. "I've known Marissa's husband for several years. He does a lot of her editing. They're good people. Are you going to work with them?"

"That's up to Lex," Krys says, casting a glance in my direction as she sips her wine. "We've told her we're fine with it, but it's her decision."

Zack's mother looks at me expectantly. "I think so," I say. "I'm a little nervous about it, but the prosecutors in New York told me they have other clients who have already agreed to take part. They won't use my name either."

She gives my hand a squeeze. "I think it will be a rather empowering experience."

"That's what I said," Krys tells her. "She's going to let them know after the holiday."

I get the hot chocolate from Jamal and bring a mug over to Zack. "I think you should do it," he says in a soft voice. The others have already moved on to another topic.

"The documentary?" I ask.

"You said speaking at the college made you feel better. Maybe this will too."

I think it will. It will also put me on a path I can't run away from—which is why I'm undecided. Still, I like the idea of being part of something.

I think of Daisy and Jaime and last Thanksgiving. Daisy sitting on her bed eating chicken wings and watching reruns. Me and Jaime on my bed sharing food in cardboard containers, laughing and talking.

"I'm thankful for you," she told me.

I swallowed the wonton in my mouth. "I'm thankful for you too."

Daisy snorted. "Get a room."

They're both gone now. And I'm still here. The idea of being part of something that might save other girls is so tempting. I'm just afraid of fucking up.

But I was also afraid of sex and love and trust, and so far that's turned out okay. I had a dream the other night—not about the motel, but about Zack breaking up with me. He said I wasn't worth the trouble. He wanted a girl that wasn't damaged.

I woke up with a hollow feeling in my chest that's still

there, though faded. It's not that I think he's going to leave. It's that I'm afraid I won't be enough for him.

I sit beside him on the couch with my own hot chocolate. "I might do it," I tell him. "Maybe."

He puts his arm around me and I lean into him. His mother smiles at us, and so does Krys. Jamal is too busy making gravy.

A few minutes later, my uncle declares dinner ready.

It's delicious. I eat way too much. Right before dessert, Jamal says, "In my family, it's tradition to go around the table and say what we're most thankful for. I am thankful to be sharing this day with all of you. I'm thankful for my beautiful wife, and I'm thankful for my soon-to-be daughter, Lex."

I blink back tears. Seriously, since I came to this house, I've cried more than I did in the seventeen years before.

Dr. Bradley says she's thankful for all of us and that Zack met me. Krys says she's thankful for all the good people in her life—raising her glass to the Bradleys—thankful that Jamal does most of the cooking, and she's thankful that she found me again.

"I'm thankful Mom decided it was finally time to leave," Zack says when it's his turn. He smiles at me. "And I'm thankful we came here." It's not a declaration of undying love, but I know what he means and it's as good.

Now, it's my turn. "I'm thankful that Mitch can't hurt anyone else. I'm also thankful for all of you, especially Aunt Krys, who saw me at my worst and wanted me anyway."

Krys's eyes are watery, but she doesn't cry. We all lift our glasses and toast, and then we dig into pie. Later, Zack falls asleep on my shoulder while Isis lies across our laps on the sofa. We're watching a movie while Krys, Jamal, and Dr. Bradley have coffee and talk—probably about us.

I think about Daisy's family. Do they miss her? What about Jaime's parents? Are they thinking about her right now? I miss her. I kind of miss Daisy too. Wherever they are, I hope it's better than what they had here. If I take part in the documentary, I'm going to make sure people know about them—especially Jaime. Not the Jaime she became, but the one I loved.

I pet my dog's head and kiss my boyfriend's cheek, and I lean back against the couch and watch the rest of the movie. I feel safe. I feel loved. I feel so full I could burst.

It's pretty much the best Thanksgiving I've ever had.

TEN MONTHS LATER

"Anything yet?" Elsa asks, handing me a cup of coffee.

I shake my head. My butt is sore from sitting on hard wooden chairs. I shift to my hip. "The jury's still deliberating."

We're at the courthouse for Mitch's verdict. It's been a long four days. I've been here every day, sitting in the crowd, staring a hole into his head as all the terrible things he's done are laid out in great detail. I've seen photos of lost girls—sold girls. Photos of Mitch with them, photos of what they looked like when the police finally tried to save them. Most of them ran back. Some are here in the room with me. A couple of them testified, like me, but the others didn't. They watch him like they still love him.

Like they want him to love them back. I can't look at them very often because it makes my stomach hurt.

They showed photos of Jaime—in life and in death. Daisy too. I cringed when I saw what he did to her. He saved up a lot of his rage for Daisy. I can only imagine what he would have done to me.

"Why are they taking so long?" Elsa laments.

"Yeah," Zack chimes in. "Not any real debate here."

I take both of their hands as I sit between them. "They'll be done soon."

Patience is something I've been working on—and channeling my energies into something positive. That something is helping other trafficked girls. I've been speaking in public more and more often, mostly for the documentary crew to capture. A year ago, I never would have thought myself capable of becoming a champion for others.

I wouldn't have thought I'd have kept a boyfriend for this long either. Zack is still there for me, a little taller and broader than he was when we first met. I swear he's going to be a giant.

We both go to Wesleyan now. I'm actually in some of his mother's classes. I'm thinking of majoring in psychology, though I can't see myself being like Dr. Lisa. I'd like to run an organization that helps rescue trafficked girls—and boys. Lonnie and I have talked about maybe running it together. We even have a slogan: *Girls Don't Have Price Tags*. She hasn't been hanging out with Amanda much anymore since Amanda got kicked out of school for selling drugs on campus. I swear that entire family is messed up in a way that makes even me shake my head.

Krys bought me a tattoo for my eighteenth birthday. It was the one thing I wanted. It wraps and twists around my back, hip, and torso to cover the scars from the motel. It took three sessions to complete, but was totally worth it.

It's vines of ivy. And right below my heart, a poppy where one of the leaves should be. Every time we have sex, Zack kisses it. Elsa came with me when I went to get it. She asked if I was certain I wanted the poppy.

"Poppy made me who I am," I tell her. "Instead of trying to forget her, I'm going to own her." In a lot of twelve-step programs, they talk about gratitude, and I'm finally able to feel that toward the girl I used to be. I can't put her in a box and forget about her. I can't leave her in that motel alone and afraid. I need her with me.

I turn my head and see Frank sitting alone behind Mitch. My mother hasn't been to the trial at all. Apparently she and Frank broke up. I haven't heard from her. The best thing she ever did for me was give up her parental rights so Krys and Jamal could adopt me. I will always be grateful to her for that, but not much else.

"They're coming back in," Elsa says. Within a few minutes, the judge is in front of us, and the jury returns to its box. I study their faces, hoping to figure out what they decided. Nothing.

I watch Mitch as the verdict is read, clinging to Zack and Elsa's hands. On the charge of trafficking: guilty. Kidnapping: guilty. Murder: guilty. I stop listening after that. I can't hear past the roaring in my ears.

Mitch looks old. Defeated. He's been beaten so many times, his nose has an entirely new shape. I wish I could feel sympathy for him, but I'm not there yet. I'm in no hurry to be.

He's going to pay for what he did to me. For what he did to all the other girls.

People applaud the verdict.

Elsa hugs me hard. Zack does too. "We have to go cele-brate!" my friend decides. "Lemme call Maisie and see if she wants to join us."

"How do you feel?" Zack asks, grinning down at me.

I smile. "Relieved. Happy. Glad it's over."

His smile fades a little. "But?"

"It doesn't change anything, does it?"

He strokes my back. "He can't hurt anyone else."

That's something. Actually, it's everything.

Elsa returns. "Maisie said she'll meet us wherever. Where do you want to go?"

I think about it. "Thai," I say.

"Great. I'll text her." She turns away again.

"You sure you want to celebrate?" Zack asks.

"Yeah. I'm sure." I look over his shoulder. "But there's something I need to do first."

He follows my gaze to Jaime's family. They're sitting two rows back and getting ready to file out with the rest of the crowd. Jaime's mother, father, and one of her sisters. The sister not much younger than me. The one who looks so much like Jaime, it hurts to look at her.

My fingers close around the bracelet in my pocket as I stand. I walk to them, say hello. Give them hugs. They're still awkward with me, and I don't blame them. Their daughter's dead and I'm alive.

I turn to Jaime's sister and offer her the bracelet.

"Your sister made this," I tell her. "I want you to have it. It's made of things that were important to her." To both of us, but I leave that out.

"Don't you want it?" the girl asks, eyes wide.

I shake my head. "I have other ways of remembering her. I think she'd like knowing you have it."

She nods, a tear sliding down her cheek. "Thank you." She pulls me into a hug. I hug her back and try not to cry, because she hugs like Jaime too.

Eventually I leave her and return to Zack and Elsa. "Let's go," I say.

Zack puts his arm around my shoulders. I put mine around his waist, and we leave the courtroom together. As we walk out, I feel like I'm finally waking up from a bad dream. Things seem clearer.

I'll carry the memory of the motel and what happened there with me forever, but it's gone now. Finally torn down. I don't need to have rooms inside my head that I can escape to. I don't need to be numb. I don't live there anymore. I don't have many nightmares anymore, but I still dream. Sometimes I wake up screaming, but most nights I don't.

I dream of other faceless girls who have come and gone before me, and those who are still out there, lost. They're why I get up every morning filled with hope. I look for them every time I speak to a room full of people, or share my experience with others.

I will never stop looking.

acknowledgments

Stall313.com does not exist in the same way it is described in this book. However, it represents many sites out there used to buy and sell young girls (and boys) for the sex trade. If you want to know more about the inspiration for this site, please check out the documentary *I Am Jane Doe* by Mary Mazzio, a truly inspiring story about the fight to end online trafficking, the effects it's had on victims and their families, and the movement that brought down Backpage.com.

There are so many valuable and amazing organizations out there that are trying to help those who have been in the life make a fresh start and heal from the abuse they've suffered. If you're interested in contributing to these organizations, I have a list at Stall313.com.

Just a quick note in case there's any confusion—the age of consent in Connecticut is sixteen, but anyone under the age of eighteen is considered a juvenile, or child, by law. So, while Lex can consent to have sex with someone older than her, the law is able to step in when trafficking is suspected. When Detective Willis comments that Jaime/Ivy is eighteen now, it's not about consent, it's about the fact that she's no longer a child and the law can't protect her as easily from traffickers. It's a horrible thing, but once someone is eighteen, if they return to the life there is always the possibility that they are no longer being coerced, and have chosen to become sex workers. That doesn't mean we turn our backs on these young women (and men), but they are now considered adults, able to make their own decisions, and the courts can't make those decisions for them. I think this is when the organizations dedicated to fighting trafficking may be needed most.

There are so many people who need to be thanked for helping this book become a reality, I'm just going to start at the beginning. I need to thank my husband, Steve, for bringing a news story about human trafficking to my attention, and for urging me to write about it. Also, for the hugs he gave me when research overwhelmed me, and for being there whenever I needed to talk it out. For eating lots of takeout, for driving me around to do research, and for talking me down when my rage over the trafficking industry threatened to burn me up. Most of all, I want to thank him for being a good man, the kind of man who knows that no one should be bought and sold.

Thanks to Detective Tanya Compagnone for doing what she does to end trafficking, and for telling me about it. You are my hero, girl. You make the world a better place. Also, thanks to Michelle C. for introducing us. And a huge shout-out to Dina St. George for just being an all-around amazing woman who has made a difference in the lives of so many girls. Also, to Christie Kelly for her caring and boundless energy. And to Taylor deGraffenried for doing so much for so many girls who need help. Ladies, you are the real-life Wonder Women of the world.

Thanks to Alicia Clancy for buying this book, and for Vicki Lame at Wednesday Books for helping me make it the best it can be. Thanks so much for your support of this project and your love of the characters. You are both so fabulous. And thanks to Miriam Kriss for selling the book, and to Deidre Knight for seeing it through with me.

Thank you to women like Kubicki Pride, Nacole Lynn, MA, and JS, for fighting against human trafficking and for sharing your stories with the world. You are true inspirations.

And last, but certainly not least, a big thanks to my girl, Madallya. You are my inspiration. Please remember you are so much more than you might think. Thank you for sharing your story, your time, and your talent with me. I have become a better person for knowing you. I'll always be your Great White, no matter what.